FORGIVE OUR SINS

THE FORGIVE ME FATHER SERIES
BOOK TWO

CAITLIN MAZUR

WPC PRESS

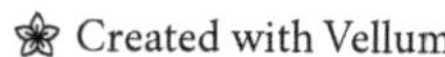 Created with Vellum

For my husband,
who helped me feel like I finally belonged.

For my husband,
who helped me feel like I finally belonged.

Decision is a risk rooted in the courage of being free.

— PAUL TILLICH

AUTHOR'S NOTE

This story takes place across New Hampshire, upstate New York, and Vermont, with the Coutts commune established in what was once White Mountain National Forest and Coutts Peak established on what was once Mount Washington. For the sake of storytelling, some details of the landscape may have been altered.

1

———

MAURA

FOR A GIRL who had never been dishonest a day in her life, I was doing well as a heretic. Four days in, I had defied almost all the Prophet's commandments.

Thou shalt not steal.

Broken on the first day after my treacherous swim across the lake. My waterlogged clothes weighed me down so much I couldn't manage more than a crawl. Sand and small rocks littered my body as I lay on the shore, letting the sun dry me out. Then I'd wandered for what felt like miles, hunger cramps crippling every movement. I tried not to think of food, but every shock of color between the green foliage was a fool's wish.

I journeyed through the afternoon into early evening, sure my limbs would give out at any point. And just after delirium struck, I stumbled across a dirt road that brought me to a metal-roofed shed tucked between two tall shrubs as if someone hoped to hide it. Motivated by hunger-driven rage, I'd broken the lock with a large tree branch. Inside, I found what I assumed to be rations for us heathens at the Island of Repentance from where I'd escaped.

I tried hard to curb my greed, but without a anything to eat for days, hunger was a difficult thing to suppress. Afraid to test my famished stomach, I ate two apples and a piece of bread, pocketing what I could carry for the rest of my journey before darting back to the trees.

Remember the sabbath day to keep it holy.

Through the chaos of my life's upending, I'd lost track of the days. But Sunday was yesterday, when I'd heard the church bells ring from where I sat on the forest floor, pulling ticks from my ankles. Sunday church bells differed from Saturday church bells because they rang six times as opposed to four. On weekdays, they rang twice.

I'd looked up through the trees, listening to the clanging. The sound that had once brought comfort now seemed ominous. Like a warning. As if Father taunted me from the top of Coutts Peak. Could he see me sitting in the dirt, separating my leg hair to make sure I'd gotten all the bugs? I knew my sister wife, Abigail, would've clucked her tongue and called me a dirty pig, reminding me how close I still was to childhood, while she more closely matched our husband Andrew in age.

Thou shalt not defy the Prophet.

There was no question of whether or not I had failed this commandment. The Prophet — my Father — condemned me to solitude, and I had escaped. If that didn't count as defiance, I wasn't sure what did. But that hadn't been all. I'd added insult to injury with rebellious thoughts. I'd voiced my mistrust of the Prophet and his actions to Eli, the man who had saved me. An Outsider. I'd helped him and his group escape Father's men. I had defied my Prophet in the worst ways imaginable, and I continued to do so now.

But what choice did I have? I'd learned that despite us sharing a bloodline, Father would not protect me. He wanted only to protect himself and the men who obeyed him. And those men only wanted to protect what they thought was rightfully theirs — their women, riches, and comforts. By any means necessary. If I wanted to survive, knowing what I knew now, defiance was essential.

Honor thy husband.

Was this commandment still obligatory if your husband was a murderer? Perhaps I just wanted to make myself feel better about my rebellion, but I thought God might give me a pass on this one.

I collected these sins, marking each one off in my head on my checklist for miscreants. It was my first collection, something I had always wanted. As a child, my sister, Morgan, had collected toy horses, hoping to get one of each breed. Mother found this so endearing that she convinced Father to give her extra allowance to visit the luxury toy shops in our commune. Morgan had been three short when she'd given up playing with them, and it had always bothered me she never completed the full set. But me? I might get close to completing my collection of sins by the time I got out of this mess.

Which wouldn't be any time soon. I was about to break a fifth commandment.

Thou shalt not bear false witness against thy neighbor.

I hid behind a thick row of blueberry bushes, picked clean by a farmer or animal. The sun hung low in what I now knew to be the west, spreading the last of its heat on the afternoon in slow, humid waves. Green and yellow hills extended into the distance, leading away from the mountains that overshadowed the land to my left. Coutts Peak. Those mountains had been my home. Where I'd once had a promising future.

To my right, a thin wooden fence enclosed a wide land perimeter, backing up to a white, gambrel-style barn with a gray roof. Only the tall sliding barn door was visible from this angle, but I was almost certain horses were inside. And if there was any chance of getting out of the commune, a horse was essential.

I wiped my hand from forehead to chin, spreading dirt and salty sweat down my face. If I guessed, I'd been watching the barn for no more than a half hour. It seemed empty, but I couldn't be sure. Urgency nipped at my heels. The longer I waited, the more danger I was in. By now, I was certain someone must've checked in on the Island of Repentance. They would've seen the damage from the storm — the downed pines, caved-in roof, and a discarded cast-iron skillet. Private radios would announce my absence, which meant I needed to steer clear of the Hunters, Father's most trusted confidants.

However, the news would not likely reach regular folk like farmers at the mountain's base. Father was too proud to admit he didn't have control. So, if I met someone inside the barn, I would lie about who I was, where I'd come from, and where I was headed. It wasn't a great plan, and it was by no means foolproof, but it was all I had.

I straightened, my back tight from hunching over for so long before I gathered my only belongings in the world: a book of matches, two rubber gloves — one filled with water, one empty — and a few kitchen utensils, all stuffed into a garbage bag. I clutched the bundle to my chest, closing my eyes as I steadied my breathing.

With as much energy as I could muster, I shot out from between the bushes and sprinted across the field. The sudden shock of exposure was like plunging into cold water, heightening my adrenaline and enhancing the colors and sounds around me. I ran the length of the fence until I reached the side of the barn, my chest burning. Breaths came in heaves, and I swallowed them silently, pressing my back against the wood siding.

Squeezing my belongings as if they were armor, I came to the corner of the building and peered around. A horseshoe-shaped driveway led to a screened-in white door, surrounded by potted plants that had wilted in the summer sun. Inside looked dark, but I still couldn't confirm it was empty from where I stood. The driveway bumped up to a thin dirt road, empty in both directions, but that might change at any minute.

With one last look down the road, I hunched and darted for the door. I was sure I would hear the rattle of bullets or shouts from a distant observer. But the only sound came from my boots scraping against the driveway as my feet hit the ground.

The barn was not nearly as nice as the one I'd used for my scavenging duties on Coutts Peak, but those material luxuries had been a show. A horse was a horse no matter the barn, just as Andrew was a murderer, no matter his title. I reached the concrete step, yanked open the screen door, and pushed inside.

It was dark inside the wide hallway, the floor washed in gray, smelling of mildewed hay and manure. Barred stable doors lined the hall, except for an archway to my right leading to the stock and feed room. Windows dotted the walls above the stables, dust particles dancing in the soft sun reflected on the floor. A low symphony of rustling, munching, and sighs filled the space, and a smile crossed my lips. The stables were full.

I turned to the feed and stock room, approaching a short wooden table, where I dumped my bag of belongings. Items tumbled from the plastic, but I was already inspecting the walls. A variety of scavenging bags hung on brass hooks, and I grabbed the first canvas backpack I saw. I repacked my meager items and remaining food before rifling through the various drawers built into the walls. I snagged a hay bale cutter, several cross ties, a crumpled water bottle from the trash, and a roll of paper towels, along with a few more apples, three handfuls of sugar cubes, and a bunch of carrots, all of which I shoved into the mouth of my new pack.

Something thumped against a wall and I ducked, spilling a few of my newly acquired items across the floor. I held my breath, squeezing my eyes closed. I hadn't made it this far just to be caught by a Hunter, had I? Disappointment dropped like a weight in my stomach as I inched forward to the archway.

The hall remained empty. No shadow crossed the door. I stilled, listening, but the only sounds were my heavy breathing, my pounding heart, and the horses in their stalls. After a moment passed, I straightened, feeling foolish as I picked up my spilled bounty. A horse had kicked the stable wall, that was all.

My apprehension hovered as I put the backpack over my shoulders and went to search for a horse. Riding gear hung on the walls beside the feed room, and I inspected each one, choosing a Western bridle, nylon blanket, and barrel saddle. The less weight I carried with me, the better. My adrenaline armed me with strength as I slung the bridle over my shoulder and secured two hands around the saddle, carrying the materials into the barn's interior, my footsteps echoing against the high, lofted ceiling. I took careful note of each horse, stopping at the end before a black Thoroughbred. A dark coat would be best to stay hidden, and his height — about 16 hands — was ideal for my size.

I rolled the stall door open, grateful for my scavenging

training. Without it, I would have had no knowledge of horses, saddles, or bridles. I would've still been stuck atop that mountain, hoping a pregnancy would come along to give me some semblance of purpose in life. Sadness accompanied the thought. I had yet to grieve the identity I'd left behind before I'd stepped into that creek.

But that had to come later.

The stallion whinnied as I approached. I dumped the saddle to the side to run my hands along his back to soothe him.

"Good boy," I whispered, sliding my fingers across his silky coat. He dipped his head back to meet my gaze and sighed his approval, lips rippling over his teeth.

My hands quickly worked as I tugged on the cinch's worn leather to buckle it tight beneath his belly. I cooed over his obedience as he followed in a half circle to face the open door of his stall. Holding my breath, I guided him into the hall, expecting Andrew or Father to come bursting through, guns drawn, at any moment.

You're okay. You're going to make it.

I didn't fully believe my thoughts. Too much of my history had proven hope was typically too good to be true. But I wasn't going to turn back now. I took a few deep inhales as we reached the back door of the barn, each of our steps seeming louder than the last.

"Stay," I instructed the horse as I pulled the barn door left on its slider, showering us with warm sunlight. We emerged into the pasture, but I stopped dead in my tracks as we crossed the threshold. Just beyond the fence, a figure wearing a straw hat stood watching us, shielding their face from the sun.

2

____

MAURA

THE FIGURE APPROACHED from the hills, head downturned, arms swinging at their sides. Broad shoulders suggested they were a man and as he came through the far gate, I better understood his height. He didn't wear green armor, and that was all that mattered. Hinges squealed as he entered the pasture, clicking the gate latch closed behind him.

I looked for an escape opportunity. Moving forward would give me less time to think up an explanation, but would make it look like I belonged there. Moving backward meant I left with no horse and had a higher chance of getting caught. Though every nerve in my body wanted me to flee, I forced my legs forward.

The man removed his straw hat as he neared, revealing a receding hairline and freckled face. His plump cheeks were raw from the sun, nose blistered from a bad burn. He slowed his pace, working to catch his breath. His eyebrows squished together as he frowned — a look of disapproval.

Was it how I looked? I glanced down at myself. Sweat and dirt stained my unwashed clothes. My scalp itched, my teeth felt fuzzy, and insect bites covered my skin. When was the last time I'd pulled my sweaty fingers through my hair? Yesterday? The day prior?

"Good afternoon," he said, giving me a once-over. I smiled as naturally as I could, but every muscle felt forced.

"Hello," I answered. "I'm terribly sorry to bother you."

He shook his head. "I don't have anyone on my roster for this afternoon." He glanced back into the barn. Always straight to business with men in the commune. They all had something to prove. "Did your husband or father contact us?"

I swallowed. "Well, I sure thought so," I said, feigning ignorance. "He told me we needed the horse for something important."

The man nodded, seemingly unconvinced. "Who's your husband?"

"My husband is, uh — Matthew Coutts." My gall surprised me. The lie fell out of my mouth so easily. Uncle Matthew was Father and Andrew's youngest brother, who seemed to be marrying quicker than all six Coutts' brothers combined. Andrew's name would have raised alarm, though I wasn't confident this would work either.

The young man straightened, his wide eyes trailing from the tips of my boots to the top of my head. "Oh," he said, his voice deepening as though he hoped to impress me. "Matthew sent you all the way down here?"

I nodded. "He's heard such *great* things about how you've trained your stallions." His brows raised at the compliment. "And the horses are running low on energy up on the peak. Because of the—" I glanced skyward, "— heat." I forced a heavy breath out, wiping my brow, hoping my lie explained my appearance.

He pressed his lips together, and I held the air in my lungs, squeezing the reins so tightly the decorative leather would imprint on my palm. Did he know? Would he believe me?

"Well, alright," he said, putting his hat back on. "I'll still need to check in before you take Chance." He glanced up at the horse, who stamped impatiently.

"Of course," I said. "If you give him a call, I'm sure he'll—"

"I know how to do my job, ma'am." He tipped his hat before brushing past me with a superior air of authority that made my insides boil. I might've been a Coutts' wife, but I had no pull here. Even the lowest-ranking man took precedence over the highest-ranking woman. Ephesians 5:23. *For the husband is the head of the wife even as Christ is the head of the church, his body, and is himself its Savior.*

But that was the least of my concerns. I'd seen our Scavenging leader, Jeremiah, use the two-way radio system when he needed an immediate answer. All the farmer had to do was press a button to alert Matthew that I was trying to take a horse, and my flimsy lie would fall apart.

I didn't have much time.

Careful not to startle Chance, I tugged his reins to get him to move with me as the man disappeared into the barn's dark interior. The call would take seconds — the response, maybe a minute.

We raced across the grazing area. The hills were too open, so the forest would be the only way. My trembling fingers made the latch tricky to release. Precious seconds snuck by as I inspected it closer, but the gate wouldn't budge. Fear slid down my neck as I fiddled with it, casting a hurried glance at the open barn door. The farmer would return any second. And if there was a Hunter nearby, they wouldn't hesitate rushing over to investigate.

Finally, it came loose, sliding free with a tired squeak. I

pushed the gate open, then, with a tight grip on the saddle horn, pulled my body up and over Chance's broad back.

I dug my heels into his side, and the stallion wasted no time. Chance seemed about as eager for the open air as I had been leaving the Island of Repentance. He broke into a trot, heading straight toward the thicket of trees.

"Hey!" The voice chased us across the grazing field and over the fence as we trotted towards the tree line. "Stop!"

My heart pounded in my ears.

Don't look back. Don't look back. Don't look back.

Bent low, I concentrated ahead, calves straining as I worked to keep them embedded in the horse's side. Chance cantered through dozens of trees, pine needles, and thick brush scraping against us as we rode deeper into the thicket. My hands shook, making the reins snap against the wind.

Getting the stallion was only one hurdle cleared. I still needed to outrun the farmer. Dodge the impending Hunters. Find the scavenging zones to guide me to the edge of the commune. From there, if I wanted any shot at surviving the world outside this commune, I'd need to find the waste center where I'd left Eli and the others.

Fear tricked me, transforming snapping branches into gunshots and shadowed brush and dead wood into waiting snipers. Chance slowed his pace as the terrain shifted, dodging rocks and dips in the earth. But I didn't turn. I wouldn't. I had to focus on what lay ahead.

The first flash of white came later that afternoon. The marking of a scavenging zone. I pulled Chance to a stop, squinting at the stapled sign on the tree. Zone 256. My zone, 16, must've been hundreds of miles away from here. The world spun. After living most of my life on the mountaintop, I found it hard to fathom how large the commune was.

I urged Chance forward again, and we left the sign behind, working our way up a slight incline through the trees. The sun was sinking quickly — a fact I could no longer ignore. We would need to rest soon. A dark forest and unsteady ground were a recipe for disaster.

As we crested the hill, a shriek of laughter cut through the quiet. Instinctively, I tugged on Chance's reins. The forest floor dipped ahead of us, a narrow, rocky brook splitting the terrain. Two small children splashed near a large boulder, their mother hovering nearby, nursing a newborn. If they looked up, even for a second, they would see us.

Terror collected at the base of my spine, the world suddenly brighter. We were so close. I could hear the ripple of water against the stones, the mother humming as she paced the water's edge. I slid from Chance's back, lowering myself to the ground. As slow as possible, we descended the hill, and I led him into a thick part of the trees, tying his reins to a thin trunk.

"Stay," I whispered, as if he had a choice. He grunted, turning his nose away from me. "Oh, don't be sour."

I knew I should remain hidden and wait out the sun's descent, but against my better judgment, I ventured back up the hill, remaining hidden in the brush. They weren't dangerous. My curiosity was justified. But as I watched the mother at the edge of the brook, I realized the pit in my stomach was much more than a wish to be intrusive. It was something more, something deeper, something I'd pushed away from the moment I'd married Andrew.

Longing.

My heart ached. The path ahead of me was set in stone. I had left not just Father, Andrew, and the commune, but my family—my mother, my sister, Morgan, and the rest of my young siblings, those who still lived in the midst of Father's lies.

Had I tried hard enough, I knew I could've gotten back on Father's good side after completing my penance — become a good girl who behaved. Returned to my simple life and pushed my memories deep beneath the surface so they only emerged between murky daydreams. But I had opened a door I never intended to close again. And though it had been my choice to make, I knew in my heart there were so few circumstances in which I would've chosen to stay.

But my God, how much this hurt.

AT DAWN, we crossed the brook. No matter how relieved I was not to share a bed with Andrew, I would never grow accustomed to sleeping on the forest floor and waking up with strange insect bites. I scratched the new one at the back of my neck as we passed scavenging zone 247.

We rode through the day, taking breaks every few hours until finally, the air shifted. The smell of rotten eggs was faint at first, but as I guided Chance downhill, my eyes watered at the stench. I never thought I'd be so happy for such a foul aroma.

The hill we traveled sloped sharply, the earth dropping away to reveal the land beyond. Though this was familiar terrain, it shocked me to see its size from this perspective. The large waste center covered most of the acreage to my right — trash, plastics, cardboard, and metals of different colors, like a vibrant mosaic, stinking in the late summer sun. In a strange contrast, flat farmland stretched across the land to my left, a thick forest beyond it, as far as my eye could see. That was where I needed to go. Where Holli had promised to leave a trail.

Navigating down the hill was easy. But another problem lay ahead.

Stationary black dots sat in neat order on the dividing line between the waste center and the farmland. Hunters' trucks.

Were they waiting for me?

Icy fear slithered through my body, making my skin clammy. My leg muscles tense against the saddle. How I despised Father and the violence those trucks represented! I knew any animosity toward the Prophet was sinful, but I was too battered and exhausted to care. I felt my features curl into a scowl, reins gripped tightly in my hands. No. I had made it this far. It couldn't be for nothing.

"We're getting to that forest," I said to Chance. "And we're gonna do it without dying." The stallion nickered. I took it as a sign of encouragement.

With a determined fire burning hot in my belly, Chance and I used the remaining sunlight to descend the hill, careful to keep off any visible path. I guided him around areas of concern, stopping halfway to massage my sore calves before continuing.

We walked through the sparse tree cover at the base of the hill. Night's dark layer took hold, shadowing our surroundings and making it difficult to see. A benefit and a hindrance. Making it across the flat farmland would require darkness and a lot of blind faith. Luckily, I had both in abundance.

As we reached the onset of flat land, I could just make out the dim lights from the Hunter's trucks. About a dozen stood between me and the forest beyond. The further into the farmland I walked, the better our chance of not being seen.

The flashy helmets the Hunters wore were not just for show or protection. They were equipped with night vision technology, and I was ignorant of how it worked as a woman from the commune. But I had to assume they could only see so far, though there was no way to test my theory without putting myself in jeopardy. I had to try. This was the last obstacle standing in my path to freedom. If they caught me, after all this, I couldn't help but believe I deserved it.

I rode Chance out into the dark nothingness of the farmlands for a few moments before I turned to look back at the trucks again. Small dots of light were visible from the waste center looming behind them, but I couldn't see the outline of the vehicles at all. Whether that was a good or a bad sign had yet to be seen.

Every muscle in my body begged me to turn around and flee. But there was nothing left for me in the commune. My departure from the Island of Repentance had sealed my fate. Father would never forgive me, and I refused to endure any more of his lies.

The thought allowed me to press my heels into Chance's flank, so he sped up into a trot, carrying us into the open ground ahead. The vile, sour smell from the waste center choked me as we moved into the open air. I considered listening for shouts, but what good would that do? It wasn't like the Hunters would announce themselves before they shot.

The blinding darkness made me dizzy. I dug my heels deeper into Chance. He quickened into a smooth canter, and I clung to his crest, trying to steady my breathing. I had no way of gauging how far we'd gone, but the horse continued forward, and I had no choice but to trust him across the dark farmland. At times, I was sure we'd wandered into a black abyss. That Chance was taking us to the world's edge, deep into nothingness. My mouth went dry.

And then, when I thought the darkness would never end, spindly shadows emerged in the distance, like fingers stretching to the heavens. Trees.

I gasped in relief, my knees releasing their tension against the saddle from exhaustion and the break of fear. Beneath my slick palms, Chance's mane was frothy with sweat. Together, we disappeared into the dark depths of the forest.

3

MAURA

I SLEPT until a sliver of blue dawn peeked between the trees, revealing my unfortunate decision of laying in a bundle of weeds. Chance grazed a few feet in the distance, still secured to the tree I'd tied him to as I picked dandelion pappus from my hair.

After taking a few swigs of the precious water I'd refilled at the brook, I took some time to get my bearings. Chance and I backtracked to the hill beside the waste center where Holli had promised to leave her mark, careful to stay hidden from the Hunters' trucks. The memory of the middle-aged woman's warm hand on my cheek made me remember her last words to me. "You'll always have a place with us. And if you ever do follow, go west. Follow our path from here — I'll mark trees as we pass them, just in case. Look for my H."

Early morning passed overhead as I painstakingly searched tree after tree, squinting at small dents and scrutinizing animal scratches, wondering if Holli had tried to hide her marks or left them more obvious. She'd never specified what they would look like. By the time the sun rose to brighten the sky, my clothing stuck to my sweaty skin, and I stopped believing there were any marks at all.

Perhaps Holli had told me she'd leave a trail to make me feel better, and I was out here wasting my time. Maybe the group had moved on without me. And why shouldn't they? Even though I'd sacrificed my safety for theirs, I was still technically the enemy. Chance munched away on stray bushes, unbothered by my plight. Defeated, I sat on the ground with the canvas tote, pulling it between my legs to get a bite to eat.

"C'mere," I said to Chance, holding up an apple. He lifted his head before trotting over to where I held it. "Glad you're enjoying yourself."

He grunted before his teeth crunched into the fruit, squirting me with juice. I closed my eyes with a heavy sigh and wiped it away. What was one more layer of grime on my soiled clothes and skin? The familiar ache of regret sank like a weight in my stomach. Had I made the wrong choice? Was God teaching me a lesson? Was this where my journey ended? I thought of what punishment awaited me next. Though divorce would not be an option, surely Andrew would banish me from his estate for good. He'd cast me off to become a permanent scavenger, like the rest of the infertile women on our bus.

I pulled my knees up, draping my arms over each before my eye caught something unnatural on the pine tree behind Chance. My body stilled, relief expanding in my chest. Carved into the bark was an H, each end leading off with a little curl. Beside it, an arrow pointed west.

I scrambled to my feet. It was here! Holli had kept her promise, and with an arrow, no less. I turned back to the canvas tote, pulling the silver dinner knife I'd taken from the Island of Repentance and chiseled away at the mark. I doubted the Hunters would think much of it, but it never hurt to be safe. Once I had skinned the bark, I stood back to admire my work. A light blemish on the dark wood. Nobody would notice. Equal parts relieved and terrified, I returned to Chance, who looked up at me, his dark nose smudged in dirt.

"We're going to make it," I said, rubbing circles on his flank. "C'mon!"

With a newfound sense of purpose, Holli's arrow led us through the forest. About a half hour after the first one, I found another H carved into a tree, an arrow leading north. Now that I knew what to look for, the marks seemed easier to find. We followed her direction until the trees broke for a long stretch of road.

We'd put a good distance between us and the waste center, but a paved street still made me anxious. It meant trucks, which meant Hunters, which made us exposed. We kept to the side of the road on the off chance we needed to retreat into the trees. Holli's arrow pushed us west with the setting sun at our backs. We would need to find a place to sleep soon.

A fork appeared around the bend. At the intersection, a wooden sign read: *Coal Creek, est. 1869.* Holli had carved another H and an arrow pointing right beneath the date.

I urged Chance down the cracked pavement, past weeds and tall, browned grass. The trees thinned, and the road widened as we entered a small town. The main road ran the length of the entire collection of buildings, ending in a cul-de-sac. A second street crossed in the middle, leading to homes built side by side behind the building-lined street.

On our left sat a church with a pointed roof and missing shingles, a small schoolhouse choked by weeds, a post office with no windows, and what remained of a looted grocery store. Glass, debris, and about a dozen abandoned cars lined the pavement. A long brick building covered the length of the right side, vines creeping up its corners. Faded black letters over a large garage door read *Coal Creek Fire Department*.

I eyed the garage. Chance could fit through it if I could somehow get it open, giving us both relief from the heat and a chance to sleep. The sun hadn't set yet, but we'd been walking for almost a full day. If I had any intention of continuing forward at this pace, we both needed rest.

I slid off the saddle, my feet stiff and my thighs sore as I willed movement into my legs. The sun reflected from the building windows caught my eye, stopping my breath in my chest. Even though Holli had pointed us this way, this place felt empty.

Eager to find cover, I approached the fire department's front door and turned the weathered handle, surprised to find it unlocked. Inside, I was met with the stale smell of neglect and warm air. A circular desk took up much of the interior space, dusty frames covering the wall behind it. But the dark invited fear to the forefront of my mind. Would someone jump out from the corner, gun drawn? Were there dangerous animals using this as a home? I locked the door behind me as I stepped across the threshold and hurried through the space.

A wooden door at the back of the room led me to the garage. An old, lone firetruck sat parked in the middle of the large, gray room. To my relief, there seemed to be more than enough space on each side for Chance to stay comfortable throughout the night.

I unlocked and opened the garage door, leading Chance through. After I secured us both inside, I wiped my hands on my jeans, feeling light with accomplishment. We had made it out of the commune. We were safe. There was a roof over our heads. The only thing left to find was water, but that was a tomorrow problem.

I turned back to Chance, relieving him of his saddle and bridle before offering him another apple. He munched it down eagerly, leaving my fingers covered in slobber. A well-deserved reward and hopefully enough to avoid dehydration until morning. I scanned the room for supplies, but anything of value wasn't obvious. It didn't matter. Being behind closed doors and out of nature woke my exhaustion, and I wanted nothing more than to rest. But where?

My first thought was on the floor until I noticed a black spiral staircase at the far end of the room. It led to a small ledge with a door. Promising. With one last pat on Chance's back, I climbed the stairs and pushed the heavy door inward.

The stench of mothballs washed over me and I wrinkled my nose, studying the small room. A ratty couch sat in the middle of a worn carpet, with a small kitchenette on the right. I darted to the sink, yanking the tap up, my mouth open and ready for the satisfying drip of water. But nothing came.

Another reminder of how ill-equipped I was for this world. Defeated, I kicked off my boots, dropped my pack on the floor, and curled up on the threadbare couch before exhaustion overtook me completely.

A LOUD CLATTER startled me from sleep. I gasped, sitting up straight and wiping away the layer of dried drool from the corner of my lips. Sleep clouded my movements, but I rubbed it from my eyes, my fingers clammy from the shock. Adrenaline fired through my veins, filling my ears with a rush of blood.

What made that sound? I stood from the couch, arching my back as I attempted to stretch my muscles back into working order. Sunlight poured through the small windows in the room, but…it couldn't be. Could it? Had I slept through the night?

Something clanged on the lower level, like metal against a pipe. I froze. Was it Chance bumping his head against the firetruck or garage door? He was probably hungry, wondering where I was. The thought filled me with guilt, but I couldn't shake the fear. The sound seemed too controlled to come from an impatient horse.

I tried to remain calm as I pulled my boots on, tugging at the laces so they were secure around my ankles. Though it was safer for me out here, the Hunters could still find me, just like they had when I was with Eli and the others.

For a moment, my heart leapt at the possibility that it *could* be Eli's group in the firehouse. That by some act of God, he'd put them at the same place I'd arrived. But the thought was foolish — a child's wish. There was no magic in this world, and the odds of ending up together were small, even with Holli's guidance.

I stood, swallowing to ease my dry throat. The door to the spiral staircase seemed too far away, but I needed to look — I needed to make sure there was no one here besides me, if not for my own sanity, then to protect Chance. He was my only companion, and it was my job to keep him safe. Plus, if I was going to survive out here on my own, I needed to be brave. What better time to start than now?

Still, my hands trembled as I brought them up to the handle and pulled the door open. I stuck my head out to peer down into the garage, but my view was obscured by a mud-crusted t-shirt, half-tucked into a pair of dirty jeans.

I shrieked, pushing myself back from the door and

letting it swing closed behind me as I backed up into the room. My stomach rolled as I frantically searched for something to use as a weapon.

The door shot open. A figure entered — a short man with thinning blonde hair and a round, white face. He grinned at me, the spaces between his teeth visible in the light. His small eyes narrowed in on me as I retreated into the room, still looking desperately for something to protect myself with.

I settled on a discarded pan that hung on a drying rack beside the sink, finding irony in my reliance on cookware. It was too light for my liking, but the man didn't need to know that. I wrapped both hands around the handle and lifted it to my ear.

"Hello," he said in a voice that made my skin crawl. He took another step into the room. A lion stalking prey.

Trouble.

"Aren't you going to say hello back?" he asked, taking another careful step. He'd reached the edge of the couch I'd slept on.

I swallowed. "Hello," I answered. Obedience was a wicked thing.

The man's smile widened. "See?" he said. "That wasn't so hard now, was it?"

I pressed my lips together and tightened my grip on the pan. The man's eyes shifted from my own to my weapon, and he frowned. "Put that thing down, will you?"

"No," I growled, surprised at my tone.

"Oh," he said, with a mocking frown, "don't be like that."

The muscles in my shoulders trembled with fear. The man took another step forward, and his features came into focus. He looked hungry.

"What do you want?"

"I want to be your friend."

"Stop," I said, frustrated at my tone of fear. "Don't come any closer."

"But why?" he asked. His eyes traveled now, drifting from my gaze, down my neck, to my chest. I knew no good came from a gaze like that. "You don't want to be my friend?"

I took a hurried breath, wishing I could cover myself. The way his eyes traveled down to my hips, across my legs, and back up to my eyes made me feel naked. Vulnerable. Like the first time I'd laid with Andrew. He met my eyes again, taking another step; he was halfway past the couch and closing in.

"No," I said, adjusting my grip, palms burning against the metal handle. I could see him more clearly now — the way his blue eyes were glazed over and bloodshot, like Andrew's got sometimes when he'd had too much whiskey. There was something wrong with him. Maybe I could use it to my advantage.

I moved, taking an urgent step to the left. The man tried to match my move, but failed miserably, steadying himself on the side of the couch. The faint scent of alcohol drifted up as he met my gaze again.

He was drunk.

"Where're you going?" he asked.

There was no use in answering again. With the pan still in my hand, I darted to the right. The man's feigned friend-liness dissipated, and he growled, attempting to scale the back of the couch separating us. His foot tangled with the cushions, and he fell forward, his body contorted in the fabric. I watched him over my shoulder, hurrying to the door, letting the pan go slack in my hands. I just needed to get down to Chance, and we could take off — the man would be hard-pressed to catch up with a *horse*.

But my thought ended there. Outside the door stood

another man — tall, bald, and much more coordinated. He wrapped his arm around my neck, pulling me into his chest with little effort. I screamed this time, mostly from shock and then again from fear. The man ripped the pan from my fingers before I could fix my grip, letting it clatter to the floor of the garage. From the corner of my eye, I watched Chance startle at the sound and flee through the open garage door.

"No!" I cried, my voice weakened by the arm across my throat. I writhed in the man's arms, struggling to catch my breath, fingers grasping at his meaty forearm that kept me prisoner. He smelled of body odor and earth, and even through my struggle, I could sense he was making little effort to hold me where I was.

"Ernie?" the man called into the room. Red-faced and sweaty, the shorter man made his way to the door, rubbing his shoulder.

"Fucking bitch." He spat on the ground beside the taller man's shoe. I winced at his words, scrunching my nose up as his face came clearer into the light. His patchy facial hair revealed cratered skin. A red and yellow cold sore had cracked open on the side of his dry lips, which his tongue absentmindedly licked.

"I thought you were lookin' for gas," the tall man said.

The man named Ernie gestured wildly toward me.

"I caught her," the tall man answered. "Not you."

"Scared her out the door, didn't I?" Ernie said.

"She was already on her way out, you useless ass."

"Fuck you, Lee."

"I'll leave you here," the man named Lee said, tightening his grip around my neck. "C'mon." He adjusted his grip and dragged me toward the stairs.

I tried to think but found I could only focus my attention on continuing to breathe, which was becoming harder by the second. He pulled me down the stairs, arm tightening with each step. My temple began to tighten, eyes bulging in their sockets. By the time we were at the bottom, I was seeing stars.

"Alright," Lee said. He shifted, releasing my neck. I gasped for a breath as his hand glided down my back, hovering just above the hem of my jeans. Until now, I'd never considered how thin my shirt's fabric was. I flinched away from his touch, uncomfortable and filled with shame. He moved his fingers, fumbling with something I couldn't see. But moments later, something cold jammed against my back.

He leaned his head down, lips flush against my ear, and I closed my eyes, wincing. Waiting. "You feel that?" he asked, letting it travel up and down my spine. I shivered and felt his cheeks rise into a grin. "That's a gun, sweetheart. So don't do anything stupid."

Panic found me, rising into my stomach and up my throat like bile. I should fight. I should at least try to break free of my captors. But what choice did I have? No weapons were at my disposal, my horse had run off, and the last of my supplies remained upstairs in my forgotten canvas bag. I had no chance.

I glanced back up at the room where I'd slept, cheeks flushing at the thought I'd had. That this place had been a gift from God. That I'd somehow find Eli and the others.

Foolish girl.

4

ELI

I REMINISCED on what sleep was like in the old world. How calm used to settle over me on a warm summer afternoon when there was nothing to do and nowhere to go. How easy it had once been to close my eyes and fall into slumber. I missed that kind of safety.

I rolled my neck, wincing as my ear scraped against tree bark; a far cry from the pillow I'd left behind at Mom's. With a sigh, I opened a bleary eye, glancing at our surroundings, the itch of frustration impossible to scratch. The sun streamed down on the trees above us, filtering through the leaves to dance across the forest floor. A gentle breeze wove its way through the branches, making them creak and snap as they shifted weight.

Holli moved beside me, bumping up against my sore shoulder as she snoozed against the tree behind us. The red in her hair had faded to gray since I'd first met her, now tied back behind her neck in a short ponytail. Purple bruises sat beneath her puffy eyes, and — even through sleep — she absentmindedly massaged her thigh.

A small stream flowed a few feet away, where my

brother through adoption, Sid, sat hunched on a rock, a folded piece of faded paper in his lap. Sweat gleamed on his dark, muscular shoulders, sunlight catching on the single diamond in his left ear. Beside him stood six-year-old Mia, her blonde pigtails bouncing as she dipped her toes in and out of the stream, hands gripped tight on her pants so they wouldn't touch the water.

I closed my eyes to see if sleep still waited for me, but it was already gone, and getting it back seemed like a chore in itself. Bringing myself to my feet, the bones in my spine cracked as I straightened, rolling my shoulders to relieve the stiffness in my body. I wasn't old — twenty-four still counted as young — but the exertion this trip demanded from us was wreaking havoc on my muscles. We needed to find a camp, and soon.

"How was your nap?" Sid asked, not looking up, his voice tinged with sarcasm.

"Spectacular," I answered with a groan.

I peered over his shoulder. He held a map we'd taken from Mom's — our original camp we were forced to leave after Maura Coutts upended our lives. After rescuing her from the creek, the Coutts Hunters sniffed us out, cornering us at the edge of their commune. Luckily, she'd returned to her people, leaving us alive but nearly empty-handed.

"I figure we're somewhere here," Sid said, drawing a circle with his index finger over a green area. "The office building was here." He pointed to a spot south of where he'd circled. "And I want to get here." He traced his finger northwest to a cluster of streets.

"What's there?"

He looked up at me, his brown eyes soft in the sunlight. "I passed through here when I came from L.A. Stayed in one of those Coutts halfway houses. It was still connected to the water grid back then."

I nodded. "You think it's still standing?"

He shrugged. "You got a better idea?"

I did not. Though isolation was ideal for hiding from the Hunters, it also meant we weren't finding any fresh supplies.

"Alright. How long?"

"Gotta be another four miles into town, maybe one more into the neighborhood. We could make it before it gets dark. Sleep in a real bed." He glanced at Holli leaned up against the tree. "I think we deserve it."

I looked at Mia, who had turned her attention to scooping up a slippery frog. "We're getting low on pretty much everything," I whispered.

"I know." Sid grimaced. "If we find a car, maybe we can go back, but we've gotta make do with what we have. We've got food, water, and bullets to last us the week. For now, that's enough."

I glanced at Holli, taking a pained breath. The middle-aged widow had worked so hard to cultivate a careful selection of supplies that would keep us alive. She'd willingly shared her resources, skills, and harvests, only asking for her protection in return. Her garden had produced essential meals, her healing knowledge had saved us from scars and infection, and she'd kept Sid and me from murdering each other, which, in itself, was a hell of an accomplishment.

And I'd made one error in judgment that forced us to give it all up. I looked back at my boots, guilt weighing heavy on my heart. I had saved Maura from that creek because there hadn't been another option. She would've died, and I knew Holli understood that. Hell, I understood that, but it didn't stop me from feeling responsible for all we'd left behind.

It wasn't just the resources or Mom's house. We'd left Mom's gravesite behind, too. Though I considered myself well-equipped to survive in a world like this, it didn't make grief any easier. Out here, we were displaced. There was nowhere to return to. We'd lost the place we called home.

"I'm serious, Eli. We can't worry about that now," Sid said, finding my gaze. "Okay?"

I nodded, pressing my lips together. But how long could we keep this up? Summer's heat would fizzle out in only a few weeks' time, and soon we'd be heading into cooler seasons. The farther north we headed, the colder the climate would get. Without a stockpile of food or Holli's healing remedies, winter was becoming a looming death trap.

"Eli! Sid!" Mia cried, her tiny hands clutching a struggling frog. She shook him at us. "Look!" Her grin widened as she held out her prize.

"You *got* him?" Sid opened his mouth in shock.

She nodded enthusiastically, her eyes bulging as she inspected her new friend.

"Remember when you were afraid of frogs?" Sid asked, nudging me on the shoulder. I frowned. During a hike with Mom, I'd fallen headfirst into a bog and gotten a mouthful of lily pads. When I'd tried to stand up, a frog had attacked — though Sid said it was just jumping away from me — filling me with an unwavering fear of amphibians until I was a teenager.

"Shut up."

"Bring it over here!" Sid encouraged Mia, and she darted forward, frog clutched tight in her grip. I recoiled, and Sid laughed so hard he woke Holli up.

BY THE TIME we reached the edge of town, the clouds had shifted from wispy white to an angry gray. Moisture filled the air with sticky humidity. The sour stench of our collective odor stung my nostrils and turned my stomach. Mia whined occasionally, bouncing along Sid's back, her head nestled against his neck, thumb stuck between her teeth. We were *all* ready to be done with this leg of our journey.

I couldn't help but be intrigued by what we were about to find. Wealth outside the Coutts commune was rare, and those who'd had money had kept to themselves in the Midwest. The Coutts Family used that to their advantage by creating a collection of what they called halfway homes commercialized to the *curious believer*. The living spaces were some of the best marketing tools the Coutts ever created. They bulldozed old towns to stand up a bunch of McMansions, with mowed lawns and white picket fences to give Outsiders the privilege to experience the luxuries the Coutts commune had to offer.

Living in poverty was an exhausting crusade. Lack of money kept us tired and unable to ask too many questions, while the absence of adequate medical care kept us too sick to fight for our basic rights. We lived frugally, scrounging together what we could for meals. Sid, Mom, and I were better off than most. There were families who lived beneath bridges, under tarps stapled to PVC pipes. There were people who died of starvation, thirst, and pneumonia. To be pulled from that reality into a cushy Coutts halfway home with access to anything you could dream of would've been enough for many people to justify their choice to join the Coutts, even if they didn't buy into their beliefs.

Though time had woven her way through these

streets, the town didn't fit with the world I knew. Its brick buildings had only experienced recent neglect. A two-way paved road ran through the center of the small town, complete with faded yellow and white lines. Concrete sidewalks ran the length of each side, with square clusters of dirt from which individual trees grew. The only new evidence of neglect was small sidewalk cracks, where the dandelions grew sideways, stretching towards the sun.

Various retail stores, including a small boutique and an organic food store, lined the street we walked. This place hadn't been free from looters, though — piles of glass in front of the shops unlucky enough to be broken into sparkled in the waning sunlight. Dead leaves and debris — remnants of another life — covered the sides of the sidewalks and cluttered up the sewers, forming shallow ponds of water.

The row of shops ended in a T at a small schoolhouse, promising education for grades K-12. A photo of Peter Coutts hung above the front door. Someone had taken a knife to it, leaving his smiling face in shreds, flapping in the occasional breeze as it drifted by.

We were silent as we walked, our footsteps echoing off the brick. I tried to imagine my life here. What it would have been like if we'd had all those resources for a better life. Mom had done her best. She'd worked her ass off to provide for her two children. And she did well as a young, single mother because she knew how to stretch her dollar. But things changed drastically as time wore on, and Peter gained more power and influence. When I'd woken up to the realities of adulthood, my outlook had been so bleak I'd turned to things that had almost killed me. Though we didn't talk about specifics, I knew Sid had been no different out in LA. It was easier to numb ourselves. If I was honest, for a while, I thought it had been the only way to survive.

"Almost there," Sid said, leading us down a road to the left, marked by a sign that read *Creek Hill Community* in wide, gold letters. Beneath, in a black script, read *A Coutts Family Endeavor.*

Dogwood trees lined the road, their dead blossoms covering almost every square inch of pavement. It was a good indicator that nobody had entered this neighborhood recently, though logic also warned me nothing was ever definitive.

We made our way through the layer of flowers, careful not to disturb them too much. It felt wrong to stomp through such a beautiful neighborhood with the state of us — smelly and dirty, some of us with blood on our hands. We did not belong here. We belonged back at Mom's.

Two-or three-story Colonial-style homes, stone paths, and picket fences lined the long street. It looked like a scene straight out of a movie — like it couldn't possibly be a real place outside of the Coutts commune. I expected the community to be trashed, or at least a little more worn, but most of the windows remained intact, the front doors shut tight. Identical trash cans sat at the end of a few driveways, overflowing with garbage bags that were never collected — a hopeless wish to maintain normalcy.

I hated how exposed we were. We were already weak — low on food, weapons, and water and I feared an ambush would eliminate us completely. I kept a hand on the gun at my hip, reassured by Sid's presence beside me. He held his gun at the ready, eyes darting from house to house.

I watched the windows, too — certain I would see a head pop out or hear the shock bang of a bullet in the distance. But only nature seemed to permeate the space

— the low hum of crickets and mosquitos and the gentle sway of the trees.

"It seems empty," I whispered, afraid to make too much noise.

"That's a good thing," Sid grumbled. "People tend to stay away from these neighborhoods. Too worried the Coutts will show up — collect what's theirs."

"Should we be worried about that?"

"We should be more worried about rest and supplies." He kept his voice low so Mia and Holli wouldn't hear. But the weight of his words made me nauseous. Sid was just as aware of the danger ahead of us as I was. There was no way around it. We were running on fumes and desperately needed rest, even if that meant not making the safest decisions.

Sid paused at an intersection, pointing to a two-story home on the corner, its foundation overgrown with neglected landscaping. A high fence rose around back — a necessary line of defense — and it faced all roads leading in. The perfect vantage point.

"This is it," he said, rolling his neck.

Holli hunched over, hands on her knees, before looking at Sid.

"Go around back with Mia," Sid continued, turning his back toward Holli. "Eli and I will search the interior, and we'll let you know when it's clear," he said as she reached for the young girl, peeling her off of his back. Mia whined but curled up into Holli's arms anyway.

Holli was never one to complain. She had made it clear over the last few months we were not to be gentle with her. She held her own — she could survive with or without us. And we both knew that neither of us would've lasted this long without her. But her exhaustion in that moment was palpable. It was the first time I'd given much thought to her aging body.

"Thank you," she whispered, throwing me a guilty but knowing smile as she gently rocked Mia. I nodded, pulling my gun from its holster to get familiar with its weight.

"We're a team," I told her. "We get through this together."

She nodded, moving toward the back gate, her walk slow and unhurried. I faced my brother, and he grimaced, wiping sweat from his forehead with dirty fingers.

"You good?"

I grunted indifferently. "I'm alive and awake and ready to cover your sorry ass."

"Good." He nodded towards the front door. "Let's go."

Sid and I entered a front foyer with wooden floors and a threaded rug beneath a gold chandelier. A set of wooden stairs led to the second-floor balcony. A formal dining room sat to our left and a small sitting room to our right. In that brief moment, I fondly thought of Mom's torn-up recliner. It was used and loved unlike the untouched, dust-covered furniture here.

I kept both hands gripped around my handgun, straining my ears for any sign of danger as we took careful steps inward. Sid jutted his chin towards the stairs, and I nodded, understanding he'd take the upper floor while I secured the bottom. We parted ways, and I entered a dark hallway beside the stairs, careful to open each door quietly — one to an empty coat closet, the other to a small bathroom.

The hallway spilled into a large kitchen with a sliding glass door that led to the backyard. I pulled the blinds aside, glimpsing an angry purple and gray sky. Holli and Mia sat on a cushioned lounge chair, both pointing toward the clouds, whispering something unheard to each other.

Same as the front of the house, the kitchen looked like it had been built and left abandoned. I searched a small pantry — laughably empty — and another room off the kitchen with a desk and a small bookshelf. There were no framed family photos or trinkets that seemed personal to someone who may have lived here. This place was a tomb. The final resting place of meaningless things that would collect dust and take up space.

"Eli?" Sid called, and I returned to the hallway to peer up at the balcony. Dressed in black, gun slung across his back, his dark face smeared with dirt, Sid looked like an imposter in a castle. "Good?"

I nodded. "Empty."

Visible tension melted from his chest as he descended the stairs. Together, we collected the girls from outside, the air cooling as it began to drizzle. I tried not to think too hard about the garden we'd left behind — the thirsty raspberry bushes or bell pepper plants drinking up the water they sorely needed as the summer lingered on.

With Holli and Mia asleep upstairs, Sid and I collected pots, pans, bowls, trash cans, plastic containers, and even the empty ash bucket for a fireplace I doubt had ever been used. We placed them all outside on the deck to capture rainwater. My body ached in places I didn't know it could — the soles of my feet were numb, and my back and shoulders were sore from my pack.

The skies opened up as I carried the containers outside, and I welcomed the freshwater against my sun-scorched skin. Showers had become such a distant thing of the past, no matter how many times we tried to jerry-rig buckets of warm water. Without much thought, I shed my clothes on the steps to the porch, stripping free of my boxers and socks. Cold rain lapped at my skin, and though I cared

little about modesty, I went around the side of the porch, pressing my hands against the siding.

The thick, sharp smell of sweat rose as the rain washed away dirt from my skin, sinking into my scalp and pores. With my head tilted forward, I watched the water drip from my hair to feed the muddy ground, removing some of the grime still clinging to me.

We were safe for tonight, a strange feeling after being on the run for almost a week. It was time to rest. And though that should've come with some relief, danger still lurked in my peripherals. We were lost. There was no camp to return to, no certainty we would find food or supplies.

Thunder rumbled in the distance. A warning. I glanced down at my bruised body, a patchwork of survival in this strange world. My body had served me well, but that wouldn't last forever. I thought of Holli. Of how tired she'd been when we'd gotten here. How another trip like this might damage her beyond repair. I hoped we could last here long enough to at least give her adequate time to recover.

"You crazy asshole!" Sid's voice caught me off guard, and I looked up, rain splattering across my cheeks and into my eyes. He grinned at me from the porch railing and threw me a towel, already wet from the rain. "Your ass cheeks are gonna get struck by lightning."

"Worth it!" I answered, wrapping the towel around my waist. Sid shook his head, retreating into the house, and I followed, scooping up my wet clothes on the way.

5

———

ELI

Hail pounded the roof through the night and into the morning. The bedrooms in the house were too empty, too *pristine* to sleep well, so Sid and I slept on leather furniture in the living room under the guise of keeping watch. His snores comforted me into a deep sleep, like when we were children.

I woke to a pink sunrise, the early morning sun spilling across the wood floors and creeping up the white walls. Sid dozed in his seat, head tilted against his shoulder, his gun within careful reach on the floor. A clink in the kitchen followed by a stifled giggle forced me upright, and I straightened, stretching in an effort to ease the tense muscles in my back.

After shaking sleep away, I ventured to the kitchen, where Holli and Mia sat at the center island, slapping each other's hands.

"Morning, ladies," I greeted them. Mia slapped Holli's hand, which she snatched backward, making the little girl erupt into a fit of giggles.

"Shh!" Holli laughed. "You'll wake up Sid."

"Oh man," I said with mock concern. "You *definitely* don't want to do that." Mia gave me a mischievous smile before hopping off her stool and darting down the hallway.

"Sleep okay?" Holli asked, searching my face.

I shrugged. "Enough. You?"

"Been up a few hours with Mia." Her jovial grin turned to a troubled frown. "Nightmares."

"She okay?"

Holli forced a laugh. "Come on. We left everything she's ever known, Eli." She studied my expression. "But she's resilient. She's alive. And she'll survive this, just like the rest of us."

I leaned against the island, resting my head in my hands, following a pattern in the marble.

"There's something else," she said, pulling my attention back.

"What?" The thought of another problem made me want to flee, to run back to Mom's and hide beneath the covers of her bed. Leaving our home behind highlighted the child still lingering within me.

Holli slid off her seat and guided me towards the office off the kitchen. The sun had risen higher in the sky, making the room golden, sunlight reflecting off the dusty wooden surfaces of the desk, bookshelf, and floor. Our backpacks sat empty against the far wall. Holli had removed all the supplies we'd carried from Mom's. We'd left a lot in the truck we were forced to leave behind, unable to pack too much to maintain our stamina.

There were a few boxes of bullets, two hunting rifles, one revolver, one pistol, and a tattered medical kit. Each of us had a change of clothes, a water bottle, and a knife. Sid's compass, Holli's collection of jars filled with herbal remedies, a faded map, three bottles of iodine for water purification, and a large baggie filled with other essentials — matches, flashlights, batteries, duct tape, and various tools were the only other things sitting on the rug beside our stock of food.

This was it. All we had left in the world. I raised my gaze to meet Holli's worried one. The line between her brows deepened as she tried to read my expression.

"There's nothing else?"

She shook her head, glancing back at the pile of food. "If we stay put, we have enough for a few days at best," she said. "Maybe longer if we stretch it. But—"

"We can't move right now. We need a plan."

Incoming footsteps alerted me to the door. Sid stuck his head in and grinned at us. "Which one of you sent the little hellion in to wake me up?" Holli and I frowned, and Sid's smile faded. "What's up?"

I stepped aside, revealing our remaining supplies on the floor. Sid took inventory, eyes darting from object to object, his features tightening as he came to the same realization.

"Okay," he said, glancing at me. "We'll scavenge the nearby houses and whatever's left in town."

I nodded, though fear gripped me tight. It was one thing to not have our creature comforts — our familiar beds, lush garden, chicken coop, and even the outhouse. But no food meant hunger, which led to starvation, weakness, and death. It was a fate I refused to resign us to. We had survived this long. The idea of perishing because we couldn't scrounge up a can of food made my stomach roll.

"Thirty minutes," Sid ordered, slipping out of the room.

I met Holli's gaze again and tried to smile through my worry. "It'll be okay," I reassured her. "We can figure this out."

She nodded, but I knew she wasn't convinced. I wasn't sure I was, either.

———

Sid emerged from beneath a heavy garage door, his dark skin gleaming with sweat. His lips curled into a smile and I looked up from where I sat on the curb, head tilted in curiosity.

"Look at this shit," he said, holding up a box of bullets. "Just sitting in the trunk of the car." He shook his head.

"Any *food*?" I stressed, stomach gurgling. We'd found only two cans so far — old tuna and garbanzo beans, whatever they were.

"A win is a win," Sid said, plopping down beside me as he shrugged his backpack off. Carefully, he placed the faded box of bullets inside. They looked old and dusty — there was a chance the gunpowder had already lost its potency, but I held my tongue. Sid was right. Considering the positives was important when we were down on our luck.

My hunger was beginning to gnaw at me, however — eating away at my patience and slowing my instincts. I was glad the entire neighborhood seemed empty. My reflexes were not at their best. I regretted ever taking our food supply for granted.

"We should split up," I suggested, eyeing the street that led into the small town. "It'll be faster that way."

Sid zipped up his pack and ran his hands up and down his face before dropping his head to look at me. "Yeah," he agreed. "You want to finish the rest of the houses, and I'll head into town? I can meet you back by the schoolhouse when we're done."

I nodded, groaning as I got to my feet. Despite the rest

we'd gotten, everything still ached. Our journey had not been kind to our bodies. We needed rest. But rest without food wasn't possible, so I pushed my discomfort to the back of my mind, heading toward the next house.

Sid saluted me before he hoisted his backpack up and over his shoulders again and took off in the distance. I walked slowly, watching him, before he disappeared at the end of the street, turning into town.

The next few houses were staged like the others, some with signs of a past life, some filled with dusty furniture and display pieces that once meant luxury. China stacked in glass cupboards, crystal chandeliers, and even fake bowls of fruit on marble kitchen counters. The whole idea of this place made me angry — they showcased their wealth and access to luxuries to people who couldn't even afford basic things to survive.

Though we had never taken the Coutts up on their offers, I couldn't blame the people who had. These houses were remnants of a world the generation before us once had. This was a taste of the other side, where the grass was actually greener. Even now, imagining myself living here, I remember how persuasive the Coutts propaganda had once been. How they'd dangled medications and clean water as an enticement for joining their cause. My heart ached in appreciation for Mom, how she'd kept us level-headed and managed our expectations our entire child-hood. She'd never given in.

I scoured house after house, dumping drawers and cleaning out garages and basements for anything left behind. I found a four-pack of sardines, a half-finished jar of peanut butter, a bottle of hydrogen peroxide, towels, toothpaste, and rope. Seven of the houses had nothing worth taking. I finally dipped into my food stash, allowing myself two handfuls of stale granola for lunch before I headed into the last house on the street.

The stench hit me as soon as I walked through the door — a sharp rot that had sunk into the walls, floors, and fabric of the place. A reminder that nothing was ever as it seemed. My shoulders tightened as I reached into my pack for a bandana to cover my nose, the same one I'd used to blindfold Maura.

Cautiously, I entered, leaving the front door open to the summer air, my focus sharpened by the idea of entering a tomb. Dead bodies were meant to rest. But the dead had no use for the things the living needed. Why let it go to waste?

To my immense relief, the downstairs was free of corpses, and I let the tension in my shoulders go slack as I entered the kitchen, rolling my sore neck, before I saw the small kitchen table in the corner of the room.

Food. Soup cans, more beans, three bags of rice, a carton of granola bars, and six bags of jerky. A small medical kit and a half-drank bottle of gin were beside a matchbook and mud-splattered lantern. A relieved sob escaped my lips as I stumbled toward the resources we so badly needed. If I'd believed in God, I would've thanked him.

I left my backpack on the kitchen chair; handgun gripped tight in my fist. Fear of a corpse was silly, but I couldn't help it. No matter how many times I encountered death, it never got easier. I could walk away, of course, but bodies with an odor meant fresher supplies. And if there was anything beneficial, it might mean life or death for us. I was responsible for three other lives. I needed to check.

As I climbed the stairs, the sour smell wafted through the thin fabric over my nose, but I pushed forward, hand at my hip, though I knew there was no threat. A narrow hallway led to different rooms. Based on the smell, I knew what lay behind the doors at the end. I tried to ignore my growing dread, but it settled like a bull on my chest as I searched through the bathroom and two empty bedrooms.

When there was nothing left but the room, I approached the doors. I could flee. No one would know I hadn't searched. But the pull of potential kept me rooted to the spot. My hand hovered over the door handle before I took a deep breath, held it, and pushed inside.

Two bodies lay in the bed, huddled beneath blankets — a gracious gift. Someone had pulled an extra mattress onto the floor, where another two huddled masses lay. My footsteps faltered, and I tried not to focus on the bodies. Four people, just like us. They had tried to survive but perhaps didn't feel it was worth the effort anymore. Or they'd gotten sick, which would've been even worse.

I tried hard to push the glimmer of resentment away. The temptation of eternal sleep had called to me many times, especially after Mom had died. There was something serene about seeing a body lie so still, breathing ceased. They no longer had to care, no longer had to fight to satiate their most human needs. They were at peace. And that was something we all craved at our very core.

On the table beside the bed lay a handgun with two bullets and three empty prescription pill bottles. I picked one up, turning the opaque blue container to read the label.

Demerol.

My eyes widened. Opiates? Access to this kind of drug was unheard of, though I supposed anything was possible in this little Coutts hideaway. But these people had recently died — not before the plague. I glanced at the mounds on the bed. How had they gotten prescription painkillers?

A shot rang out in the distance, muffled through the trees and the windows, and I dropped the bottle, heart racing. Sunlight filtered through the curtained window, warming the corpses' blue soles.

Sid.

Without another thought, I ran from the room, down the stairs, and out the door.

6

ELI

I RAN TOWARD TOWN. Anxiety made the world too big and bright and the street too long. My chest burned from exertion as I turned the corner out of the neighborhood, retracing the steps we'd taken to get here. The thuds of my feet hitting the pavement matched my pounding heartbeat in my ears.

A shot didn't necessarily mean danger. Perhaps Sid had shot an animal for dinner. But as I entered the town, I wasn't greeted by my brother's triumphant face, grinning at me from the sidewalk, holding his bloody prize high. If Sid had gotten fresh meat, he'd be the first to shout about it.

Eerie silence followed me down the street. Yesterday, the town had seemed like a refuge, but now, it felt like a death trap. Had someone watched us arrive? Had they waited for us to come out to look for supplies? All it took was one sniper shot to take me out for good. The thought of leaving Mia and Holli alone plagued me, so I clung to the sides of the buildings, keeping a steady grip on my handgun.

I was too exposed, but I couldn't stop imagining Sid lying in a pool of his own blood. Careful not to disturb the broken glass scattered around sidewalks, I entered the first few shops, eyes scanning the dark interiors for any sign of life. My chest tightened as my search of the first few shops turned up empty.

I gulped a breath and tried desperately to hold my panic at bay before entering the next store — some boutique promising sustainable cleaning products. My heart pounded like it was going to burst from my chest. Even if he was hurt, Sid would've heard me coming and announced his presence by now. Not hearing his deep voice made my throat dry.

Neatly stacked cleaning products sat on some of the shelves, organized by size. Debris and signage covered the shop floors, sticky from the promised product on the shop's welcoming sign.

"Sid?" I hissed into the small space, my voice bouncing off the walls.

Silence.

I took another step forward, boots crunching against shattered glass. The sound brought fire to my senses, and I spun around slowly as if expecting someone to appear through the shadows.

No one emerged. I sensed I was alone, as badly as I didn't want to. That meant Sid was gone or, worse, lying dead somewhere, and it had been my fault for suggesting we split up. Frantic panic erupted in my chest.

"Sid?" I cried.

Silence.

I surrendered my stealthiness, scrambling through the store, looking for a clue, signs of a struggle, anything that explained where he'd gone.

"Sid?" I yelled this time, overwhelmed by the fear of Sid

being dead. "SID?" My heart beat in my throat, my chest on fire, fear bubbling in my stomach until it overflowed into full-blown panic. My mind raced, ping-ponging between the need to be quiet and the need to find my brother. So what if someone heard? Let them. Let them come out so I could question them. So I could *hurt* them. I couldn't lose Sid. Losing Sid meant…

The familiar feeling of helplessness overtook me as I reached the back of the store. A window faced a gated, brick courtyard. I squinted, my heart leaping as I saw the gate's iron latch unhooked. A door behind the register led me outside and down brick stairs.

A dumpster sat in a corner, two chairs beside it, but the rest of the space was empty. And then, I saw it. Sid's single diamond earring sparkling in the sun, still attached to part of an earlobe, lying in a pool of blood.

I COULDN'T BRING myself back to the house. Having to face Holli and tell her I'd failed Sid, that he was lost or potentially *dead* was the worst thing I could imagine. Our group was small enough as it was. Losing a crucial member of our team not only hindered us but might condemn us to death. Our marksman, our protector, the man we relied on to hunt for food, to prep our guns, to fight for us 'til the death, was gone.

Gone.

The heavy guilt I'd carried with me for so long grew, following like an unwelcome companion as I dragged my heavy feet back to the house. I convinced myself Sid wasn't dead. How could he be? His larger-than-life presence made it impossible to imagine. Sid was a survivor. He could be violent if he needed to be. He was smart. The guy could weasel his way out of anything.

I spent the rest of the afternoon digging through dumpsters and wandering through basements, looking for fresh blood, hoping he'd hidden from whatever or whoever attacked him. But the town was empty, silent, and still. And that scared me more than anything.

Nothing but endless forest stood beyond the main road, and though part of me wondered if I could search there to find a clue or someone with answers, I knew the journey would be futile. I could no longer ignore my exhaustion or the fading sunlight. My pace was unsustainable, and I feared for my safety. If both Sid and I didn't come back, Holli and Mia would be at risk. I needed to return to them before dark.

My thoughts consumed me as I left the town behind. I hadn't found his head or a limb. I'd simply found an earlobe. If anyone could survive something like that, it was Sid. The lack of blood in town was also encouraging. A mortal gun wound would have produced liters of blood. That meant he'd either crawled off to somewhere I couldn't find him — unlikely — or someone had taken him.

I trudged down the street, the house looming ahead as the last remnants of dusk fell away. The onset of night transformed the neighborhood, filling once bright spaces with shadows darkened by tree cover. I approached the door, hands curling around the straps of the backpack filled with supplies I'd found — necessities — but at what cost?

A light flickered behind drawn curtains like a lost firefly, and I tried hard not to think of Holli pacing back and forth across the front foyer, worried. She would be. There was no way around that. There was no way around delivering my bad news, either.

Before I turned the doorknob, Holli threw the door open, candle in one hand, the other on her hip. Deep purple circles puffed beneath her swollen eyes, and the familiar weight of guilt and shame threatened to bury me on the spot. I felt like a scolded child, coming back hours after curfew, like someone with something to hide.

But I knew Holli. She wasn't there to scold me. As I stepped forward, she ushered me in, eyes scanning the distance, expecting Sid to follow. When she met my eyes, I shook my head, careful to keep my face stoic.

"What happened?" she asked, closing the door.

I shook my head. "We split up," I croaked, my voice hoarse from yelling all afternoon. "He took the town, and I took the houses. I heard a gunshot, so I took off, but by the time I got there—"

Holli's features stiffened.

"I don't think he's dead," I grumbled, reaching into my pocket. My only intent in picking up the piece of flesh had been to show Holli. I wrapped it in a piece of paper I'd found behind one of the store counters, staining it crimson. I unwrapped the bloody package for Holli, holding it in my hands like some precious heirloom. "I found this."

She gasped before looking back up at me, eyes wide with worry.

"I know," I said, wrapping it back up.

"And you looked—?"

"Everywhere. And now in the dark…"

Holli nodded in understanding, her gaze far away, before she put her arm on my back and guided me toward the kitchen. "Come on then," she said. "Mia and I made dandelion tea. Want some?"

The gesture was small, but it was her own way of processing the news. We had been gone all day, missed the unspoken curfew of sunset, and only one of us had returned. I took protecting this group seriously, but we all did in our own ways. Sid was the muscle. I was the planner. And Holli was the one who kept us all healthy and level-headed. No matter where we were, she filled our group with warmth. She reminded us of our humanity. She'd never had kids of her own, but she'd have made a great mother. She helped fill the deep hole Mom's death had left behind.

We sat in silence in the kitchen, sipping earthy tea from a pair of coffee cups Holli and Mia had found. Crowns and bracelets made from threaded flower stems lay scattered across the counter — remnants of a tea party. Mia had probably been in heaven. My heart ached as I thought of having to explain Sid's absence to the young girl.

"Eli." Holli searched my face, pulling her mouth tight as if unsure of what to say next.

"He's out there," I said with certainty. "We have to find him." She nodded slowly, but I could see the wheels turning. "We don't have a choice," I stressed. *I can't keep you both alive by myself,* I wanted to say. *I can't do this without him.*

"Tomorrow, we'll go back to town," she said, fingers tapping against the ceramic cup. "We'll look for clues, something that could tell us where he's gone. Okay?"

"And then what?" I pushed. "What if there's nothing?"

"Then we'll keep looking." I could sense the *but*, the urge she felt to maintain my expectations, but was relieved when she ended the sentence there.

"Fuck," I said, pushing the tea away and placing my head in my hands. There was no solution, but it didn't stop my brain from trying to find one. I had to fix this. There had to be a way. The alternative was unthinkable.

"You should get some sleep," Holli pressed, touching her fingers to my wrist.

I peered at her from between my fingers. With Sid missing, I knew sleep would never come.

"You go," I said. "I'll stay down here. I can't…" I stopped before my voice broke.

"Eli." Holli looked on the verge of tears too. "This isn't your fault."

I stared at her, studying her wrinkles, the dark sun spots on her skin, and the way her brows furrowed. Did she really believe that? Or was it something she was saying to me to ease my pain?

"You've got to stop blaming yourself for things," she whispered, easing her chair back and stood. She squeezed my shoulder and gave me a sad smile before leaving the kitchen. After a moment, I got up and followed her.

I settled in the living room again, avoiding the leather recliner where Sid had slept the night before. The candle Holli left on the coffee table flickered off the white walls and over the framed generic artwork hung on the walls. I tried keeping my thoughts away from Sid, instead inspecting each piece of furniture, how many small intricate details were threaded into the rug, and even picking up the ostentatious coffee table book that outlined the Coutts Family's history and accomplishments throughout generations.

I flipped through its thick pages, filled with black-and-white photographs of the Coutts men that had come before Peter. They had sold so many pieces of propaganda like this, likely to counteract the many stories not painting them in a favorable light. Money and power guarantee you can drown those things out with showpieces like this, casually reminding onlookers *hey, we're not so bad.*

It made me think of Maura. I hoped she was safe and free from punishment. I hoped they had given her grace. She deserved that, at the very least. But I knew deep in my heart that she'd likely been punished for staying with us — for even getting swept up in the creek in the first place.

Saving Maura had been instinctual but also a complicated event that spun our lives out of control. I hadn't meant any of us any harm, but in my pursuit of being a savior, I'd displaced my entire group and caused Maura a lot of pain. I couldn't help but wonder if I'd actually saved anyone at all.

7

MAURA

A GRAY PICKUP truck was parked outside the garage door, with a mud-splattered frame and paint peeling from its edges. The mangled front bumper was squished in on one side, where it met a broken headlight. A blue tarp covered the truck bed, filled with various items I couldn't distinguish. Lee pushed me toward the driver's side door, the gun still pressed up against my spine.

"Get in," he ordered. I eyed his pale, shaved head and narrow nose. He looked like he'd never smiled a day in his life, like the world had been so unjust to him that he'd simply never learned.

With no other option, I pulled the door open and climbed past the steering wheel and into the single bench seat. Though the windows were open, the truck reeked of body odor and alcohol. I breathed through my mouth as I considered my options. I'd never driven a vehicle before. Perhaps I could pull at the steering wheel and make us crash. But that risked my wellbeing, and I couldn't run, let alone survive out here, if I was injured.

Ernie clambered in through the passenger side door,

breaking me from my thoughts. Despite his prior anger, he now looked like a giddy child, excited by a new toy. He looked at me in that same way, wetting his lips with his stubby tongue as though he wanted to unwrap me. Nauseated, I closed my eyes as Lee got into the driver's seat, cramming me in the middle.

"We can drive back around to the rest of town later," Lee said, his gun still gripped in his left hand, aimed at me over his lap. He turned the key in the ignition, bringing the truck to life. "First, we'll get her situated." He pressed on the gas, lurching the vehicle forward. I pushed my hand out to steady myself as he peeled away from the fire department.

A bullet of panic rose in my chest as the town whipped by. I thought of Chance, spooked and alone in the forest beyond. Emotion welled in my throat, and I worked furiously to swallow it.

"Let me hold the gun," Ernie argued, leaning over my lap to grab the weapon. Lee and I both flinched, likely from the same fear that the drunken man would accidentally shoot us both.

"Abso-fuckin-lutely not."

Ernie stuck his middle finger at Lee before leaning back in his seat. He hiccuped, burped, then fumbled with something on the truck's floor. He produced a silver flask, unscrewed the top, then took a long swig of something that smelled sharp and foul — like whiskey, but worse. Ernie scrunched up his nose as he screwed the cap back on, releasing a sharp breath as he swallowed.

"Fuckin' moonshine," he said.

"You're a fuckin' alcoholic is what you are," Lee answered, his tone heavy with annoyance. "I don't even know why I bring you out anymore."

"Because *I'm* the entertainment," Ernie slurred, leaning

against the far window. "Some booze would do you good, man. You're too on edge. Two shots of moonshine and ten minutes with this one." He whistled. "That'll loosen you up good." He leaned into me, turning his nose into my cheek. "Bet you'd like that, wouldn't you?"

I recoiled, my shoulder bumping up against Lee's. He leered at me, and I straightened, pressing my back against the bench seat.

"One of us has to have our heads on straight. Otherwise, you'd be as good as dead. I bet you don't even know how to get back from here."

"Oh, shut up," Ernie retorted, his breath sour. "I could figure it out without ya."

The men's bickering turned to muffled noise as I worked hard to focus on my predicament. The pit in my stomach threatened to swallow me whole as I counted my failures. By now, there was likely a widespread manhunt after the incident at the barn. I'd lost my horse, my backpack, and Holli's marks. I'd already been uncertain about finding the group, but now, the task's impossibility made my insides curdle.

Tires screeched across pavement as Lee took a sharp turn out of town, taking the truck through grass and plowing past the sign I'd seen before entering Coal Creek. The truck groaned as we straightened on a new road, the engine humming as the truck sped up. Faster, then faster still, until the landscape outside the windows began to blur. I took a sharp breath and squeezed my eyes shut, frightened by the speed, terror combing through every nerve.

"Oh," Lee said with a gentle laugh. "I think she's scared."

"Think she might be," Ernie answered, so close I felt his warm breath on my face. "You scared, sweetheart?"

I pressed my lips together. I would not give them the

benefit of responding. Surely, this is what Father meant when he spoke of Outsiders and sin. These were the men he'd warned us of.

"Are you gonna *scream?*" Ernie chortled, his throat rattling with mucus.

The engine thrummed, whining as Lee continued to increase our speed. "Here," Ernie said. "I've got something to calm your nerves." I kept my eyes closed but heard him unscrewing the cap of his flask. He waved it beneath my nose, the aroma stinging my nostrils. "C'mon, girlie. Drink up. You'll be glad you did."

I opened one eye. Ernie pressed the flask's opening to my lips, his eyes fixated on my mouth. The wet metal made me want to gag. I pushed my head against the seat as far as it would go, but it wasn't enough. There was nowhere to go.

"Open up." He pushed it between my lips so the tin connected with my teeth. I kept them clamped together. "Oh, c'mon," he growled, eyes flashing with irritation. I looked up at him. Fear bubbled in my stomach, but I was frozen. Trapped. Alcohol was forbidden for women in the commune. I had never touched a drop in my life.

Ernie twisted the flask, and the grooved mouth slashed painfully against my gum. I tasted blood. On instinct, my teeth parted, and he took no time wasting his opportunity to force it inward. He tipped the small bottle, pouring pungent liquid into the back of my mouth. It burned, and I choked, dribbling some down my chin.

"Don't *waste* it!" Ernie pressed his hand against my lips, squeezing them against my teeth. His brows furrowed, nostrils flaring in frustration. He looked angry. Animalistic. Time seemed to slow. Trees flew by the windows, a blur of lush green. Lee's arm hung over the steering wheel, his features pulled up into a tight grin.

I wanted to spit it out, to bite his fingers, but before I could even attempt to, Ernie took his other hand and pinched my nose, cutting off my air supply. My eyes bulged, tears leaking from the corners at the vile taste and sudden lack of oxygen. Panic erupted in my limbs, and my heart took off, pounding wildly against my ribcage. I writhed in my seat, shifting my shoulders as I tried to pull away from his grip, but it was no use. I was sandwiched between the two men. Bile inched up my throat as I struggled with the liquid's burn sloshing in my mouth.

Against my own free will, I swallowed.

Fire coated my throat. I was sure whatever he'd poured into my mouth would burn holes into my flesh. It would kill me. It would rip apart my organs and fry my insides, destroy my vocal cords, my tastebuds, and tongue.

"That's it," Ernie said, giving me a wild grin. He clutched my cheeks in a vise grip and shook my head before releasing me. I gasped, gulping a breath before I started coughing. My chest burned. My cheeks flushed with shame. I could still feel the imprint of Ernie's dirty fingers on my mouth and nose. Lee laughed beside me, his foot still heavy on the gas, driving so fast I feared he no longer had control of the vehicle.

I tried forcing my tears back, fingers gripping the edge of the seat as I trembled. Did these men want to kill me? Or worse, did they know I was a Coutts? Were they going to force-feed me alcohol until I died? I thought of Eli and the first time we'd spoken, when he told me there were people out here who'd want me as bounty.

And they'd do worse things to you than not tell you where their camp was.

I had been so terrified of Eli's existence that I hadn't ever paused to consider how lucky I'd been to encounter someone kind. The incline shifted. Lee slowed the truck, and I forced myself to open my eyes again. The world spun, but I could just make out distant hills between the trees from Ernie's window.

"Call Hank," Lee said, guiding the truck up the crest of a hill. He glanced at Ernie, who grumbled something incoherent as he opened the glove compartment.

I leaned into Lee as he slowed the truck enough to turn, the items in the truck bed shifting with a loud clang. He pulled onto a dirt road lined with more pines that blinked out the sun. Wherever we were going was hidden away from the main road, possibly deep within the expansive forest that covered these hills. My stomach sank. There was no way I'd find the group now.

As the truck bounced along the unpaved road, we passed a small wooden sign that read Maple Hill Lodge in faded red paint. The tires dipped where the earth had given way, its mirrors scraping past brush. Ernie produced a black and yellow radio, turned the dial, and static filled the space.

He pressed a button. "Come in, Hank?"

The static returned for a minute before another gruff voice answered, "Hank here."

"It's Ernie," he responded. "We've got a new arrival. Coming in hot."

"Opening."

A high, chain-link fence appeared through the trees, its top wrapped in barbed wire. Both edges disappeared into the distance. A squeal echoed through the windows as some mechanical thing slid the gate open.

Lee drove the truck toward a distant wooden structure supported by thick stilts. A flimsy set of stairs led to a wrap-around porch, which enclosed the entire building. Moss and leaf clumps covered a low, sloped roof. Lee rolled the truck to the rear of the building, parking it beside two other trucks in similar conditions. He pulled the keys from the ignition and let the gun in his hand go slack. In the distance, I heard the gate pull shut.

Six large machines roared beneath the building. Wires snaked up the sides of the stilts, porch, and building walls like vines — black, orange, and green. Ernie opened his door, falling out onto the dirt on the other side.

Lee rolled his eyes before he exited the truck, too. He turned, wrapping his hand around my bicep to tug me across the seat. I landed on the solid ground outside, a shock radiating through my calves as I found my footing.

"C'mon," he grunted, pushing me toward the flight of stairs. I stumbled forward, my limbs somehow slower, the world a little unsteady. I righted myself, glancing back at Lee as he raised his thin brows, hand resting on the gun now at his hip.

"Climb."

Rot made the wood soft against my boots. The railing was slimy, missing supports in areas, so the entire thing wobbled at the slightest touch. Careful not to put too much weight on the places that looked untrustworthy, I made my way to the top.

If there was ever a polar opposite of the Coutts commune, this was it. Bottles, ashtrays, pieces of clothing, magazines, cans, food wrappers, a stray toolbox, mismatched shoes, old electronics, and what looked like thousands of cigarette butts covered the cluttered porch and lawn furniture. Men and women of differing shapes, sizes, and skin colors dotted the area, some lounging on furniture, others hanging over the railing. The woman who stood closest to me was wrapped in a sheer pink robe that fluttered in the wind, wearing only a pair of underpants beneath, unashamed by her nakedness. She flicked a cigarette over the railing as I looked away, my cheeks hot with embarrassment.

The porch itself sagged with neglect, likely as rotted as the stairs. But the property must have once been a desirable place. In the distance, parted trees gave onlookers a spectacular view of Coutts Peak, a shadowed, purple summit. I paused at the top of the stairs, waiting for further instruction. People had taken notice of my arrival and drifted toward me like moths drawn to a light, their thin faces filled with curiosity.

The people varied in age — some young enough to be my siblings, while others who looked as old as Sister Abigail or even Mother. But just like Ernie back in the firehouse, there was something deeply wrong with their tired, lifeless eyes. Some had wounds in the crooks of their arms, others were missing full sets of teeth. One had a purple, angry-looking vein that snaked around her neck, up behind her ear.

"Fuck off," Lee spat at them as he came up the stairs, as though they were disobedient animals. They scattered like birds, returning to the porch railing or the ratty lounge cushions. I kept my gaze on my shoes. Lee's grip found my neck, and he pulled me along like a rag doll toward the screened front door.

We entered together, the door banging against the wall. He pushed me inside, and I stumbled, catching myself on a wooden end table. We stood in a small room lined with oak. A long desk covered most of the space on our right, with a sign that read *Maple Ridge Lodge* hung from a linked chain secured to the ceiling.

There was a door behind the desk and a large wall covered in photographs and magazine clippings. I immediately regretted bringing them into focus. As I scanned them, I realized they were images of naked people doing some very sinful things. I gasped, looking away at the other side of the room, which had a stone fireplace and a few wooden chairs. The room stank of dirty socks, and I fought to keep the liquor in my belly, horrified when I remembered it was the only thing I'd consumed today.

Lee pulled me through an archway into a hallway with numbered doors on each side, guiding me down the hall until we reached the last door. He pulled a brass key from his pocket, slipped it into the lock, and turned the handle. The door opened into a small, dark room that smelled of old floral perfume.

"Behave, Bev," Lee said before he shoved me forward and slammed the door behind me.

I caught myself on the wall. Bev? Was Bev a form of punishment? Was he using some kind of code language I didn't understand? The thought made me shudder in fear, and I stood stark still, waiting for what would come next. Only nothing did. My eyes began adjusting to the darkness.

Something moved within the room that startled me. I jumped backward, my back against the door. The shadowed figure struck a match, dragging the flame to a candle wick, where it danced for a moment before catching.

"Hi," said a small woman sitting in a chair. "Who're you?"

8

MAURA

I PRESSED myself against the door, hand fumbling for the handle. It slipped past my fingers, and I grasped it desperately, tugging on the knob. It twisted only slightly before sticking. Locked.

The candle's flame danced in front of a woman's face. Small scars covered her skin like something had taken small bites of her. Deep, tired circles made her eyes look sunken, giving her round, red-tipped nose prominence on her face. My eyes finally adjusted, bringing shapes into focus — two beds, a doorway to my right, and the woman, sitting in a chair beside a desk. The far wall looked like it once featured a window, but something obscured the sunlight.

"I'm Bev," the woman continued, seemingly unbothered that I hadn't responded. "Want some?"

The woman gestured towards the desk with her candle. Narrow blue containers, plastic baggies, and rolled-up pieces of paper littered the surface. Bev pointed at a small tray covered in what looked like white sand, then picked up a container and shook it at me. "What's your poison?"

I opened my mouth, then closed it again, shaking my head. I didn't want to be poisoned. I wasn't supposed to be here. This wasn't how my escape was supposed to go. Then again, I wasn't sure what I'd imagined this looking like. Me, with freedom under my arm and no plan, running off into the sunset? I had been so, so stupid.

A sob fell from my lips as regret pummeled my chest, and I sunk to the floor, hands threaded between my curls. I tugged at my scalp, frustration getting the best of me as I bit my lip to hold back tears. What was God trying to teach me now? I'd escaped from one locked prison only to be thrown in another.

"Aw shit," Bev said. Candlelight wobbled across the room as she inched towards me, her movements unsteady and slow. "Don't do that," she soothed, sitting with her legs crossed on the floor beside me. "Don't cry."

She wore a sheer robe similar to the woman outside. Thankfully, she wore a thin camisole and a pair of shorts underneath. Like Eli, she had tattoos on one of her shoulders. She smelled sharp, like a sterile wipe or the doctor's office. I looked up at her young, cratered face lined with worry. Her eyes were bloodshot, like the women outside, like Ernie in the firehouse. But she didn't smell like alcohol. And there was something else behind her empty eyes — a spark of gentleness, of genuine concern that reminded me of Holli. I pressed my palms into my eyes and continued crying.

"I didn't mean to make you cry, honey," Bev said, her hand resting on my knee. My first instinct was to recoil, but it had been weeks without another human's show of comfort, and despite her strangeness, I welcomed it. Her thumb rubbed me through my dirty jeans.

"You didn't," I said through my tears. "I just don't want to be here." It sounded so childish and willful that my chest felt heavy with shame. I wiped away my hot tears with the back of my hands as I pulled my knees up and wrapped my arms around them.

"Baby, none of us wanna be here," she said. "But the men have what we need. They're heavy on booze, pills, and coke, but they've got the hard stuff for your arm, if you wanted it."

I peered up at her, past my knees, trying to understand, but she might as well have been speaking another language. She smiled, showcasing a gap in her front teeth.

"I promise, if you can get past the idea that sex means anything, it's actually not so bad." She glanced over her shoulder. "We got beds and food, all the uppers and downers you could need. They like to keep us that way, and I think most prefer it. There ain't no shame in it. There's nothin' out there worth a damn, anyway."

But I'd hardly heard the last part of what she'd said. The word sex had cut through the noise, ringing in my ears — the forbidden act, the one I had waited many years for, one that had brought me nothing but pain. To hear it said so casually, to be cast aside as something to ignore, prompted a roll of nausea in my stomach. Certainly not sex with men like Ernie and Lee. Certainly not sex with these half-dead women I saw lounging around outside or trapped inside these rooms.

"I don't—" I shook my head, trying to find the right words. "I don't want any of that."

"Uppers? Or downers?" Bev tilted her head to the side. "You a booze girl?"

I smacked my lips, rolling my tongue as I fought to get rid of the horrendous liquor Ernie had forced me to drink.

"No," I said. "I don't want anything. I just want to get out of here."

Bev squinted at me, leaning forward over the candle so

close I was afraid she might burn the loose shirt over her chest. "You don't use?"

"Use what?"

Her face fell, eyes widening as though she were seeing me for the first time. "Drugs? Pills?"

I tilted my head in confusion. "Like medicine?"

Bev frowned, silence filling the space between us before she asked, "Where did you come from?"

I squeezed my fists, trying to form a lie, but none came to me readily. Sid, Holli, and Eli, initially recoiled from me when I'd shared my family name. Would Bev do the same? Did someone who lived in these conditions, someone with dead eyes and a careless attitude towards sex, care where I came from? Would she tell the men who'd thrown me in here?

She glanced at my hands, eyes landing on the simple gold ring Andrew had given me on our wedding day. There was no gem — those were reserved for first wives, but it had an ornate C etched into the side. Would someone on the Outside understand what it meant? Where it had come from?

Her fingers traveled upward to touch it, the pads of her middle and pointed finger resting gently on my knuckle. Our eyes met.

"Are you a Coutts?"

I snatched my hand back and cradled it to my chest, twisting the wedding band. Bev kept her eyes on me.

"So what if I am?" My voice sounded strange and distorted in the stale air of our small room. I waited for her to yell. To tell me I was a monster.

"You have to take that off," she said, eyes returning to the ring. "You have to hide it. If they find out where you're from…" She shook her head. "You don't belong here." Her voice deepened, filled with edges of worry. "You have no idea what they'll do to you." She shivered as if the very idea disturbed her. My body felt cold and foreign, like I was in a dream.

"What is this place?" I hadn't wanted to ask the question, but it was necessary. Lee and Ernie wouldn't keep me locked up in this room without purpose. I knew something was afoul here, something terrible. But I needed Bev to say it.

Bev looked at her dirty toes, her hands gripped tight around her calves. "I've been here from the start," she admitted, her gaze drifting to a memory that existed only in her mind. "The lodge is full."

"Full?"

"Of people. The men in charge, they keep us here for their own fun. You know how men are." She shrugged. "Some of them were raiders after things went to hell. They went after the pharmacies and the medical centers for the pills. Some of the others were in drug or prostitution rings — sex traffickers, pimps, you know?" She looked up at me. "Or maybe you don't." She looked at the floor. "Anyway, after the world turned upside down, it was hard to find things that made you feel good. These guys are animals, but somebody leading them was smart. Men will always want sex. Addicts will always want drugs. Even when the world stops turning."

I remembered Lee's gun at my back. The way the people had looked and behaved when I'd first come up the stairs. Ernie's flask. The desk was filled with things Bev offered me when I first came in.

"So they offer you…what exactly?"

"Drugs," Bev said, glancing back at the desk. "Substances. Things that make you feel good." She rubbed her hand across her face.

I thought of Andrew after a few too many whiskeys

— the way his body relaxed and his speech slurred, the way his eyes got watery and lazy, the way he held my body in ways that made me sick to my stomach.

"Like alcohol?"

"Sure," Bev shrugged, then narrowed her eyes. "You've had alcohol?"

I tugged my wedding ring off my finger and held its weight in my right hand. "No," I said on instinct before tears welled up again. "I mean...yes. They forced me to," I whispered, meeting her eyes. "In the truck when they were driving me here. They forced me to drink it, but—"

I could hear Abigail's voice when I was in purpose training. *Alcohol puts the devil inside of women. Drinking it will make them behave indecently and expose themselves. It turns them into demons. Such shame! Such contempt for our Lord!*

"—I'm not supposed to have it."

"Shit," Bev whispered, giving me another once over. "You really are the real deal, then?"

I didn't answer.

"Well, you make sure you keep that information to yourself," she said, lifting herself off the floor. "They treat us regulars like animals. I'd hate to think what they'd do with you."

"What's that mean?" I asked, getting to my feet and following her toward the beds.

Bev sat in the chair beside the desk. "I mean, they might use you as leverage to get something they want from the Coutts. But knowing these guys..." She glanced up toward the door. "They'd use you like a trophy. Imagine saying you'd slept with a Coutts wife." She sucked in a breath between her teeth.

"No!" I cried, sitting on the bed closest to the door. It

bumped up against the wall, and I leaned against it, terror settling in my chest. "I don't—I can't—"

"It's not a question about whether you can or you can't," Bev said, her tone somber. "That doesn't matter to them."

"So that's what they're going to do to me then?" I asked, hating the waver in my tone. "Give me drugs and ask me for..." Heat rose to my cheeks.

"Sex?"

I nodded.

Bev pressed her lips together. "They're not going to ask you," she said. "They'll just...do it. And I'm sorry about that."

A wave of heat poured over me, and I felt like my chest had caved in. I struggled for air, gasping for each breath. I couldn't get it into my lungs fast enough. The room spun. I held the wall for support, closing my eyes as I tried to make sense of my situation.

"I can't stay here," I gasped, looking at Bev playing with the wax dripping from the candle's wick. "I have to leave. I have to get out of here." The ceiling began to spin. I pressed myself harder against the wall, trying to ground myself.

"Mmm," Bev said, her eyes brightened by the flame she was now inspecting. "But how?"

"I don't know!" I said, frustrated by her aloofness. "Have people left here before? Isn't there a way to get out?" I stood from the bed, approaching what might have once been a window. But where there should've been glass, there was only a material that felt like rubber. I pushed against it with both hands and pounded with my fists, but it didn't budge.

I yelled in frustration, spinning on my heel, annoyed that Bev seemed only interested in moving around the little pieces of paper on her desk in the candlelight.

"There's been people," she said as I sat back on the bed.

I looked up. "People?

She nodded. "People that were here, and then they were gone. But…I don't know what happened to them."

A breath bottled in my chest. "But they escaped?"

She shrugged. "I don't know. They could've been sold. Could've been killed. Could've escaped."

"You don't know?" Panic rippled through my tone. "You didn't ask?"

"Who'm I gonna ask?" she said, meeting my eyes. "A question like that would get me in trouble."

"Haven't you ever tried to leave?"

She looked down at the candle. "No." The word felt heavy and final before she took her bare fingers and waved it over the flame. I watched as it licked her skin black.

"Why not?" I whispered.

"I already told you. There's nothing out there worth a damn. So I have to put up with a bunch of men treating me like shit — what else is new? At least they feed me. Give me a roof over my head. All the drugs I could ever want." She met my eyes. "At least in here, I know what I'm getting."

WITH THE WINDOW COVERED, it was impossible to tell whether it was night or day. Eventually, I succumbed to exhaustion and fell into a few hours of dreamless slumber while Bev muddled around the room. She woke me when food appeared — a slice of bread and an expired can of tomato soup. Even though I didn't trust these men, I inhaled it like an animal, cross-legged on the bed. My stomach contracted painfully as I digested it, but I didn't care. I was too terrified about what was to come.

Bev, on the other hand, seemed perfectly relaxed,

humming tunes to herself as she ate her meal with slow bites. She brushed her fingers through her long, dark hair, braiding it, then shaking it out and starting over again.

Why hadn't she tried to leave this place? Was this how she wanted to live? Had the drugs been such an excellent incentive she'd never considered it?

"Bev," I said. She looked up. "What happens…when they, you know…come back?"

"Oh." She frowned. "They usually come collecting a few hours after we eat." Her gaze shifted to the discarded soup can on my bed. "They'll bring us down to the showers."

"The *showers?*"

She nodded. "They want us clean. A shit and a shower, as they say." She chortled, but I tensed at her words. "There's a place out back — I think it used to be a shed or something. They give us soap, water buckets, and towels. Once we're clean, they line us up on the porch and take their pick. If you're not picked right away, you're supposed to wait around 'til the night is over." Her gaze traveled over me again. "But I don't think you're going to have that problem."

I swallowed. My throat was dry.

"Will it hurt?" I asked.

Bev's features softened, and she looked down at her lap. "It might. I try to numb myself as much as I can before. It helps." She gestured toward the desk. "I can give you something, if you want."

I relived the sharp, violent taste of the alcohol Ernie had given me. How my head had throbbed afterward. How sick I'd felt. The thought of a strange man touching me while feeling like that seemed worse than the alternative.

"No. I can't."

"It's nothing," she soothed. "Just a pill or two. It'll just make everything softer. More manageable."

Tears sprung from my eyes before I could stop them. Would this be my life from now on? Sitting here, debating whether or not I should take a pill that would make this nightmare more palatable? Was I destined to become like Bev? A slave to these horrible men?

Bev didn't ask again. When she finished eating, she climbed into bed, not bothering to use the covers, and fell asleep, lightly snoring. I used the time to inspect our room with the candle — the cracks and crevices, any weak point of entry. But there was none. Like the Hunter's truck that had whisked me away from Eli and the others, it was a solid prison.

After some time, a commotion started outside the door — muffled sounds of yells, whoops, and laughter. Fear forced me to straighten as I looked over at Bev, who was startled awake, her eyes wide and frightened. She sat up, squeezing her eyes closed with a pained moan, before she stumbled over to her desk, crashing into the side so everything rattled or scattered.

Her hands shook as she sat down, her hair tangled in a bird's nest at the nape of her neck. I wanted to ask if she was okay, but words wouldn't form past the terror in my throat.

I flinched as a nearby door slammed. Bev looked at our door, then back to the desk in an urgent scramble to ingest whatever it was she thought would numb her enough. I studied the room, desperate for a way out. Maybe if I stayed put and didn't stand up, they'd leave me alone. Maybe I could climb under the bed and hide. Would they remember I was here? Would they look for me?

But there was no time. The door to our room burst open with a slam.

A large man ducked beneath the frame to enter, his hands almost too big for the small source of light he held between thick fingers. The lantern reflected off the gun strapped to his hip.

Time stilled. He could've been a Hunter without his helmet. The man carried the same air of authority, the same weaponry, and the same expectations as the men I'd tried to run from. The end result may have been different, but was it? Obedience was a language all men seemed to speak.

"Get up," he ordered beneath a bushy beard, holding the light to his face.

I stood obediently from the bed, clutching my hands behind my back. I yanked my wedding band off my hand, slipping it into my back pocket. I had no marriage to go back to, but the idea of losing the only thing I had from home frightened me. Better to hide it until I figured out what to do with it.

"Let's go, ladies," the man said.

Bev got to her feet as if she was moving in slow motion. An empty blue bottle rolled off the desk and onto the floor. She looked at me with a soft smile before heading toward the door.

I followed.

9

MAURA

I FOLLOWED Bev past the large, leering man out into the hallway. About two dozen people stood in a single file line — men and women — though there were far more women than men. A red lightbulb was the only source of light. It hung from the ceiling at the far end of the hall, the wire disappearing out of the window behind it. It made everyone look like they existed in shades of red and black.

The man who'd come to our room brushed past us, meeting a slimmer man by the archway who I recognized as Lee. They spoke in a hushed whisper, backs faced toward the line of us in the hallway. Bev turned her head, speaking to me from the corner of her mouth.

"Idndea," she mumbled.

"What?"

"I had'n *idea*."

My eyes widened. "About?"

"I did something," she said. "You'll see."

"Let's go!" Lee barked from the archway, slamming his hand against the frame. The line moved toward the front of the building in a slow shuffle. Moonlight shone through the lobby's dirty windows, spilling across the floor and furniture. Men sat in chairs or near the front desk, drinking from mugs or plastic cups. The white substance I'd seen in Bev's room lay in different areas, on trays and magazines. Two girls, wearing only sheer robes, sat behind the desk, heads lolling, as the men beside them laughed at them, their hands poking and prodding their bodies.

A short man pushed open the door behind the desk, and for a brief moment, I saw shelves of the same blue bottles Bev had on her desk — what looked like *thousands* of them. It was enough to keep the people here forever. The door slammed closed behind him before I glimpsed anything else.

The whole place stank of sweat and liquor, filled with men's belches and jeers. I looked for Ernie, but he wasn't lingering in the lobby. My stomach jolted in revulsion as I thought of where he probably was instead.

We exited the building, the night air a welcome refresh I recognized but couldn't enjoy. Everything, including my own movements, felt numb. Like I was walking on autopilot. A familiar feeling. Similar to how I felt every evening I'd laid with Andrew.

The realization hovered over me before it crashed through my nerves. Clarity struck like a knife, twisting into my heart. The actions of Andrew, Father, and nearly every man in the commune were not so far off from what was happening here, was it?

No.

I shook it from my mind, unable to carry the full weight of what it meant. I needed to focus on what was right in front of me. Bev said she had an idea, and I hoped it would help us get out of this mess. I needed her to tell me the details before it was too late.

Despite the pleasant, warm air, I shivered as we paused

on the porch. Lee came through the door, gun drawn, pointing it at two shirtless men heading up the line. He glanced at his companion as his towering figure trudged onto the porch behind me and Bev, showering us in the light from his lantern. His weight shook the structure, and for a moment, I was sure the wood would crack. That would be a mercy in itself.

Instead, he turned to Lee and said, "That's the last of 'em."

Lee grunted in response and led us down the stairs. We passed the rumbling machines and emerged at the back of the building where the three trucks were still parked. Lee led us past them into a wide field. The overgrown grass nearly reached my waist. We followed a clear path of trampled overgrowth to somewhere in the distance.

Ahead of me, Bev occasionally splayed her hands out as if she were about to lose her balance. The men seemed undeterred as if this behavior was normal. I supposed it probably was, but that didn't stop me from searching for clues about the idea she'd mentioned. What had she done? And how would I know she'd done it?

The grass thinned, revealing the shed Bev had mentioned. A wide, wooden structure was elevated on cinder blocks, one side fully concealed by a patchwork of tarps. In place of a door hung a cloudy shower curtain, split in the middle. Two lanterns hung on either side of the door, providing meager light. A trail of water cascaded from the tarps downhill to our right and out of sight.

Lee stopped outside the shower curtain door. "Wash up," he said, sounding bored. "You all got twenty minutes."

A slow procession through the curtains began. I rocked back on my heels, squeezing my elbows with my hands. One by one, each person entered, swallowed by the small space. Bev disappeared inside. I moved to grasp the curtain, but before I could, Lee stepped in front of me.

"Ah," he said, turning his nose up like a dog catching a scent. "You again."

Lantern light silhouetted his face, blotting out his features and making his eyes black. I tensed, startled backward on unsteady feet. He grabbed a fistful of my hair, forcing my head to look at him. With my scalp on fire, my brain struggled to fight the movement — run, fight, kick, *anything* — but every nerve betrayed me as my body went slack from shock.

He leered at me, a grin finding his lips as he drank in my fear. As though it were something to be celebrated and collected, like treasure.

Like a trophy.

"I'm gonna have so much *fun* with you tonight," he hissed in my ear, his breath hot against my skin, and I whimpered.

Just as quickly as he'd grabbed me, he released his grip, shoving me forward so I stumbled into the shed. Terror shot up my spine as I tried to catch my breath to steady my pounding heart. Despite the dark, everything seemed too bright and much too loud.

I'm gonna have so much fun with you tonight.

I gagged, leaning against a spare beam to my immediate right, trying to find a place to focus in the midst of chaos. The shed was packed. There was no privacy, simply a few stools, buckets of water, and a bucket full of soap bars. People had started stripping off their clothes, kicking them to the side as others carelessly trampled over them to use what I assumed were toilets at the far corner.

The space reeked of unwashed bodies and defecation, and my stomach roiled. I gagged up my dinner, spewing it into the corner, down the wooden beam, and across my shoes. I heaved again, squeezing my eyes closed, fingernails sinking into the wood, splinters inching beneath my nail beds. Tears streamed down my face from the force of my vomit. I didn't care. I couldn't care.

I should do something. Run. Make a scene. Go for help. But where? And how? Helplessness overwhelmed me and kept me rooted to the spot. It was no different from the commune. I'd been ordered to do something and so I'd do it. Like I always did.

I bit my tongue — both in an effort not to scream in frustration and in some kind of sad hope to wake myself up from the nightmare before me. But this was real. All of it. Including the dark-skinned man walking toward me in the distance, a frayed towel draped over his arm. He was tall, shirtless, and muscled — a thin scar on the side of his nose.

I'd seen that scar before. The day I arrived at Eli's camp. The night Sid pointed a gun at us. I blinked and wiped my mouth with the back of my hand.

"Maura?" the man standing before me asked.

Slowly, I brought my gaze up to meet his, my jaw dropping at the impossibility of it all.

It was Sid.

I WAS DREAMING. Hallucinating. There was no way it could be.

But the grip on my arm was very real, and before I knew what was happening, Sid pulled me toward the back of the shed and made a show of grabbing a bucket of water and two bars of soap. He handed one to me.

I couldn't tear my gaze away from him. Mostly to convince myself he was real, but also because something was wrong with his face. One of his eyes hid beneath a swollen lid, and when he turned, I saw a fleshy wound where his ear should've been, covered by a thin layer of gauze stained with fresh and clotted blood.

"What the hell are you doing here?" he hissed as he dipped the soap in the water and scrubbed his hands.

"I ran from the commune," I answered, copying him. "Doesn't matter. Do you know what this place is?" I whispered with urgency, glancing around at the others. "What they're doing here?"

Sid's jaw tightened. "Yes. Do you?"

I nodded, keeping focus on the spot on my wrist I was starting to rub raw.

"How long have you been here?" Sid asked.

"They brought me in this morning. I think. You?"

His shoulders sagged. "Since yesterday."

I stopped scrubbing, searching his face as though it would show me his damage. But his steel armor remained locked in place, his scruffy jaw in a constant scowl. I wanted to ask him if he was okay, but some part of me understood he would only respond to that as an accusation.

"You need to get out of here," he said. "We both do. They fucked up my ear, bad. I thought about running alone, but I'm weak. I lost a lot of blood. But together—"

"How?" I asked. "They said we only have twenty minutes."

Sid eyed the front of the shed for the guard before he moved to the tarp wall. He pressed against it and it shifted. "I can tear through the bottom," he said. "We can slide through. Hide in the grass. But we need a distraction."

I nodded. "Okay. But I have to get Bev."

"What?"

"My roommate."

I glanced over my shoulder, trying to find Bev in the sea of bodies. As the people moved from side to side, I made her out in the distance, sitting on a stool, unmoving. Her head lolled against the wall behind her, black stringy hair getting caught in the wood.

Sid shook his head. "No. Maura. We don't have—"

"It'll only take a second," I promised as I took off across the room. My heart lifted in hope as I approached my roommate. Her head tilted backward, mouth open. I nudged her, but she didn't move.

"Bev!" I said, tugging her shoulder. She blinked her eyes open, and they took a moment to focus.

"Sorry," she mumbled.

"Come with me," I said under my breath. "C'mon." I started to walk, urging her to follow, but she didn't budge. I fell back on my heels, observing her. She seemed to be trying hard to keep her eyelids open. They drooped down. Her breathing slowed. "Bev?"

Her eyelids fluttered open. "What?"

No. This wasn't right. Her words were too sluggish. Her body sagged so much. She was now barely upright, reliant on the stool and wall to keep her in a sitting position. Her eyes closed again, mouth opened, a little moan escaping from her chest.

"Bev!" I grasped both shoulders and shook her, but her head merely rocked back and forth on her neck like a rag doll. I looked around the room. Nobody seemed to notice, nor care, that Bev wasn't responding. I needed to wake her up. But how? Pinching? Yelling? A bucket of water? But nothing seemed right.

We were running out of time.

I looked back at Sid, who hovered by the tarp, his eyes narrowed in on me.

"Bev," I tried again. Her eyes didn't open. I touched her

face, her skin cold and clammy beneath my fingers. I nudged her cheek, and she nuzzled into my touch before her body collapsed again.

"Please," I whimpered, my tone heavy with desperation, but I already knew she was too far gone. She folded, head dropping forward, limbs collapsing, before she fell to the floor with a *thump*. I knelt, heart pounding, shaking her shoulder. "Bev!"

No response.

I tried slapping her cheeks with both hands. "Bev! Wake up!" My shouts rang through the small space, and I looked up at the huge guard who'd collected us as he stormed through the shower curtain. He eyed Bev, took a deep sigh, and rolled his eyes.

"For fuck's sake. Again?"

He nudged me out of the way to kneel beside her, rolling her over like a limp rag doll, her legs and arms at all the wrong angles. I wanted to scream at him, to move him with urgency to get her help — get her to a doctor — before I remembered they didn't have those resources here. The man used two fingers to check her neck, leaning in over her face, listening for her breath. I took a step back toward Sid, terrified.

And then I realized what Bev had done.

Her *idea*.

Cold horror drenched my entire being. Had this been it? A distraction so I could figure out how to get out of here? I shook my head, lip between my teeth. I hadn't wanted this. I would never want this. Not for anyone. Not for any reason. She looked so frail. Lifeless. Dead.

The crowd of people who were all in some form of bathing or relieving themselves stopped, leering over heads and shoulders to get a good look at the body on the floor. I brought my hand to my mouth, afraid I would retch again. There was a hand on my shoulder. I looked up at Sid, following his gaze to the guard who knelt over Bev, the radio to his lips. It was now or never. Sid and I needed to make our move — and fast.

We moved to the end of the shed. I forced myself to look away from the gathered crowd to focus on what came next. Sid had found a shirt that was too large for him — it hung from him like a curtain. He stuffed the towel in the waistband of his jeans, then reached for the tarp's edge, where he ripped it free from the structure.

"Come on," he said, pushing it out so it was taut against its holds. The gap was plenty big for me to slip through, but I couldn't stop looking at Bev. The large man tucked the radio into his belt loop, then threw her over his shoulder like a sack of potatoes before leaving through the flaps. The whites of her eyes were just visible through her dark hair. My chest felt like it was being crushed. I couldn't breathe.

"Maura!" Sid hissed. I looked at him, steadying myself in his gaze.

With a firm nod, I slid my legs through the opening, slipping down the side of the wooden building and into the scratchy grass below. Then I held the tarp for Sid as he mimicked my movements, falling into the grass beside me.

10

MAURA

WE CROUCHED in the tall grass, our shoes squelching against thick mud. From this vantage point, the rear of the lodge loomed over us, a dark, two-story prison. Bass boomed from somewhere inside the building, blending with the humming machines beneath it.

We were well hidden in the untrimmed pasture. Above us, the clear sky held twinkling stars and a sliver of the moon. It seemed too wide and open, too large to be possible, and for a moment, I froze, convinced the darkness would swallow us both. I felt every muscle in my body, every fried nerve, every shock of adrenaline that struggled to fire after the past few days.

Sid faced away from me, holding his hand out to show I should stay still as he charted our path. Between the grass, the dark was so deep I could barely make out the entirety of his shadow. He turned, finger at his lips, and began to move.

The sounds from the lodge dulled as we crawled forward at an excruciating pace. As the meager light from the showers faded, my eyes adjusted to the punishing darkness. Adrenaline crackled beneath my feet. I wanted to run. I wanted to ask Sid why we weren't running. Someone would be on our heels in minutes. The more of a head start we had to get over that fence, the better.

A shadow beside us moved, followed by a grunt and a zipper. I caught the silhouette of Lee's face as he turned to the side, eyes closed, urinating. He was so close. Too close. I hadn't even seen him. Frightened, I grasped Sid's upper arm, and it tensed beneath my grip.

Sid froze. I teetered on my heels, pressing my lips together, desperate not to make a sound. Sid's breaths were slow and measured as he studied Lee. If he turned around, he'd see us, possibly even walk directly toward us. We had no choice but to move.

I looked at Sid, anticipating his movement, but he shook off my grasp instead. Something about him had changed. Tension radiated from his lithe body, and before I could understand our next step, he stalked forward, approaching Lee.

Sid's dark, elegant limbs made him look animalistic, like a predator gliding through the grass. My muscles tightened, and I lowered myself down to the ground quietly, fingers sliding through warm mud. We had no weapons. Would he try to knock him out with his fists? Tackle him? Punch him until he couldn't speak? I thought of what Lee had said before I'd entered the showers. How he was, even now, anticipating our evening together. It made me hope that whatever Sid did to him hurt.

Fear rooted me to my spot. Sid inched into the dark until I could only make out the tip of his head before I lost sight of him. My chest felt like bursting. I couldn't blink away Bev in the showers, the way the large man had carelessly removed her from the floor as though she were nothing more than a dead rat. The sound of a zipper broke the silence, and suddenly, Sid popped up, whipping the towel he'd tucked into his pants around the man's neck.

I gasped.

I knew I shouldn't have made a noise, but I couldn't help it. My brain felt slow. In seconds, Sid pulled Lee into a chokehold with the piece of fabric, tightening both sides of the towel in a death grip until it couldn't stretch further. The towel yanked his milky skin taut, deforming the natural elongation of his neck. Lee's eyes bulged, the whites visible even in the dark.

He clawed at the towel, at Sid, stumbling backward, so Sid had to regain his composure against the soggy terrain. Lee reached over his head at an impossible angle, tugging at Sid's dreadlocks, trying to gain leverage over his attacker. But Sid was too quick and had the advantage of being taller. Despite his injury, he dodged his hands, shoving his elbows into Lee's shoulders to keep him from getting too close.

Lee stumbled again, trampling the overgrown grass, grunting and gasping beneath Sid's force. As he turned, I saw his fear — his oval mouth and lolling tongue desperate to gain air, the way the muscles in his neck, shoulders, and arms struggled against the force of Sid's hold. Lee's form shadowed the man behind him, but even from where I lay, I saw Sid's face screwed up in concentration.

There was some part of me that knew I should turn away, aware I was watching someone's life being choked from their body. I wanted to tell myself I was a helpless witness to the scene unfolding, but there was no shaking away my horrible fascination. *Devil's curiosity*, Abigail would call it. There was a cruel kind of satisfaction in watching a man who had punished so many receive punishment in return. Men like Lee would always take what wasn't theirs.

Sid released a monstrous growl, gripping the towel tighter until the threads began to tear, making impossible indents on Lee's neck. He gurgled, snorted, and gagged before his movements slowed. He lifted his hands, fingers dragging across the towel before his arms fell limp at his sides.

The man's body went slack, flattening against Sid, who stumbled backward with a gasp. They collapsed into the grass with a heavy thud. I lifted my head, still watching Sid, his lip curled in a snarl, eyes wide as he pulled the towel tighter. Lee's features had softened, eyes closed, mouth still open. His neck was at an odd angle, forced by the taut towel. I was no Hunter. I had never hurt anyone. But even I knew Sid wasn't just trying to hurt him. He was going to kill him.

At last, after what felt like both a single second and multiple hours, Sid propelled himself backward through the mud and grass until he bumped into me. With a sharp breath, he turned as if surprised to see me, his eyes wide in horror. I matched his panic, unsure of what to say or what the next step was.

It didn't matter. There was nothing to say. Sid closed his eyes and covered his mouth with his hand, gagging behind it for a minute before sucking in a lungful of night air. He stuffed the towel in the back of his jeans, then pulled out Lee's holstered gun into his grip.

His eyes found mine, and he waved me forward. But I wasn't sure I could move. Everything felt numb.

"D-d-did you—?" The words came out muddled, hushed. Terrified.

I saw Lee's boots in the grass. Worn leather. An untied lace. Was he dead? Unconscious? Would anyone find him?

"Maura, please!" Sid's voice shook.

I bit my lip. It didn't matter. The alternative was worse.

He would've caught us running. And if we hadn't run, he would've defiled my body. Hurt me and countless others. This was the only way. Still, the wrongness of killing plagued me as it had when I'd seen Andrew shoot a helpless man. But that had been different. Andrew hadn't been under threat. He'd shot him for convenience.

"C'mon Maura!"

I forced my thoughts away, focused instead on getting my limbs to move forward. With Sid's shadow ahead of me, we skirted Lee's body, plunging deeper into the high grass, away from the lodge and into the dark. Did the fence enclose the entire property? My adrenaline skyrocketed at the thought of having to climb it.

A metal chain-link fence topped with barbed wire grew in size as we approached; a monstrous barrier reinforced with chains in its weak areas. Sid spent a minute walking along it, looking for a break wide enough to slip through.

"Fuck!" He hooked his fingers between the links and looked up. "We have to scale it." His eyes traveled up over my head. "There." I followed his finger, pointing to where two posts met unevenly.

A man roared in the distance, yelling something unintelligible. A fist or a foot met wood. Someone screamed. I could not catch my breath. Every inhale felt painful and forced, like trying to breathe underwater. I met Sid's gaze, his eyes wide.

"You're going to climb up the higher side," he said, his urgent voice muffled by my racing heart. "Grab the top of the pole on the shorter side and swing yourself over carefully to avoid the spikes. Okay?" He tugged the towel from his pants and handed it to me. "Wrap this around your dominant hand that'll hold the fence. Just in case."

"Okay," I said, taking the towel and doing as he said.

Still shaking, I straightened, hooking my fingers and

tips of my boots into the wire grooves. The barbed wire leered at me as I climbed. Shouts still came from the shed, but I ignored them. The movement felt good. Purposeful. I focused on my upper body strength, adrenaline fueling me forward. It took four long pulls to reach the top.

I placed my hand on the shorter pole, eyeing the rusted barbs curled too close to my flesh. One wrong move, one slip, meant danger. I shook it away, making careful work of swinging one leg, then the other before I let go. The spike closest to me snagged my shirt sleeve, tearing the fabric as I fell.

My arm met the ground first, a sharp pain shooting up my shoulder and neck. I rolled to the side, sitting up, rubbing it, the world spinning. Sid gave me a determined nod from the other side. I held up the towel to see if he wanted it but froze.

Someone had turned a floodlight on. It came from the lodge, somewhere near the trucks, shining over the shed and high grass. My stomach cramped, scalp prickling as light invaded the darkness we'd crawled through. They would find Lee. They would see us.

"Sid!" My throat tightened as I watched him scale the fence hurriedly, his face shadowed. From here, I saw his festering ear wound in the sudden brightness. The light traveled over us, then stopped. I squinted, desperate to find Sid between the white spots in my vision. Already halfway up, Sid nearly slipped, grasping for the top of the pole.

My breath came in shudders as I got to my feet, pressing myself against my side of the fence, tapping on the wire, desperate for him to get over.

"Please! Hurry!"

"YOU!"

The voice thundered across the high grass. I tried to find it, but the light was too bright; headlights bore into my corneas. I blinked away tears, not wanting to lose sight of Sid.

"Get back here, you stupid assholes!"

His silhouette became visible in the light as he raced forward, a large gun clutched in one hand as he ran. He pulled it into his body, wrapping his arm around it, fingers dangerously close to the trigger.

My heart lurched. Sid groaned in pain as he flung his body over the fence, knuckles bleeding from his climb. He released himself from the fence, boots meeting the earth beside mine. We needed to run. Now.

"STOP!"

A sudden crack rang out, impossibly loud. Too close. I screamed as I ducked, knees hitting the earth, Sid's arm at my back. Shrapnel scattered the landscape, ricocheting off of bark, off the fence, the leaves, and the earth beside us. Somehow, we still moved forward. Sid kept his grip on the back of my shirt, forcing me along with him as we crawled for cover.

Another shot came. My ears rang, head throbbing from the deafening rattle. I waited for pain, for bullets to shred across my body. But none came.

We stumbled forward. I was all limbs and tight muscles, a bundle of blind anxiety.

"Get up!" Sid said, his tone weighted from exertion. He pulled me to my feet. My legs were heavy and foreign, and unable to move. But Sid kept a grip on my arm and tugged me forward as he moved deeper into the dark, into the trees, away from the blinding light behind us.

Our adrenaline-fueled running bled into a jog, then, before long, a slow walk. And when we couldn't push ourselves forward, we settled beneath a rocky overhang. Stopping to rest was no longer a choice but a necessity. Everything ached.

It was difficult to discern what areas needed tending to more — my battered arms and face, scratched raw in places from the thick brush we ran through, or my sore legs, feet, and lower back from carrying my weight for so long.

Exhaustion made my head throb, eased only slightly as I sat in the dirt. My chest and throat burned. We needed water but would need to wait until morning. The night blinded me. I couldn't see Sid, but I felt him plop down beside me.

"Do you think we're safe here?" I asked him, my breath ghosting across my bruised shoulder.

He gave a non-committal grunt. "We shouldn't even be alive," he finally said. I felt him lean away from me to lie on his back. "Can't keep moving at this pace though. Have to rest."

I listened to Sid's breathing slow as he fell asleep. Worry plagued me, but I would have to save my questions for tomorrow. I leaned back, head finding the earth as I curled up to his warmth, close enough to feel it but far enough away not to touch him. We had managed a death-defying escape together, but I didn't think that made us friendly.

I tried not to think about how, only weeks ago, he'd held a shotgun to my chin.

11

MAURA

I woke to Sid moaning.

His deep tone made the pained groan almost melodic, like he was humming. As I blinked sleep away, I watched him roll back and forth against his left shoulder, hands pinned to his face, the wound on his ear a startling red and yellow mess of what was once cartilage and skin. Old blood stained his fingers.

Daylight brightened the small cave we laid in. Outside, trees extended as far as I could see. Things slowly clicked into place. The lodge. Scaling the fence. My sore muscles, my aching back, the heat on my neck from where Lee had likely bruised me. I froze at the thought.

Lee. The dead man.

I swallowed, rotating my head to look back at Sid. The killer. Our savior. His knees came up to his chest as he continued his slow roll, back and forth against the earth. The back of his oversized t-shirt was stained black. He had saved our lives. But there was something wrong with him.

My muscles tensed in protest as I sat up. "Sid?" My voice came out in a low rasp. "Sid?" I tried again, clearing my throat. "Are you—" The *okay* faded on my tongue. He was quite obviously not okay.

He turned onto his back, pulling his hands down so they rested on his nose. His wide pupils took me in. A thick sheen of sweat coated his forehead, wetting the dirt stuck to his skin from sleep. I let my eyes travel over what was once his ear. The wound seemed to have worsened overnight — whatever gauze had been stuck there had fallen away, and yellow pus leaked from its puckered edges.

"This hurts like a bitch," he growled, rolling onto his shoulder before he brought himself into a sitting position. He winced, gingerly swiping his fingers around the sensitive area with a hiss. "I think it's infected."

He looked at me, eyes swimming with worry. "We have to get you to Holli," I said. "She can help you. She'll know—"

"I don't even know where the hell we are, Maura. I've been missing for days. They probably packed up and moved on already. I don't..." He paused, closing his eyes with an inhale before he spoke again. "I don't know if we'll be able to find them."

I hugged my knees, resting my head against them as I studied him. The things I knew about this man were minimal. He was strong. Scary. Ruthless. His survival instincts were almost unnatural. I think he hated me, yet he'd saved my life. Of course, his injury also made him need me, and that could've been the reason for his kindness. But I also needed him.

"They wouldn't leave you," I whispered.

A small, condescending smile crossed Sid's lips as his eyes traveled over me. "Yes, they would've. And they should've. We were already low on food, low on ammo. Waiting for me would've been stupid." He laughed to himself. "It's certainly not something I would've done."

"Well." I straightened. "We have to try. We can go back, we can—"

"What part of *we might not be able to find them* don't you understand?"

"So, what do you want to do?" I asked. "Sit here until your ear gets worse?"

"No."

"Okay. So you're planning on *what* exactly? Starting a new life without ever thinking about them again? Are you kidding me?" My cheeks flushed with anger. "After all that? You're just gonna *give up*?"

"I'm not *giving up*."

"Sure sounds like it."

Sid's mouth dropped in disbelief. "What the hell's gotten into you?"

"What's gotten into me? Oh, I don't know. I left everything I've ever known behind because a tree fell on my house, and I thought it was a sign from God. I lost my horse, got kidnapped into one of the most horrible places I could imagine, watched you kill a man, and then we nearly got blown apart trying to escape!" My voice rose. "I guess *that's* what's gotten into me. And now, after all of that, I'm sitting with someone who just wants to give up. Fantastic." I nodded my head. "Really, really wonderful."

Emotion welled in my throat, furious tears threatening to fall. I clenched my hands into fists as I stared at Sid, nostrils flaring, every ounce of anger, frustration, and pain surfacing since I'd left the Island of Repentance.

He started to laugh.

"Don't," I warned, getting to my feet. The cave was so small, my hair brushed the top. "I'll leave you and your infected ear here."

"No," he said, breathing a laugh through his nose, "you won't."

Grunting in frustration, I turned away and exited the cave. He was infuriating. No wonder he and Eli fought so much.

I wandered away from Sid, eager to put some distance between us. The humidity had lifted overnight, and I breathed in the cool air, welcoming its refreshment. In the quiet, I closed my eyes and allowed myself to drink in nature in all its glory — the rustling leaves, the hum of a bullfrog, the babble of water.

Water.

My eyes flew open. I turned over my shoulder to look at Sid, who leaned forward, massaging his calves. The fury I felt toward him faded. Slightly.

"Sid," I hissed.

His eyes caught mine. "What?"

"Water."

He brightened at my words, groaning as he got to his feet, ducking beneath the rock overhang. We followed the sound down a hill, where brook water weaved between large boulders, disappearing beyond more trees. We kneeled in the mud, cupped our hands, and drank.

Once he'd had his fill, Sid ripped a piece of fabric from his oversized shirt and dipped it into the cool water, sighing in relief as he pressed it to his head. We sat side by side, watching the brook travel in silence.

"I wasn't laughing at you, you know," Sid finally said.

I glanced at him. He held a stick in his free hand and drew squiggles in the earth before the water lapped them up. I forced a laugh. "Could've fooled me."

"Maybe you're easy to fool." I narrowed my eyes at him. Sid sighed. "You've been through a lot. I was laughing because you surprised me."

I lifted my brows. "Surprised you?"

He nodded. "I guess I thought you'd go back to your

people and stay there. All those luxuries up there? Three meals a day? A warm bed?" He whistled through his teeth. "You gave that all up for *this*?"

"Not for *this*," I said, gesturing around us. "I wanted—I mean, I hoped I'd find you and the others." The admission sounded even more outlandish when it came out of my mouth.

"It's a big world out here. You just hoped to stumble across us?"

I wrinkled my nose. "That's what happened, didn't it?"

A flash of surprise crossed his face as if he hadn't considered it. "I suppose it did."

"Holli promised to leave me some signs. I followed her marks into Coal Creek, where those men found me."

"She left you marks?"

I nodded. Sid looked incredulous, his lips in a flat line.

"We could backtrack," I suggested, looking over my shoulder. "Go back into the town, follow from there?"

"It'd be too dangerous to try to pass the lodge again. Those men were loaded out of their minds, which won't bode well for us if they find us. We need to find our bearings and get out of their vicinity."

"How'd you end up there, anyway?"

Sid settled his chin between his knees. "We were staying in one of those Coutts halfway home neighborhoods. Big town, lots of shops. Eli and I split up — he went through the other homes, I went through the town. I got ambushed. I think they were trying to shoot my shoulder to slow me down but blew part of my ear off instead." He winced. "By the time I realized what happened, they had two guns on me."

"So they took you back to the lodge, too?"

"Sure did." Sid's mouth twisted as though he were

searching for the right words. "One of them liked what I looked like."

His dark skin? Strong muscles? The way he manicured his trimmed beard and eyebrows? His height? He sighed impatiently, then struggled to get to his feet. I mimicked his movements, uncertain if I should've helped him.

He peered at the sun through the trees, hands on his hips, before looking back at me. "We should move before the sun gets any hotter. If we can find a road or a landmark, hopefully we can figure out where we are."

"Okay," I said, confused at his sudden switch of subject. It had seemed, for a moment, that he was opening up, only for him to clam back up again. Sid checked the gun, sliding out different compartments, then sliding them back in.

"Three bullets. C'mon." He waved me along.

We walked through the trees in silence, stepping over rocks and dead brush, the sun making its hazy rotation above us. The quiet made it too easy to dwell on our situation. Two people stuck together who couldn't be more different. What if we never found the others? What if I was condemned to live with Sid until — until, what? I tried imagining what our life would be like together. Silent, tense, and rugged. It was nearly as bad as having to live with Abigail and Joanna forever.

"What did you mean before?" I asked, my voice breaking through our silence.

"What?"

I rolled my shoulders, hurrying forward to fall in line with him. "When you said one of them liked what you looked like?"

Sid slowed his gait. "Why do you think they took you?"

I tilted my head. "Because I'm a woman."

Sid nodded. "And not everyone wants to sleep with a woman. Whether or not your commune approves, gay people exist, Maura — good and bad, we're all still out here."

I had heard the term before during Father's sermons as he preached about what an abysmal place the Outside was. How such sins were being committed by men who lay with other men when their rightful place was beside a woman. I found it hard to imagine — hard to fathom, really. All I had ever known were the family dynamics within our commune. A powerful man who provided for his wives.

"Oh," I answered, unable to think of anything to say to his proclamation.

This time, he forced a low laugh. "What, you're not going to pray over me? Try and save my sorry soul? Condemn me to hell?" The edges of his voice rippled with defensiveness.

"No," I said, searching his face. He looked so hardened, so angry. What kind of reaction was he looking for?

He shook his head as if I didn't understand. I swallowed, words escaping me, and as the silence wore on, everything I thought to say sounded forced. We walked quietly for a few moments before I said, "I'm sorry."

This time, Sid did stop. "For what?"

"I'm sorry this happened to you. I'm sorry it happened to both of us. I'm sorry you had to leave your camp. And I'm sorry you're so angry at me and my community." I swallowed, forcing myself to hold back tears. "I wish I could fix that."

He turned and studied me from head to toe, eyes narrowed in suspicion before he released the tension in his shoulders and nodded. "Thanks," he said, almost as if he was uncertain he meant it. He began walking again.

"I mean it," I said, trotting after him. "I know you hate me—"

"I don't hate you."

"You don't?"

He shrugged without turning to look at me. "I mean…I thought Eli was an idiot for bringing you back to our camp." He sighed, glancing up at the sky, continuing to move forward. "But after what you did for us by the office building…I think I was being unfair."

"How's that?"

We skirted a large mud puddle. "I guess I've been angry at the Coutts for being so awful for such a long time, I never really considered there might be another side to things. I just assumed you all thought the same. What the Coutts did to my community — it was unforgivable. The propaganda against the gay and trans community was so deeply evil, it was impossible to escape it. Even people who weren't completely bought into the Coutts ideals were afraid of us. For nothing more than who we loved or who we longed to be.

"You probably didn't know, but people were hurting us. Beating us up on the street in broad daylight. Shooting us. Torturing us, our families. Children. So many people went into hiding, or, like me, went out to California to be far away from it all, even though there was nothing out there but a wasteland. Your people used religion as an excuse to be hateful. All in the name of God.

"It's hard to see and hear and feel that kind of hate and not want to return it in full force. We were condemned to be monsters and pedophiles. The way the Coutts spoke of us was as if we weren't actually human. It didn't matter who you were, what good you'd done in the world, how much money you had, nothing. If the wrong person found out you were gay, trans, or anything different from what they perceived as *normal*…that was it."

I bit my lip, my stomach sinking.

"So I've been angry for a long time. A real long time.

But hate tends to blind you. Even if it's hatred for the people who hate, I suppose." He paused. "So, I'm sorry too. I lumped you into a group. I wrote you off before I knew you, ignored your past and your traumas, and what your life might've looked like before we met you. So really, I was doing the same exact thing to you that I hated someone doing to me and the people I love."

I swallowed, turning his words over, realizing it very well might have been the first time I'd ever heard a man admit they were wrong. Right there, out in the open, out loud. I longed to say something profound, something to articulate how deeply meaningful his words were.

"I didn't know," I whispered. "My God. I am so, so, sorry."

"It's not your sin to atone for, Maura. You're just part of the system, same as me, same as Eli, Holli, Mia, all of us. None of us chose this. We're all just trying to survive. And maybe live a little, too."

AROUND MID-DAY, we found a road. It was better maintained than others I'd seen, with a thick yellow line running through the center. We followed it north, remaining hidden along the tree line. Sid and I agreed not to expose ourselves. Now, not only did we have Hunters to worry about, but the Coal Creek men too.

Hunger pains ached deep in my belly, and I wondered how much longer we'd last without getting some sustenance in our bodies. Sid's wound didn't seem to be healing, either. In fact, there was now more pus than blood, though it was hard to tell with the myriad of colors spread across the small piece of fabric he'd torn from his shirt. I wanted to recommend switching it out for a clean one, but every time he moved the wrong way, he hissed with pain. We needed Holli.

We walked slowly, and every half-hour or so we stopped. As the day wore on, I watched Sid's strength fade. He gritted his teeth when he stood and squeezed his eyes closed as he walked. Exhaustion plagued him mere minutes into the next leg of our journey. Weeks ago, I'd seen him run full speed up a steep incline with a child in his arms like it barely winded him. The wound was seeping into his body, infecting him. And there was nothing I could do to help.

The road made a sharp turn west, and we followed it across a bridge and beyond until finally, a dirt drive intercepted our path. At the edge hung a mailbox. Someone had painted a now faded sunflower on its side in delicate strokes; a reminder that this had once been someone's home. A place someone had once cared about. I approached cautiously, peering up the drive. It disappeared over a small hill.

"We should check it out," Sid said, his hand at his hip, taking sharp breaths. His eyelids fluttered, and he swayed.

"Lean on me." I offered him my shoulder.

A flicker of hesitation crossed his features before he hobbled over, resting some of his weight on me. Together, we climbed the hill. Sid kept the gun gripped tightly in his free hand but didn't seem to have the strength to point it. I hoped there was something worthwhile at the end of this drive — it had been the only break in the road we'd seen since we started walking.

As we came up over the hill, the driveway came to a single-story wooden home with a red metal roof. Two dusty windows framed a slim front door with broken stones leading up from the dirt path. I noticed the driveway split, curving around the house, leading to a red tractor covered in high grass and weeds where another distant structure stood.

Sid shifted his weight, bringing the gun into both hands as we approached the dwelling, but there was no need. The interior was dark and quiet. After a few long, heavy breaths, Sid lowered his aim and looked at me. Weariness painted his face. I didn't know how he was still standing upright.

"Sit," I demanded, pointing at the grass.

He shook his head, instead leaning up against the side of the house. Stubborn man. I went to the front door, but the handle wouldn't budge.

"Here." Sid lifted himself from the wall, pulling the towel from his waistband. He wrapped it around his hand, then with a heavy grunt, smashed through the window. The glass shattered inward. Sid reached inside, unlocked the window, then pushed it up. "Can you climb through?"

I nodded, dusting away glass particles before I heaved myself up and over the sill into the small house, careful not to catch on any shards. The dark interior smelled of rot and mildew. It was a cluttered home, with cobwebbed bookshelves, stacked newspapers, and neatly labeled boxes. Even the walls were crowded with photographs and framed newspaper clippings. Everything was covered in a thick layer of dust.

Waning sunlight spread across the wooden floor as I unlocked and opened the door, allowing Sid to enter. He stumbled inside, and I helped him to the single gray recliner tucked in the corner of the room between a disorganized coat rack and a worn cat tree, still covered in hair. He sighed as he sat, one hand fanned out protectively over his bad ear.

"You'll need to check the building out back," he said. "I'm sorry, I can't—"

"Don't be sorry. I'll check."

He forced a smile before holding out the gun. "Take this."

I stared at it. "No," I said, shaking my head, eyes wide. "I can't — I don't know how to use it."

He sighed, then shook it at me. "Take it." He met my eyes. "I'll show you."

I inched forward, gaze focused on the weapon. I'd never held a gun. I'd never studied someone shooting one. All I knew was how dangerous they were. I let my fingers dust the black, textured surface.

"This is a semi-automatic pistol," Sid said, sounding tired. "Some people call it a Glock. The most important thing you'll learn about a gun is to point it in a safe direction. Never at anything you don't want to accidentally shoot." He looked up, and I nodded. "Go ahead." He extended his arm.

I reluctantly picked the weapon up and turned it over in my hands, surprised at its weight.

"Good." He sounded relieved. "Now, you'll want to keep an eye on your ammo. On the left side, you'll find the mag release. That pushes the magazine out so you can see if it's loaded."

I found the glossy button and pressed it. The weight fell out of the bottom and clattered onto the floor. I gasped, then sheepishly looked up at Sid. He gave me a weary smile.

"It's okay," Sid said. "Sorry. I should've warned you." I picked the magazine of bullets up and held it in my free hand. "Now, that's how you unload the gun. But there could still be a round in the chamber, so you'll have to check for that too. There's a button above the mag release. Push it up, then pull the top of the gun — the slide — back."

I did what he said. The gun clicked, opening up the empty interior.

"It's empty," I said.

"Good. Now, let's practice your stance before you load it up."

I nodded, gripping the weapon tighter. He took a deep breath, wincing as he shifted in his seat.

"Okay, so imagine a line at your feet. Your feet should be touching that invisible line, a little wider than shoulder-width apart."

I looked down at my feet and adjusted, keeping both hands on the gun. Even without the bullets, it felt foreign in my grip. I wanted nothing more than to put it down. I'd seen what these weapons were capable of. How quickly they could kill someone.

"You want to feel light in your knees, a little bounce," Sid said. "Now, lean forward just a touch."

I felt stupid trying to follow all the directions at once. "Like this?" I asked.

"Loosen up a little bit," he said, a ghost of a laugh on his lips.

I tried releasing some of the tension in my muscles. "Like this?"

"Better," he said, still gazing at me critically. "Now, lengthen your arms, stick them straight out, both hands still in your hold. Angle your shoulders away from your target in case they start shooting back at you. Then, you'll pull the trigger. Just remember, only shoot if you need to. If you can hide, do that. We only have three bullets."

I froze. I turned my head to look at him. "How will I know if I need to?"

Sid's eyes darkened. "You'll know."

I pressed my lips together and nodded, looking back at

the gun in my hands. If only Abigail and Joanna could see me now.

"Now, let's put the magazine back. Numbers are on the back, facing you, bullets on the top, facing forward. Slide it in until it clicks. You'll see the bullet in the chamber."

I followed his instructions. The brass bullet gleamed at me from inside the weapon.

"You see it?"

I nodded.

"Good. Press that slide release again. That will chamber the round, and you're ready to shoot. It's going to click," he warned before I pressed it. "Don't get spooked."

I swallowed, pointing the heavy gun at the opposite wall, away from Sid. Then, I closed my eyes and pressed the slide release.

"Maura!" he shouted. I jumped, turning. "Please," he said, pressing his fingers to his forehead. "For the love of God, don't close your eyes when you shoot."

"Sorry."

He waved me off like it wasn't a big deal, but my cheeks flushed all the same. I was terrified of violence. The thought of shooting someone made me want to run for the hills, but I didn't want to disappoint Sid. My heart pounded against my ribcage. I let my arms go slack, placing the gun carefully on a side table facing the front door. Sid had enough to worry about. I could certainly follow his instructions and inspect the building myself. He was hurt. I wasn't. For the first time in a very long time, someone actually needed me.

"Is there any food?" he asked, his eyes closed.

I went to work pulling out everything still left in the cabinets. I found six cans of expired cat food and a half-finished jar of peanut butter. I carried the jar to Sid, taking a glob out with my fingers. We ate in silence, but I couldn't stop looking at Sid. His skin had taken on a gray shade. His eyes were bruised with exhaustion. The side of his face was angry, purple, and swollen. I could feel his fever sitting beside him. Whatever this wound was doing to him worried me. How long could he last like this? Worse yet, how long did I have to get him to Holli?

Defeat crept up behind me as Sid slumped over in the recliner, succumbing to another deep sleep, peanut butter still caked across his fingers. I used a dish rag to wipe them off before taking the gun into my grip and heading back outside.

12

MAURA

THE GUN WEIGHED down my right side as I walked up the dirt driveway, my muscles tight with tension. One wrong movement from my fingers and I could brush the trigger. Set off the gun. Accidentally shoot myself. I assumed I would feel safer with the weapon in my hands, but if anything, I felt even more afraid. My mind bounced from the idea of shooting someone or something to the fear we would never leave this place. Sid would die in that ugly gray recliner.

No.

I owed him. He'd gotten me out of that horrific lodge in one piece. Killed a man in the process. I would not sit here and wait for him to surrender to his infection. I had to get him to Holli. I just had to figure out how.

The sun was barely visible above the structure in the distance. Night would fall soon, covering us in darkness. I tried not to think of Sid lasting through the night. The building had three openings — two wide garage doors and a side entry. All of them were locked.

I returned to the house and grabbed Sid's towel to

break the glass on the side door. It was becoming our most useful tool. Wincing from the sound, I paused, my back up against the side of the building waiting — for a shout, a sound, something that told me we weren't alone. My hands shook, jostling the gun in my grip. How could I be expected to shoot anything if I couldn't even control my tremors? I closed my eyes, head against the solid surface behind me, and reminded myself to breathe. My ears strained for any unnatural sound, but none came. I reached carefully through the open window, fingers grasping for the lock on the other side. With a pop, the door unlocked and I pulled my hand back through to open it.

Glass crunched beneath my boots as I entered. The interior reminded me of the firehouse, made from concrete with exposed brick on the far wall. A small wood-working station, a large tool rack, and various gardening tools hung from the back wall. In the center of the space sat a silver four-door car, a four-ring emblem attached to its front.

I circled the car, pulling at each handle to see if it was unlocked. No luck. Dust coated the vehicle, dulling its color and obscuring the interior. I wiped the grime away from the driver's side window to peer inside but saw nothing remarkable. Still, the car kept me hopeful. Another opportunity to find the others. A way to get Sid to Holli.

Losing Chance crippled me, and I'd forgotten there were other means of traveling on the Outside. The only problem? Sid wasn't strong enough to drive for a long distance, if at all. Just the thought of helping him cross the backyard to this building made me sweat.

In the commune, women were not allowed to drive. But the weight of the gun in my hand reminded me that out here, all things were possible. Even driving a car. The idea was terrifying, but if that was what it took to get Sid to safety, I'd do what needed to be done.

With a new sense of purpose, I set to work, scouring the room for anything that looked like a car key. After the garage turned up empty, I ransacked the house, careful not to wake Sid. Halfway through my fourth drawer in the kitchen, I found a blocky set of keys with a logo that matched the one I'd seen on the car's hood.

Dusk shadowed the land around the house. Tree limbs climbed high into the night sky like dark tendrils, looming over me as I ventured back to the garage, keys and gun in a tight grip. I was no longer shaking. Fear took a backseat to my determination.

The keys unlocked the driver's side door, and I let it fall open, smelling the stale interior. I had only ever witnessed other people driving vehicles and hadn't paid enough attention to grasp all the mechanics. Carefully, I lowered myself inside, placing the gun on the passenger seat before I studied what lay ahead of me.

In the dark, I searched for a place to put the key, finding a key-sized hole on the side. I stuck it in and twisted, holding my breath. The engine roared to life, sending my heart galloping in my chest. Something beeped. Different colored lights flashed. Numbers and letters came into view behind the steering wheel.

Okay. This was good. Startled at my success and terrified for what came next, I moved on to my next barrier. Using the last of my remaining strength, I unlocked the garage door and lifted it, opening the building to the pleasant night breeze. My head throbbed as I got back into the driver's seat. I tried hard to ignore the pounding of my heart in my ears. One thing at a time. Just move the car out of the garage and onto the driveway. That was all I needed to do.

Sweat made the steering wheel slick in my hands. I ran my fingers up and down the worn leather, feeling stupid. I had to move the car — but how? The bus driver always hung his arms over the large steering wheel, but turning the wheel didn't seem to prompt any movement. I thought of Lee accelerating the truck, his leg muscles tense beside mine.

I tilted my head to look at the car floor, inspecting two pedals. I assumed they had one of two options — stop and go. Just like riding a horse. Pull on the reins to stop. Squeeze calves to go. Surely this was just as simple?

Straightening in my seat, I stretched my legs until my feet found the pedals, pressing my foot against the stiff, larger one. Red light swam through the garage interior and I startled, hand fumbling in the passenger seat for the gun. I pulled it into my grip, sinking down in the driver's seat, my heart in my throat.

The light disappeared as I eased my foot from the pedal. Hot shame rushed to my cheeks as I adjusted to look around the empty garage. Red lights meant stop, didn't they? I had seen those lights on vehicles before. My goodness. How foolish was I?

Irritated by my fear, I replaced the gun on the side seat and tried the other pedal. This one stirred the engine, but as hard as I pressed it, the car didn't budge.

"You're worse than a stubborn horse!" I exclaimed to no one, slamming my hands against the steering wheel.

I pulled at levers. Wipers dragged across the dusty glass, making me wince. I twisted something and lights at the head of the car bathed the driveway. Headlights. My heart lifted momentarily. But the car still wouldn't budge.

After exhausting all options on the steering wheel, I turned to the center of the car. A large handle emerged from the middle, with different letters beside it on a track.

"Oh!" I exclaimed, remembering the bus I took to scavenge. I'd watched the driver pull a large lever to park the bus, put it in reverse, and make it drive. With my foot situated against the stop pedal, I pulled the level away from the P, down to D, and lifted my foot.

It was a mistake. The car lurched forward, and I panicked. My feet scrambled for purchase on the floor. I slammed my foot against the large pedal, and the car immediately jolted to a stop, throwing me against the steering wheel. The car honked, the sound echoing into the evening air. I screamed, unable to help suppress my fear. Half of the car hung out in front of the garage, and I stayed there for a moment as I collected myself, fear fluttering in my stomach.

As my panic dispersed, I released the pedal, letting the car roll onto the driveway. Headlights washed across the grass, and I tried turning the wheel, following the curve of the drive. Too sharp. I came to a stop, corrected the tire angle, and continued inching forward to the house. After a few minutes, I'd driven the car down the rest of the driveway, stopping it in front of the house. I pulled it into park, removed the keys, turned off the headlights, and re-entered the dark house.

Sid was still asleep. I had half a mind to wake him up to celebrate my victory. I wanted to jump around the room and scream to the heavens. I'd done it. I'd figured it out.

I settled on the floor, finding a thin blanket to use as a pillow, settling in for the night. The dark shadowed Sid's face, but even in the black, I could see the sweaty sheen against his exposed skin.

"Hang on," I whispered. "I'm going to get you to Holli. I'm going to get you help."

Sunlight spilled through the windows, nudging me awake. My back and legs ached so bad I wasn't sure they would move. I stretched my limbs out on the floor, blinking away sleep. My stomach growled, and I brought my knees to my chest to ease the pain. Squinting, I brought my tired gaze to Sid, who sat in the chair, his eyes wide open.

Unblinking.

My body went cold with dread. Horror rose in my throat. I shot up, scrambling to my knees, a scream waiting on my lips. Was he dead? Had his fever taken him?

"Sid?"

He tilted his head, and I fell backward, landing on my rear, hands at my mouth.

"Yes?" He gave me a pained smile.

"Oh!" I curled into myself, relieved.

"Good morning."

"Morning." I got to my feet, dusting myself off from the floor. "How are you feeling?"

"Like shit."

"Better than yesterday?"

"A little. Sorry, I fell asleep." His eyes scanned me from head to toe. "Did you make out okay with the gun?"

I shrugged. "I didn't shoot it."

"That's a good thing. Did you manage to find anything worthwhile? Painkillers, by any chance?"

I shook my head. "No painkillers. But something, maybe, equally as good?"

"I assure you," he said, groaning as he shifted his weight, "*nothing* would be as good as painkillers right now."

I reached into my pocket and pulled out the car keys, dangling them in front of him. Sid's eyes crossed as he focused on the keys before his gaze drew up to me, mouth slightly open.

"You found a car?"

"I found it *and* drove it from the garage to the front yard," I said proudly, glancing at the door over my shoulder. "It runs just fine."

"You? Drove a car?"

"I just thought…given your…condition…" I looked at the floor, not wanting to disrespect him. "It might make more sense if I figured out how to get us out of here." I looked up, worried he might yell at me or demand we figure out a new plan.

But Sid leaned back in his chair, closed his eyes, and laughed. "You sly bitch." He cracked an eye open. "You just keep on surprising me, Maura Coutts."

I didn't fight the smile that crossed my lips.

We spent the rest of the morning collecting anything we could from the small house and garage. Together, Sid and I peered into the small trunk where we'd collected our treasures — a few tools, a small tarp, three blankets, two pillows, the nearly empty jar of peanut butter, the cat food, and a pair of scissors. Sid held the gun in his hand while I held a faded yellow map we'd found in what Sid called a glove compartment.

After a determined nod, I slammed the trunk shut. I helped Sid hobble to the passenger side door, where he climbed into his seat and collapsed in a tired heap. He was too proud to admit how pained he felt, but I could tell from the way he spoke through his teeth that he was doing everything in his power to remain awake.

A few weeks ago, the barriers ahead of us would've convinced me to give up. I would've waited for Sid to tell us what to do, probably until it was too late. But as I got into the driver's seat and began easing the car down the steep driveway, I swallowed a bittersweet realization.

The girl I used to be no longer existed.

13

ELI

THREE DAYS PASSED with no sign of Sid. The odds were not in our favor. I tried rationalizing what this meant, that some outside force had taken my brother and done something awful to him. But even that was difficult to understand. Sid was a *survivor*. He couldn't be dead. He would fight his way back to us. I was sure of it.

On the first day, we set out on a mission to find a working vehicle. Four houses down, I found a mini-van with a quarter tank of gas, and we took it through the neighborhood, shouting into hollow homes with no response. We returned with a bulging bag of canned food and the heavy weight of defeat and regret.

On the second day, we drove further, through wide stretches of trees, to neighborhoods beyond. But found no signs of struggle, no signs of campers, and certainly no sign of Sid.

On the third day, we drove in the opposite direction through two small abandoned towns. We stumbled across a day-old campfire, but nothing suggested the existence of someone who was injured or putting up a fight. Still, it was a lead, and we returned that evening with the first spark of hope since Sid had first disappeared.

But on that third evening, after Mia had fallen asleep and I'd carried her to bed, Holli sat me down in the kitchen and looked at me sternly through the candlelight.

"We can't stay here forever," she reminded me, glancing around the kitchen. "Resources are scarce. We have no clean water source, and we need to find a place with a wood stove or fireplace. Not to mention, we're in a place that could attract the Hunters."

Holli's forward-thinking had saved us so many times in the past — preparing for the seasons, starting a garden, remaining in an area with easy access to water — but in that moment, she thoroughly annoyed me.

"I know. But we can't leave," I answered. "Not yet. I know he's out there, Hol — I just need to keep looking. We'll find him. Or he'll find us. We can't just…leave him."

"Eli." Holli touched my arm gently. I couldn't look at her, so I focused on her fingernails instead. "We have no leads. He could be anywhere by now."

"Yes, we do! What about the campfire?" I searched her face for understanding. "That was a lead. That was something!"

"That…doesn't tell us much."

I inhaled, trying to contain my frustration. "It's a *sign*. Even if it's not Sid, it means there's someone else in the area who might have seen or heard something. They might know something that could help us find him. We have to at least try to find them."

"Eli." Holli's heavy tone made me pause. She looked so tired in the candlelight. New lines weaved through her face, a white chin whisker standing out in the glow as she spoke. "We have no idea where he might have gone. Even if we spend time looking for this person, there's a good chance they know nothing and are just passing through."

I shook my head. "But they *might*—"

"I know this is hard. I know you don't want to think about having to leave Sid. But fall is coming. Winter will be on its heels. If we could find somewhere closer to water, we could start a garden and start rebuilding. We need to find wood — blankets, somewhere we can hole up for the winter. We have to think about Mia. We have to think about ourselves."

"But *Sid*—"

"You know Sid," she said kindly, dipping her head to catch my gaze. I swallowed. "He wouldn't want us to stay here and let our situation worsen. He would be furious to know that's what we were doing in his absence."

I snatched my hand away from her. "You don't know what he'd want," I said but faltered. My words sounded like Sid's had when we argued about Maura's presence in our camp. I knew I was being unreasonable. But Sid was the last family I had left.

"I love Sid as much as you do," she continued.

"No!" I said, heat flushing my face. "You think he's dead." Holli paused, and it felt like someone had knocked the wind out of me for a moment. "You think he's dead?" I repeated as a question.

"I don't know what I think," Holli said, her face falling.

"He's not dead."

"You're letting your emotions cloud your judgment."

"He's my *brother*."

"I understand." Her clipped tone set my jaw straight. "Just…please consider what I'm saying. We'll be fine here for another day or two. But if there's nothing new by then, we *need* to come up with a plan, Eli. Okay?"

I chewed my lip, my skin tingling as sweat formed on

the back of my neck. I was too angry to respond. How could Holli give up hope? How could she make peace with Sid's absence?

After a few moments, she stood from her chair and left me in the dim candlelight. Anger hovered above me like a black cloud. I knew it was misguided. It masked my fear and the unbearable idea that I might never see my brother again.

MORNING ARRIVED WITH A STEADY GLOW, the sun bursting through the trees with bright rays reflecting off the sides of houses and glass panes. I slouched in one of the armchairs, fiddling with the side of the rifle, trying to stay awake. Even inside, I could already feel the heat.

The light pitter-patter of footsteps marked Mia's arrival, and she peered at me from the top of the stairs with a wide yawn.

"Good morning, Miss Mia," I said, waving her down. A smile crossed her face as she bounced downstairs and climbed into my lap.

"G'morning," she drawled, chewing on her fingers before she looked up. Her big eyes searched my face. "Did Sid come back yet?"

Her hopeful gaze nearly cracked me.

"Not yet," I said in what I hoped was a convincing tone. "How'd you sleep?"

She shrugged. "Okay." She looked back towards the kitchen. "I haveta pee."

I allowed myself to smile. "Well, okay," I said. "Let's get that out of the way, then."

Mia padded barefoot across the foyer, pulling the front

door open. Sunlight spilled into the entryway, and I closed my eyes for a moment as I embraced the warmth on my face. The small girl ran down the concrete walkway toward the bushes that were eating their way through the house siding.

"Just make sure there's no poison ivy," I called to her as she disappeared between the brush. Holli had taught us how to identify the hairy vines with three shiny green leaves.

A shimmering reflection caught my eye in the distance. Was I hallucinating? Something ambled toward us, crawling across the road. Once, seeing a car driving down a neighborhood street would have been normal. In fact, it would've been strange not to. But now, I was sure it meant only one thing.

My heart hammered. I raced into the house, holding the rifle in one hand as I ran back out the door. The sunlight forced me to squint, and I placed my hand above my eyes before I gripped the gun in both hands, aiming.

A small, silver sedan inched up the road, moving at a zig-zag down the street. The sun reflected across the windshield, blocking the bodies inside.

"Mia," I hissed.

She rustled in the bushes.

"Mia," I called again, trying to steady the rise of panic in my voice. "Come out now, please. I need you to go inside."

My vision tunneled as the car crept closer. I closed one eye to get a better aim and wavered between opting to lower the gun to help Mia inside or waiting here to shoot. Had they already seen us? I glanced over my shoulder as Mia climbed from the bushes, her goofy little grin making my fear explode.

"Eli?"

"Come on," I said, jutting my jaw towards the front door. "Get inside." Her face fell, worry painted across her features. I turned, keeping one eye on the approaching car. They were already too close.

"Mia!" I couldn't help but shout. "Get inside!"

"Eli?"

She was at my side. "Inside," I said, keeping my gaze on the car, steadying my hold. I took a few steps backward, Mia following my movements until she scurried over the threshold.

"Stay there!" I shouted. "Don't come outside." Then, turning toward the stairs, I called, "Holli?" My voice bounced against the high ceiling. Silence. "HOLLI?"

I could hear the engine now. I was certain whoever was in the car had already seen us. There was no time to run. No time to get into the shitty van. No time to grab our meager supplies. We were sitting ducks. Holli had been right. We'd waited too long. My selfish hope that Sid would come back to us had driven us straight into a death trap. Well, there was no way I'd let us go down without a fight. I turned, barely feeling the weight of the gun, my finger resting against the trigger, ready to shoot.

"Close the door, Mia," I said. She whimpered before the door snapped shut and my terror swelled.

The car rolled forward, bumping up against the curb in front of the house and scraping the front bumper. I squinted, trying to see who the driver was. Hunters? Scavengers? Someone who needed help? And then I realized how strange it was that the car seemed to know where to go. It was as if someone inside had been here before...

I shifted forward, down the concrete walk, toward where the car parked. All I needed was a glimpse. I'd know my brother's face anywhere. My heart leaped in relief, but as I looked at the driver — the hero who had brought my brother home, I couldn't help but gasp. Dark features and a mop of curly hair — a face I was sure I'd never see again.

Maura Coutts.

14

ELI

THE DRIVER'S side door fell open as I let the rifle go slack in my hands. My jaw dropped. I could taste the humid air on my tongue, but my gaze remained fixed on the small woman climbing out of the car. She didn't pause to look at me. Instead, she came around to the passenger side door where Sid sat.

Maura had been driving the car, which explained the haphazard movements coming down the street. But how? And why? Questions spiraled, bouncing around the tired corners of my brain, each one fighting for attention. I pushed them away. My relief coincided with a pit of worry settling deep in my stomach. I reached the curb and peered at Maura over the top of the car.

She hunched beside the open door, offering her shoulder to the dark arm that emerged. Sid's massive figure rocked forward before falling back in the seat with a low grunt. Maura looked up, her brown eyes swimming with concern. My stomach dropped.

"Can you help?" she asked.

Something was wrong. I dumped the rifle in the grass,

my heart picking up its pace as I pulled the door fully open, part of me terrified at what I was about to see.

My brother looked relatively intact — two arms, two legs, a solid torso. But as he turned, I saw a piece of fabric stuck to the side of his head where his ear should've been. My blood ran cold, but it was relief that came to the forefront. I ducked beneath the roof and embraced him in an awkward hug.

He grunted as I squeezed him. This close, I could smell the sickly sweet aroma of a new infection.

"You okay?" I whispered, pulling away to look him in the eye. "You fuckin' scared me."

He winced, then nodded.

"C'mon." I offered my shoulder, slipping my hand beneath his armpit and around his back.

Judging by his dead weight, I knew Sid was in bad shape. There was no way in hell he'd allow me to lift him up and out of the car. The stubborn ass would've rather walked on two broken legs than accept help. He hung on my shoulder as we cleared the curb, limping to the front door. I could feel the fever beneath his skin.

"It's infected," Maura said, following on our heels. "He's had a fever for a few days now and I knew we just needed to get him back to Holli because she'd know what to do. I cleaned it and put the cloth on it, but I didn't have the supplies to do much more—" She spoke a mile a minute, barely stopping to breathe as we approached the door.

"Oh, my!" The front door flew open. Holli's frazzled face emerged, her wild hair sprouting up from her crown like unruly grass. Mia peered curiously out from behind her legs. Holli's eyes widened as she glanced between the three of us before she burst into tears.

"Sid!" Mia cried. "And Maura!" She giggled in delight,

clapping her hands together as she jumped around for joy. "They're back!"

"What's wrong?" Holli breathed, blanching as she inspected Sid, glancing at me, then Maura. She hastily wiped away her tears.

"My ear," Sid said, tilting his head.

"And my—" Holli drew Maura into an embrace, smoothing out her hair with her hand. "My goodness," was all she managed to whisper before she stepped inside the house, moving so we had enough room to enter.

I strained against Sid's weight, easing him into the recliner. Maura hovered at his side, nearly as tall as he was sitting down. She kept her hands on her hips, biting her lip as she looked up at Holli, waiting for her assessment.

Holli's silence was a clear sign she was as shocked as I felt. Both Maura and Sid were covered in dirt and blood, cuts and bruises up their legs and arms. Sweat and mud stains were caked into their clothing, dirt coating their hair, clashing with the pristine house decor around us. They looked like they'd been to war.

"What. Happened?" Holli asked the question that danced on my tongue as she moved forward to inspect Sid.

"Later," Sid moaned. "Please tell me you have something for pain, Hol. Please."

"Of course," she whispered. "Take him up to one of the beds," she ordered me before she took Mia by the hand and ran off toward the kitchen. I glanced at Maura, who nodded, understanding. Together, we lifted Sid from the recliner and helped him to the stairs.

Sid gritted his teeth through every step before we got him to the second floor, into the first bedroom in the hall, and onto the twin-sized mattress. He collapsed face up, spread-eagle, on top of the comforter, a plume of dirt rising from his added weight. Maura and I hung back as

Holli returned, Mia beside her, both carrying several jars, baggies, and a pot of water.

"Here," Holli said, scooping a clean jar into the water and handing it to him. She pressed two pills into his hand. "They're expired. They won't work as well, but they're all we've got."

Sid stared at them before he leaned up on his elbow, threw them in his mouth, and swallowed a gulp of water before collapsing backward again. Holli groaned as she got to her knees on the side of the bed, inspecting the piece of fabric on his head, wet with pus and pink with blood. She took a deep breath, settled her hand on Sid's forehead, and ripped.

Sid's pained yell was unlike any sound I'd heard him make before — pure agony. Torment. Maura covered her mouth. Holli winced but wasted no time dipping her head down as she looked at the pus-covered flesh on his face. She took a clean rag and dipped it into the pot of water.

"I'm so sorry this is going to sting, love. But I have to clean it," she said before she began to wipe at the wound. Sid's back arched as she pressed the rag to his flesh. He squeezed his features together as he fought through the pain, his fist pounding the comforter as he groaned and whimpered every time Holli moved the towel an inch.

Having an audience for this was not a good use of anyone's time or attention. I threw my arm around Mia and scooped her up, tilting my head toward the door. Maura found my gaze and nodded, following me out.

"Let us know if you need us," I said to Holli, who waved me away with her free hand as I closed the door. The barrier muffled Sid's cries. I hoped Holli and Maura assumed my departure was for Sid's privacy. That was certainly part of it. But I was too ashamed to admit the guilt I felt.

I carried Mia downstairs and into the kitchen. Maura followed, stopping every so often to inspect the artwork on the wall. This place was so far from home, so unfamiliar. It felt strange to think it might feel familiar to Maura. She was used to luxury. Peter Coutts had spared no expense for his most devout followers. The thought made my jaw clench, but as Maura entered the kitchen, I let the tension fade.

It was beyond reason, beyond comprehension, that she was here, standing in front of me. Add the fact that she'd somehow brought Sid with her was another puzzling fact I longed to unravel. Even though it'd been mere weeks since I'd seen her last, there was something about her that seemed different.

She bent down to untie her dirty boots, her collarbones a sharp angle beneath her bronzed skin. Her hair had grown longer and more unkempt, impossible to tame. Her t-shirt hung loosely over her frame, a purple bruise swelling from her left shoulder up behind her neck. Scratches and scabs littered her arms like freckles. She peeled off two foul-smelling socks and stuffed them into her boots, massaging her feet in slow circles. I remembered meeting her after we'd climbed out of the creek. How that one wound across her cheek had been her only blemish.

"How?" I heard my voice as though it were someone else's. Maura looked up, then straightened fully. "How are you here?"

Exhaustion made her eyes puffy. She sighed as she found a seat at the kitchen island. Mia sat on the stool beside her, spinning.

"I left," Maura said, not meeting my gaze. I walked around the counter and leaned forward on my forearms, listening. "They took me back after I left you, but, Father, he—" She pressed her hands to her face. "He didn't listen to anything I had to say. Which I'm sure you all could've predicted. I mean, you tried to tell me." She lifted her gaze, brown eyes welling with tears. "And I didn't listen."

I shook my head, tracing the swirl on the marble counter with my eyes. "It's one thing to hear it, Maura. It's a whole other thing to experience it. You needed to see it for yourself. There's no shame in that."

She hung her head before launching into what happened during our time apart. My jaw dropped as she outlined impossible feat after impossible feat.

"And then I found Sid at that...*place*," she finished, pressing her lips together. Tears cleared a wet path down her dirty skin.

"What place?"

She wiped her palms across her face, smudging her tears into the lingering dirt. Her eyes flickered to Mia, who was pulling apart the stems of the dandelion necklaces she'd made with Holli, none the wiser.

"Hey, Mia," I said. The little girl looked up, and I pointed toward the small study. "Would you go play in there for a few minutes? So Maura and I can talk?"

She frowned, then looked sideways at Maura. "Are you sad?" she asked.

Maura's lips spread into a sad smile. "How can I be sad when I get to see you again?" She reached forward and scurried her fingers up Mia's arm.

Mia broke into a wide grin before nodding, hopping off her stool, and scurrying into the study. I turned back to Maura, brows raised. She pressed her fingers into her eyes before she spoke again.

"The place was full of people," she said, glancing at the room where Mia had disappeared. "They were...given drugs. Or alcohol. Stuff that made them feel good. Things they were addicted to." I watched her swallow, fighting for her next words. "The men kept us locked in rooms. Made us strip and shower, and that's when I found Sid. They were using all those people in there for…" She winced. "… sex." The word came out in a whisper, so quiet I wasn't sure I'd heard her correctly.

She closed her eyes, folded her arms on the counter, and sobbed into them. Her cries jolted me, and without thinking, I let my hand rest on her arm. Maura was still innocent, still so naïve beneath her bumps and bruises. The journey back to us had changed her. I was sure of it. Gooseflesh appeared under my fingers as they brushed against her soft skin.

Of course, it made sense. There was no such thing as law enforcement, no legal recourse to answer to. Men with nothing to lose and everything to gain thrived in this world. Yes, there was illness and animals, and the off chance you'd die from the common cold. But man was the biggest threat of them all. Maura glanced up, and her breath shuddered.

I touched my hand to my forehead, letting my fingers drag across my mouth as I considered the scenario. Rage boiled beneath my chest, bubbling to the flush in my cheeks as I thought of my brother and Maura being assaulted. Being abused. I looked at Maura, eyes falling on the bruise beneath her shirt.

"Did they hurt you?" I asked, unable to ask the real question. *Did they do the unimaginable? Force themselves on you? Rape you?*

Maura brought her hand to her shoulder, touching the bruise that disappeared at the back of her neck. "Not that way," she whispered. A spark of relief helped ease some of the tension in my shoulders, but I found myself gazing upward at where Sid lay in a bed with a deadly injury. "Sid was there longer than I was, though," Maura continued, following my gaze as if she understood what I was thinking.

I felt my nostrils flare as I tightened my hands into fists. "So you escaped?" I croaked through my rage.

She nodded. "I…He…Sid, he…" Her mouth moved without sound before she looked back at me.

"It's okay." I gave her an encouraging nod. "You don't have to—"

"He killed one of the men." Her voice was steady and certain, eyes dark. She inhaled before letting her shoulders sag as if she could no longer hold them up. "I know there wasn't another choice, but it was horrible. I've never actually seen…someone…you know." She took a shuddering breath before breaking into a fit of tears, hands at her face, cupping her cheeks, her shoulders shaking as she sobbed.

Her sorrow and shock were so palpable. I came around the counter and embraced her, wrapping my arms around her small frame as I held her to my chest. She leaned into me, pressing herself against me hard enough I bumped up against the counter.

I knew Sid had done things to get here. I'd always assumed he'd killed, though we'd never sat down and discussed it directly. Crossing the country to return to Mom's must've been brutal. And now this? Shame crawled up my spine. I'd never paused to ask. I had been so focused on Mom's death, on how Sid would react to my failure to protect her, I'd never stopped to consider what he'd gone through. Perhaps I'd justified it by assuming he wouldn't want to talk about it. And maybe that was true. But it still was a piss poor excuse.

Maura's cries slowed, and she pulled back from my hold, wiping her hand across her face and nose in her shirt. I leaned against the counter, eyeing the room Mia had disappeared into.

"We're running low on supplies," I said, massaging my temple. "And if Sid killed one of their men, there's a good chance they're going to come looking for us. Men like that…they'll want their revenge."

Footfalls on the stairs announced Holli's arrival. She entered the kitchen, wiping blood from her hands, her eyes distant in thought. She looked up and swiveled her gaze between me and Maura.

"How is he?" Maura asked, a quiver in her tone.

Holli took a seat at the island and looked at her hands. "The wound's infected," she said matter-of-factly. "I used the Gotu Kola ointment to help the tissue repair, but I'm not confident it's going to do the trick. And it's certainly not enough to draw out the infection. I needed to apply it two days ago. His fever's up, and that's a bad sign."

"How bad?" I asked.

She met my gaze, her eyes heavy with worry. "Even years ago, an infection of this magnitude was extremely dangerous. I need something to stitch up his wound. And…" She sighed, shaking her head.

"What?" I pressed.

"He needs antibiotics, Eli. He…probably needs them to survive this."

15

ELI

EVEN WHEN THE world was still operating, though its structure, order, and government hung by a thread, finding antibiotics had been tricky. It was another of the many necessities the Coutts stripped away, hoarding humanity's best defense at fighting infections in the name of God. On the Outside, the doctors added us to a waiting list, a risky gamble. Something as common as a dental infection or strep throat could kill you if left untreated. I was sure people died waiting for their prescriptions, agonizing over when more would be produced. I was also sure Peter Coutts didn't care.

Now, trying to find antibiotics was not only impossible but dangerous. Cities meant the possibility of meeting more survivors, and encountering desperate people meant we needed to be incredibly cautious. I met Holli's gaze and tried not to panic.

"Antibiotics," I repeated with a forced laugh. "Where the hell do you think we can find antibiotics?"

"I know you searched the towns nearby for Sid, but maybe you missed something. Maybe—"

"Maybe what? Antibiotics will just appear out of thin air? After decades of shortages?"

"I don't know!" Holli shouted, slamming her fist down on the counter. Maura and I drew our shoulders back, surprised by her sudden rage. "I'm sorry." She looked shocked herself. "I'm just telling you what the reality is right now. I hate it as much as you do."

"There's nothing else? Another remedy? What if we went back to the truck? To Mom's?"

Holli shook her head. "I don't think the trip would be worth it. I can only do so much with herbal remedies. Infection is tricky. It'll get into his bloodstream, and then he'll become septic, and his organs will start shutting down. He needs antibiotics. And he needs them yesterday."

"Okay." My mind raced. Sid was the decision maker. He stayed calm under stress. He always knew what to do. I was the younger brother. I'd follow him to the ends of the earth. How was I supposed to get us out of this?

I turned away from the girls and circled the kitchen island, running my fingers through my beard. Antibiotics. If there were antibiotics anywhere, they'd be in…

"East Lockwood," I said. "It's one of the larger towns, maybe a few hours from Mom's. She took us there when she needed to see a specialist. We were pretty young, but I remember there being a pharmacy."

I closed my eyes to cling to the memory. Mom, Sid, and I had walked the sidewalks, waiting in a long line wrapped around the block. It was cold. Mom had played tic-tac-toe with us on a spare piece of notebook paper she'd found in her purse. She adjusted the scarf around my neck, tucking it up over my nose. "Just a few more minutes, baby," she'd said. We took the bus home.

"East Lockwood," Holli said, her voice distant. "You're

right." There was a lightness to her tone. Hopefulness. "There's a map in the office," she said. "Can you—?"

Maura moved first, hurrying into the room where Mia had disappeared. She returned a moment later, opening the map and spreading it across the center counter. We crowded around it, and I traced the path with my finger. A major thruway ran north to south, just outside the neighborhood. Coal Creek sat southwest of us. Southeast, I found East Lockwood.

"Thirty miles or so," Holli said.

"We could leave in a few hours and get there tonight," I answered.

"That's good. Packing up should be easy. We can take a van. Lay Sid in the backseat."

I nodded, confident in the plan. I wanted to ask Holli the hard questions. How long she thought Sid had left. What the signs of sepsis were. But I couldn't bring myself to go there. Not yet. Not until we exhausted all options.

"I'll get started on packing," Maura said. I gave her a small smile before she retreated into the office with Mia.

I patted my hand against the map. "This will work, Holli. Won't it?"

Holli lifted her chin and caught my gaze. "It's our best shot, E."

It had been quite some time since I'd prayed for anything. Any inkling of faith I had fast turned to anger after Mom died, and despite trying to ignore it, I felt some kind of comfort in my rage. If there was a God, they'd made it clear they were uninterested in my well-being and very likely hated me. Perhaps they enjoyed seeing me squirm and suffer. Whatever the case, I had no allegiance to any higher power — only to myself and the people who had helped me survive.

With Maura needing time to rest and Holli needing time to tend to Sid, I ventured out on my own to siphon gas from neighboring houses so we had enough to get to East Lockwood. By car, the journey would only take about an hour, but that was only if we didn't run into any hurdles on the way.

I picked three houses with garages still holding cars I'd seen when looking for Sid. Siphoning made my mouth taste bitter, burning my throat as I carried the spare water jug at my hip. It was the best container I could find, but it did a poor job of containing the fumes well. By the time I returned to the house, late afternoon had settled, and my head spun.

Holli, Maura, and Mia had packed the van. I left the gasoline with Holli to drain into the tank while Maura and I helped Sid downstairs.

His bedroom was warm and thick with a sour smell. Sid lay curled in the fetal position, blankets askew, fresh sweat coating all of his visible skin. As I approached, I could see a slight shiver in his shoulders. His hands crossed over his chest, subconsciously trying to keep his fever at bay.

I hovered over him. His eyes flickered behind his lids, urgent with whatever dream they kept up with. I grasped his shoulder and nearly gasped — his boiling skin was so hot I couldn't help but think the fever would melt his insides. He inhaled sharply, startling himself awake with a wince and a moan.

"Hey," I whispered, letting my hand trail up and down his sticky bicep. "We've gotta move."

"Where?" His voice came out as a rattling breath. Maura's arm stretched out beside me, gripping a jar of water. Sid grasped it and brought it to his lips with shaking hands, gulping it down like he'd never drunk anything before.

"We've got to get you some medicine," I said, worried if he asked too many questions, he'd insist we not go. But as he pushed the half-drank jar into my hands, I knew it wasn't what I needed to be worried about. He could barely keep his eyes open; when they were, his gaze was unfocused and confused. He pressed his hand into his face before collapsing onto the mattress. I glanced at Maura, who looked like she was about to cry.

"Sid?" I tried again, tugging on his shoulder. He lifted an eyebrow and rolled to the side, nuzzling his face back into the pillow.

After a few attempts, Maura and I got one of Sid's arms over each of our shoulders. We lifted him onto unsteady feet, and he groaned as we half carried, half dragged him out of the room and down the stairs.

Holli scurried to the passenger side door, sliding it open wide so we could ease Sid inside. It wasn't easy. He bumped his head on the roof, prompting a slew of curse words and tears from both my brother and Maura. Finally, we managed to get him into the back row and pile ourselves in, with me in the driver's seat.

I was grateful for the minivan's space. Sid could lie almost flat in the back seat. Holli and Mia sat in the rear captain seats. Maura sat in the passenger seat, holding the map. With one last look at the house we'd found refuge in, I gripped the steering wheel and drove us away from the Coutts halfway homes toward the major thruway. The spark of hope from this morning had begun to fade, making way for an empty pit of desperation that settled deep in my stomach. I clutched the steering wheel tight beneath my fingers, gritting my teeth to calm myself.

Please, I begged whoever might've been listening. *Please let this work.*

16

MAURA

WITH THE MAP laid across my lap, I drifted in and out of sleep, a humid breeze washing over my face through the open window. My calves ached, my head throbbed, and I stunk to the high heavens. But I was grateful to be with Eli and the others.

Every so often, I snuck a glance at Sid. He was a solid, shadowed mass in the back of the van, shifting his weight to find comfort that seemed to never come. Eli did his best, but with every bump or sharp turn we took, Sid groaned in pain, which prompted Holli to lean back every so often to check on his bandages and vitals.

Oblivious to the urgency of our trip, Mia sang songs and pointed out things she saw from the window. A part of me was thankful for this little girl's innocence during this drive. What was happening to Sid was ugly and unthinkable. Her moments of joy gave us moments of refuge from the despair I was sure we all felt.

As we got closer to East Lockwood, I began following our route on the map, giving Eli directions as he drove us down a desolate, tree-lined highway. Thick foliage hid the mountains, but I knew Coutts Peak lurked beyond, teeming with Hunters. I hoped they wouldn't be worried about East Lockwood.

As the road widened, the trees thinned until they were gone completely, leaving us on an overpass with guardrails on either side. Stunning mountainous landscape covered our view to the left. Coutts Peak was a purple shadow in the distance. I tensed in my seat, wondering just how far Father and his Hunters could see from their mountain. Would they spot us? Or were we a blur, blending in with the terrain?

The road curved, and Eli drove the car to an exit ramp, giving us a bird's-eye view of the largest town I'd seen so far on the Outside. Large brick buildings spotted the outskirts, but the structures closest to the heart of the town were marred by scorched earth, exterior walls and windows stained black. A deep crater sat in the center — a dark blemish on a town that had once held history, traditions, and families. Blown-apart cars, shattered glass, and building debris surrounded the immediate hole, the extent of damages impossible to see. Eli slowed the car, tension rising in our small space. Holli released a small gasp, her hand covering her mouth.

"No…" Eli's voice was quiet and strained, almost pleading as he hit the brakes, jolting all of us forward in our seats. "No, no, no, no…" The quiver in his voice felt like a gut punch. He slammed his hands down on the steering wheel over and over again with such force he accidentally turned the turn signal and windshield wipers on.

"Maybe this is a good thing," Holli said, reaching her hand out to pat his shoulder. "There could be supplies left. If someone saw this, maybe they avoided the town completely."

Silence. Eli glanced at her.

"We have to try," she urged.

Eli nodded, then turned back to the steering wheel and began guiding us into the belly of the small city. But my heart wouldn't stop pounding. I couldn't shake my horrible feeling. Eli claimed Father had been involved in so many atrocities on the Outside — could it be possible he'd been involved in *this*, too?

"What happened here?" I whispered, unable to help my curiosity.

"The government often bombed cities or towns they deemed *a lost cause*," Holli said, her voice heavy. "I knew they'd done this in the larger cities, but I didn't think they'd bother with a place like this."

I shuddered, a sinking weight settling in the pit of my stomach. I looked out the window again as we reached the end of the ramp. "All the people here were all sick?"

"No," Holli said grimly. "They weren't. But if the US military had too much of anything left in their arsenal, it was bombs. With the lack of medical care, I think they just figured it was easier this way."

I inhaled sharply. Lack of medical care was because of Father. They bombed people to death because we had kept medicine and doctors within our borders. Because Father told us we were the only worthy ones. Because, according to him, we were too holy, too *devout* to get sick. God would never plague us with illness.

None of that made sense anymore — another puzzle I had yet to figure out. Eli had brought up the absence of sickness in our commune back when we were still in the trailer, and at the time, I'd been certain God helped us survive. After all, that was what Father had proclaimed. Now, I wasn't so sure. Even with doctors and medicine, it was strange the sickness hadn't affected us.

Cars packed the streets: some stalled on the road,

others parked on the side of the street. Eli navigated us around them until we hit an impassable intersection beneath a partially collapsed bridge. With a heavy sigh, he pulled the van into park and leaned back in his seat, shoulders lowering in defeat.

"This is good," Holli said, though I sensed her frustration with Eli's attitude. "We're out of the sun, hidden from anyone who might be looking at the town. Leave the car here. You and Maura go. I can stay here with Sid and Mia." She hesitated, looking out the window for a moment. "There's *got* to be something here we can use for him."

"Holli," Mia whined, unbuckling her seatbelt as she tugged on Holli's shoulder. "I'm hungry."

Holli busied herself with her bag, producing a small baggie. "Fruit rolls?" she said, handing them to Mia, who tore open the bag and began eating. Eli eyed her before catching my gaze. My stomach gave an unsettled grumble, but I wasn't hungry enough to eat yet.

"Maura," Eli said sternly, opening his door. I opened mine too, stepping out in sync. He moved to the trunk, removing one of the rifles and a backpack, which he handed to me. I slung it over my shoulders, pleased to find it almost weightless. As we entered the middle of the intersection, Eli's dark eyes studied the world around us, hand on his holster, ready for any dangerous movement in the distance.

The thick air stunk like sulfur. Eli stayed silent, his gaze distant. I followed his gaze. The landscape beyond the broken bridge was hard to make out — everything was coated in black soot, making the buildings, the sidewalks, the cars, and whatever else was out in the streets blend together.

"The pharmacy should be about six blocks from here,"

Eli said into the empty air, his eyes fixed on a green street sign in the distance. "C'mon."

He waved me along as he began to walk. My calves cramped in protest, but I forced myself to fall in step with him. Tension radiated from his body, his grip tight on the rifle as though he hoped to crack it.

"Are you alright?" I knew the question was futile, but I also knew how damaging an emotional explosion could be.

"Fine." His curt tone suggested otherwise, but I was not about to contradict him.

Most of the car windows or doors were shattered, suggesting someone had been here scavenging at some point. I'd expected as much. A year was a long time for medication to stay in one place. Still, my heart sank. If someone had broken into the cars, they'd broken into the pharmacy, too.

Eli stepped up on the sidewalk, kicking an empty box so it went sailing through the air. Black soot flew off its edges as it hit the side of a brick building and dropped to the ground. He ran a hand through his hair.

"We're not gonna find anything here," he grumbled in frustration, adding extra emphasis to each word he spoke through gritted teeth.

"We *have* to try," I said.

"I know!" Hysteria clung to the edge of his tone, and I saw his jaw clench as I glanced sideways at him.

"Okay."

"No." He sighed, then shook his head. "I'm sorry. I'm just...God, look at this place!" He gestured to our surroundings. "It's a wasteland."

I could practically hear Holli repeat herself. This was our best shot. This was the only way. Didn't he understand that?

"Well, stranger things have happened, haven't they?" I

said. "We've all made it this far. It can't have been for nothing."

"That's what I'm afraid of."

His words echoed off the empty buildings as we crossed another intersection, this one with an overturned car, its frame gray from the flames that had devoured it. I longed to remind him that God had a purpose and plan for each of us, but the gesture seemed wrong. That wasn't what Eli needed. It wasn't what he believed. I felt a moment of pity for what kind of grief that brought.

The walk was shorter than I expected. Eli hurried around a corner, and I followed, stepping through the settled black debris until we reached a slim brick building. Behind the bars in its window, a sign read Pharmacy.

Had Eli not pointed it out, I wouldn't have noticed it. The building was dingy and weathered, evident even beneath the black soot. Nothing like our sterile, bleached white pharmacies back in the commune. He tugged the door open, but it caught before it swung wide, secured to the building by a thick chain.

"We can climb under," he said, inspecting the space before squatting. He shoved the rifle in first, ducking beneath the chain and disappearing inside. I followed suit with a deep breath and one last look over my shoulder at the empty street.

I blinked away daylight as my eyes adjusted to the dark interior. Shelves lined both walls of the narrow store, with one long aisle splitting the space in two. Most surfaces were empty and dust-covered, but the occasional cardboard box or plastic wrapping still lingered. Eli towered over the top of the shelves, beelining to the back.

A long desk and a single door stood at the far end of the room, separated from the rest of the space by a half-hanging lopsided plastic barrier. Eli made quick work of pulling the barrier off, leaning it up against the desk before he heaved himself over the counter with a grunt.

Though my body protested, I hopped up on the desk, sliding into the carpeted back room behind the counter. White shelves filled most of the small space, almost as bare as the ones we'd passed in the store. I glimpsed a few unopened boxes at Eli's fingertips. He scrutinized them before throwing them over his shoulder, where they landed, crumpled, on the ground behind him.

"Look for anything with '-cillin,' '-cycline,' '-oxacin,' or '-mycin' in the last part of the name," he said without looking at me. "Anything with 'cef' at the start of the name could work, too. And anything with paracetamol or aceta-minophen would help his pain."

Despite our meager pickings, I detected an ounce of hope in his voice. I only nodded, inspecting the boxes and bottles on the shelves. Eli emptied his shelf quickly, his desperation more palpable by the second.

"Anything?" he asked. I met his worried gaze and shook my head. His nostrils flared, but he nodded before moving to a new shelf. My heart sank as I scanned the remaining boxes. There was nothing worthwhile. Still, I made a show of taking the boxes off the shelf and discarding them one by one.

When I finished, I glanced back at Eli, who threw the last medication into a haphazard pile at the corner of the room. He leaned his forehead against the shelf, eyes closed, his white-knuckled grip on the edge of the now empty structure.

"We should just double-check," I said, moving toward the pile. "In case we missed something." I kneeled, sorting through them, looking for the names Eli had called out, but none matched. The stack dwindled, and as I placed the last box to my side, I looked up at Eli.

He sat on the counter, staring at the floor, eyes lost in thought, his shoulders hunched forward. The heels of his boots tapped against the shelves beneath the desk like a rhythmic heartbeat. I stood, brushing my jeans off, and approached him. Eli looked at me, and even in the shadows, I saw tears well in the edges of his brown eyes.

"What the hell are we going to do?"

"We'll keep going," I assured him, even though all I could hear was Holli's urgency. "Maybe there's another pharmacy — another building we can check."

"I can't—" He choked before looking down at his hands in his lap, fiddling with his knuckles.

"You *can*."

"No." His tone deepened, and he met my gaze. He was crying now, his tears spilling over the edges and down his cheeks, soaking into his beard. Beneath his dark whiskers, his pink lip quivered as he searched for a more suitable explanation. I straightened, approaching the counter, before hoisting myself up to sit beside him, careful not to touch him.

"I can't lose him, Maura," he whispered, touching his chin to his shoulder, his eyes avoiding mine. "I don't know what I'll do."

I inhaled, searching for the right words, the things I was supposed to say in someone's moment of need. I thought of prayer, of words of comfort, of Father's sermons in which he preached *God has a plan for us all*. But I pulled them back from the tip of my tongue. Those things hardly offered comfort. I knew that. I always believed the things people said in moments of grief were to make themselves feel better. Many people looked to offer some semblance of comfort to ease the uncomfortableness that accompanies sitting in someone else's pain.

"He's not gone yet," I said, hoping it was the right thing to say. "He's still here, Eli. And we have to keep trying until we can't anymore."

Eli's eyes met mine, and I felt like I'd been turned upside down. There was a depth to his gaze beneath the surface I found I wanted to explore. He was more than a protector or a survivor. He was human and hurting — an emotion I found almost everyone related to in some way. Even here, on the Outside of the commune. Those emotions didn't end at the borders of our community like Father had led us to believe. These people out here were just as human, fragile, and capable of love as the rest of us.

I placed my hand on Eli's arm, letting the pads of my fingers gently trace along his forearm, grasping and squeezing in an effort to provide a bit of comfort. It was something I'd sorely missed after leaving Mother's home. Human touch. A squeeze of affection. Just enough to know someone else was there and listening. That someone else understood you were in pain. It didn't take away the grief. But it was better than some forced lecture about God that would mean little to him.

He tilted his head and gave me a sad smile, bringing his other arm up to wipe the tears from his face. "There's nowhere else," he whispered. "There's nowhere else to go."

"Then we'll make him comfortable," I answered. "We can do that, at the very least."

He held my gaze, breathing so deeply I saw it build in his chest before he deflated. "Let's get back," he said. "Before it gets dark."

Together, we climbed back over the counter and out into the waning daylight. Terror held me tight in its grip.

Losing Sid might destroy Eli. It might annihilate his hope. And though I knew I was still ignorant to many of the truths out here, I did know that losing one's hope was more dangerous than anything else we were destined to stumble across.

17

ELI

By the time we rounded the corner to the bridge, the clouds had shifted their color from wispy gray to pink, orange, and purple, announcing dusk's arrival. Humidity came in waves, but without the sun, it lost its thick edge. Maura and I trudged across the cluttered street together. I was brutally aware of the backpack's lightness on my shoulders.

Disappointment hung from me like chains, something I couldn't shake. I had tried so hard not to get my hopes up, but the pharmacy was still standing. There had still been pills on the shelves — much more than I'd even anticipated. That glimmer of hope had been so cruel.

Holli and Mia sat in the middle of the street, playing a game of pretend Maura and I weren't privy to. The trunk and the van's doors hung open to a dark interior, providing Sid with some airflow, though I couldn't make out my brother's figure in the backseat.

As we approached, Holli got to her feet. Guilt flooded through me as she glanced at our empty hands. She brought her gaze to mine, and I slowly shook my head. No words were needed. Disappointment was a shared pastime for our group.

"Come on, then," she said, leading us to the van's trunk.

From this vantage point, I was relieved to see the back of Sid's shoulders rise and fall as he slept. He was still breathing. But that was only half the battle. I didn't know where to go from here.

Holli produced two cans of soup that we opened and passed between the four of us — a rationed dinner. From the looks of our stock in the trunk, we were running dangerously low on food. Leaving our camp behind had been a matter of life or death, but part of me wondered if we'd just dragged out our demise. Dying from starvation was surely worse than dying by gunfire.

I pushed the thought away, horrified at its presence. We ate in silence, save Mia's giggles as she ran around the crowded street, kicking tires and debris and stomping in shallow water puddles near the clogged sewers. Holli swirled what was left in our last can, then stood, climbing into the van. She wedged herself between the rear captain seats to try to feed him. From where I sat, I watched him swat her away, groan loudly, then turn on his side.

Come on, Sid.

I groaned, getting to my feet to approach the car. Holli leaned behind the seat, her body at a strange angle as she gently spoke to my brother.

"—just try," she said. "Please."

"Water." His agony-laced voice sent shivers through me. Sid was no stranger to pain. When we were kids, he'd waited three days to even mention to Mom he'd thought he'd broken his arm. I'd watched the man rip his own molar out last winter because of a toothache.

"Eli." Holly gestured towards me, and I went to the trunk to fish out a half-filled water bottle. Another quick glance reminded me we were only a few liters away from being without fresh water.

I handed the bottle to Holli and watched as she brought it to Sid's lips. He suckled at it, barely able to take more than a few sips between shallow breaths. I tensed. Guilt followed as I went to close the trunk. It was an excuse. I didn't want to watch Sid struggle to drink or eat.

I pushed the trunk down so it clicked in place, but the world spun beneath my feet. The buildings were too constricting, ruining our vantage points, and seemed to be closing in around us. This wasn't where we needed to be. I knew it the moment we rolled down into the belly of East Lockwood and saw the bomb's aftermath. And then the disappointment at the pharmacy. There was nothing left to find here.

With a sigh, I ran my hand down my face, trying to think of what came next. Sid would know. Sid would've had all the answers. He would've already made a plan by now, and we'd be off in the car to our next destination.

Holli came around the back of the car, pulling me away from the others by the arm. We walked a little ways away before she turned around, keeping her head towards the ground and hands on her hips as she paced in circles.

"We have to leave," I said, breaking the silence.

She glanced up. "Yes," she breathed. "We need to find some fresh water so I can try to clean the wound again. But…Eli." She caught my gaze and shook her head. Her eyes were devoid of the hope I'd seen earlier that day. "I don't know."

"Don't know what?"

She looked down again. "I don't know how much longer he's going to hold on. His fever is worse, and the wound isn't getting any better. I just don't think our time is best spent searching anymore. I think he's septic."

"What does that mean?" I asked. My gut twisted, threatening to eject the soup from my stomach.

She met my eyes. "I think we need to get him comfortable," she whispered. "And wait for the inevitable."

"You want to give up?" I could hear an edge of hysteria in my tone.

"Eli." Holli's voice was gentle and kind, filled with pity I didn't want. I wanted Sid to live. I wanted her to fix him. I wanted her to give me the solution we so desperately needed. "I love Sid. And I wouldn't suggest it if I thought there was another option but…we're running out of time here. If we can do anything for him, it would be best to make sure he doesn't die in the back of that van."

The words pierced through me, threatening to bring me to my knees. I'd always admired Holli for being straightforward. She wasn't one to beat around the bush. But now, all I wanted was a lie. A far-fetched possibility that could change this outcome.

But I knew it was futile. My gut was heavy with regret. I had failed once more to protect my family. Sid's stamina and strength had always made him untouchable in this horrible world. He made it back to us from the other side of the country, and somehow, I'd never doubted that he could. The potential of losing Sid meant that none of us were ever safe — not really. We were all just an injury away from death's doorstep. Fragile little beings with egos too large for our own good.

"Okay," I heard myself say to Holli, my voice empty, foreign, and small. "Maybe somewhere near water. Somewhere nice. Peaceful," I choked. "He'll like that."

"Eli." Holli took my hands into her own and squeezed them. "I'm so, so sorry. Really, if there was anything I could do—" She choked on her words, then fell silent.

I shook my head, turning away from her, emotion

welling in my throat, so tight and forceful I couldn't swallow it. Losing Mom had upended my entire world. The hole in my heart was so big I wasn't sure it would continue beating. If we lost Sid, I feared I'd lose myself completely.

WE CAMPED in the city for the night. The road out of East Lockwood had minimal tree cover, and using headlights in view of Coutts Peak was a danger we couldn't risk. Sleep came in fits. I woke, my head against a threadbare blanket on the pavement, desperate to make sure Sid was still breathing. At times, I found Holli and Maura doing the same.

Morning rolled over us slowly, dark clouds leading to a brighter gray as the sun rose behind them. A chill wove through the air as we packed up what little belongings we had and piled back into the van.

Sid no longer had the energy to speak, addressing us with grunts and moans. Mia had stopped asking questions about his condition, probably because we'd stopped trying to give her answers. Sid was going to die. There was no way around it.

I focused on the drive as best I could, trying hard not to glance at my brother in the rearview mirror every few seconds. Holli and I had identified a town near a small river on the map, maybe twenty miles northwest, and, according to the gas gauge, we'd have no trouble getting there on our remaining fuel. Before I knew it, we were back in the thick of the trees, driving down a winding road toward another unfamiliar place. Unease plagued every inch of me.

Finally, we rolled into a small town, *Trahohill*, that

promised fresh water at the edges of its borders. The scene was as familiar as any other. Dilapidated streets, buildings, and homes. Neglected roads, stalled cars, and debris in the road. We followed the map closest to the river, hoping there was a structure within walking distance.

At the far edge of town, a small dirt road led us to *Trahohill Lodge Motel*, a riverfront resort that once promised Wi-Fi and a continental breakfast. The single-story structure was made from weathered wood, the edges green with moss. A sagging roof covered an exterior walkway leading to numbered rooms. A few of the doors had been left open, but for the most part, the building looked deserted. Still, I pulled the car off to the side, apprehensive about turning into the gravel lot.

"I'll scope it out," I told Holli, who was already loading bullets into the semi-automatic. "Pull the car up when I give you the sign."

Holli gave me a curt nod before handing me the loaded gun. I bounced the weight in my hand as I exited the car. My lack of sleep appeared as a sharp pain behind my left eye. The summer air had shifted overnight. Cool moisture hung heavy in the atmosphere, matching my anxious mood. We'd put distance between ourselves and the Coutts. Less between us and the men who had taken Maura and Sid. But we were on borrowed time. Holli didn't seem to think Sid had much of it left at all, so we'd be well on our way after…

No. I couldn't go there. Not yet. I needed to remain alert.

I crossed the graveled lot to a once-landscaped walkway leading to a door labeled Office. Pausing before it, I took inventory of the empty surroundings. No shadows. No sounds. With a deep breath, I reached for the handle and twisted, pushing the door inward.

The interior smelled like mothballs and antiseptic, but it was silent. Someone had left a mess on the front counter — an old coffee cup, a half-eaten, now moldy sandwich, and a pile of scattered paperwork — suggesting they'd taken off in a hurry.

A pegboard with numbered keys hung on the wall behind the desk, against which a lone chair leaned. Beside the desk stood a dark vending machine, snack food beckoning me behind the glass. I gasped in relief. This was something. The first glimmer of hope I'd had in days.

I took to the rooms next. I collected all the keys in my pockets, unlocked each corresponding door, and scoped out the rooms and bathrooms. Each room had a large window on its far wall overlooking a picturesque river. But Room 8 had the best view. And I decided that was where Sid would rest.

I wanted to swim in my relief, to find the joy in our discovery and relish in it. I wanted to kick off my boots and sleep. I wanted to laugh and feel the intoxicating feeling of being carefree, if only for a moment.

But I couldn't. I knew what came next. I was still struggling to climb out of Mom's loss, still trying to make sense of it. How could I greet Sid's death with any kind of courage? The idea of carrying on without him *and* Mom frightened me. I saw no way forward — no understanding of how to remain strong once my entire world was gone. A life without Sid seemed unfathomable.

I focused on my breathing as I returned to the gravel lot, gesturing the van forward. Holli turned at an angle, following my wave to Room 8, so the passenger side door was closest to the rooms.

"Good?" Holli asked.

"Yep. Let's get him settled," I said, my voice strained. The engine died as Holli, Maura, and Mia exited the vehicle, leaving the passenger sliding door wide. I ducked into the van, hovering over the rear seats. Sid reeked of sweat and sour infection, his features screwed up in pain. Gently, I placed my hand on his leg.

"Up," I commanded.

Sid opened one bleary eye and groaned, inhaling deeply, before he forced his body forward. I caught him beneath his armpits, feeling his sweat coat my skin, clutching my hands together around his back for support. Steadying my feet, I used both arms to pull him from the backseat into my grasp, careful to avoid his injury. His legs struggled to gain momentum, but I managed to get him out the door into a wobbly stand.

His skin was dark with infection, traveling from his ear down his neck and to his shoulder. An impossible heat radiated from the spot, warming my neck as Sid leaned against me. His balance faltered as he tried keeping both eyes open. I gritted my teeth against his added weight, straining my aching muscles to keep him steady.

"C'mon," I said, taking slow steps across the gravel toward the concrete block leading to the room. Holli hovered beside us, her hand on Sid's back.

"Where're we?" Sid mumbled. "Weren't we going to the city?"

I froze at his words and glanced at Holli, whose eyes widened in worry. "We went," I said slowly, inching us forward. "But there…wasn't much to find. So now we're about twenty miles outside of it. We found a nice place to rest near the river. We'll get you some fresh water, okay?"

"Oh yeah," Sid said, a lazy smile beginning across his features before being pinched out by his pain. He groaned, his head rolling on his neck.

"Come on," I urged as we got to the edge of the concrete. "Not much further."

We stepped painstakingly slow onto the walkway toward Room 8's open door. It was nothing much to write home about— a useless television, a queen-sized bed, two nightstands, and a lamp. I got Sid to the bed, where he sat first before falling backward onto the pillows.

"We should undress him," Holli suggested, studying my expression. I nodded, beginning to untie my brother's boots, afraid to look at the rest of him. It was unreasonable, I knew, but there was comfort in ignoring his pain for as long as I could manage. I had confronted reality for so long, but I knew the grief that would come was something I would struggle to bear.

After helping me with Sid's shirt, Holli left me to finish the task alone, closing the door behind her. I stared down at him in the bed, the dim light from the window shining across his sweaty, bloated face.

"Sid?" My voice sounded tender and young, like it once had when I'd called his name after having a nightmare. He would've peeked his head out from the bottom bunk to look up at me, eyes bleary with sleep but worried nonetheless. This time, though, he didn't answer.

"Let's get these off," I said, hoping he could hear me as I came around the side of the bed, tugging on his pants. He let me remove them without protest — something a healthy Sid would never do. He shivered as I threw his dirty clothes to the floor, pulling down the bed blankets so he could climb beneath them. Finally, he laid his head on a pair of pillows, his injured ear facing the ceiling, before he blinked, focusing his gaze on me.

"Thanks, E," he said as if he were drunk before he closed his eyes and fell asleep. I watched him for a moment, eyes tracing the scar along his nose and the small blemishes in his skin. His dark lashes dusted the circles beneath his eyes, lids twitching as he fell deeper into slumber. There was something startling about how his breathing started and stopped, a small snore forcing its way through his chapped lips.

I choked back a sob and wondered if this would be the last conversation we ever had.

18

MAURA

ELI SCRAMBLED out of Room 8, pressing himself against the door as if trying to hold an invisible monster at bay. I remembered the tears he shed at the city pharmacy from the mere thought of losing his brother. He leaned his head back against the door, shoulders sagging in exhaustion as he wiped his hands over his face. He looked distant, lost in a memory or a fear yet to come.

It was fascinating to watch him in the midst of his grief. Never had I seen a man express feelings so openly. Even the women in the Coutts commune were encouraged to hold back their emotions, suppress them, or ask God to relieve us from them. It was considered weak or improper to share feelings too readily. Somehow, that had never felt quite right.

Tearing my gaze from him, I checked the trunk for our remaining gear. Scooping up our collection of water bottles, I returned to the office area, where Holli used a knife on the corner of the vending machine, trying to get to the snacks. A thought had crossed my mind as we drove out of the city. Finding no medicine wasn't shocking based on the details I'd gathered of the Outside world, but the remaining antibiotics must have gone *somewhere*. Medicine hadn't just disappeared. If pharmacies existed, even if they didn't have much, they would have had something. Someone must have taken it.

And I was confident I knew who.

A thick crunch broke me from my thoughts as I made my way to the front desk. Holli pried the edge of the vending machine's glass away in one thick piece before she reached in, handing the snacks to Mia, who stood dutifully beside her.

"That's the last of it," I announced, situating the remaining water bottles on the front desk counter.

"Thanks, Maura," Holli said. "Did you see Eli?"

"I think he just needed a minute."

"M&M's!" Mia squealed as Holli handed her a few bags.

"Dessert," Holli said, winking, before turning back to me. "Would you check on him?" she mouthed.

I went back outside, holding a hand up to shield my eyes as they adjusted to the sunlight. Eli had sunk to the walkway floor, head in his hands. I closed the door and approached him, shoving my hands in my back pockets as I tried to think of comforting words. I knew there were none. No prayer would save Sid, and no Bible verse would heal Eli's fear. But perhaps…

"Hi," I said.

"Hey." He looked up, his face weary.

I lowered myself to sit on the walkway beside him, not meeting his gaze but looking for the best way to voice my dangerous idea.

"Is Sid—?"

"He's sleeping. At least, I think." He sighed. "He's in *really* rough shape."

I hesitated, studying his features. His hair had grown,

curling over his ears, matching the growing whiskers on his cheeks and chin. Purple bags sat beneath his brown eyes, making him look worn and tired. After what we'd been through, I supposed I must have looked the same.

"Eli," I said, "I…was thinking about something."

"Hm?"

"About the medicine for Sid."

He raised his head slowly, draping his arms over his knees as he shifted his gaze. His eyes darted back and forth across my face as he waited for me to speak.

"The empty pharmacy got me thinking…where did all the medicine go? It didn't just disappear. Someone took it." I bit my lip. "I wondered, maybe, if it was the men from Coal Creek? They had a whole stash of drugs. Not just illegal ones, either. I saw those little prescription bottles, like the ones still on the shelves at the pharmacy. The Coal Creek men had a whole closet full. Maybe…"

"They have antibiotics…" Eli's features stilled, eyes glazing over as they left my face and focused somewhere in the distance. He straightened, pressing his back against the wall before scrambling to his feet. "Holy *shit*," he said under his breath before looking down at me.

In one swift movement, he leaned down and picked me up from the ground, his arms tight around my middle as he squeezed me. My nose pressed into his shoulder, and I yelped in surprise as he spun us around the walkway for a minute in an effortless dance of relief.

"Maura," he said, releasing me, his hands on my shoulders as he held me at arm's length. "You're a genius."

My jaw dropped. I grasped for words I couldn't articulate quick enough. Regret flooded through me at his excitement. I'd expected him to push back against the idea — to tell me it was impossible. That there was no way we could return to that dangerous place. That we'd end up disappointed, or *worse*. But as Eli brushed past me toward the office, I knew there was no taking back what I'd offered. I hurried after him, heart beating wildly. He rushed into the office so fast that the door slammed against the opposite wall.

"Holli," he said breathlessly. She turned from her perch in front of the vending machine, pulling her hand from the innards. Mia looked up guiltily from the bag of sweets she'd opened. "Coal Creek. They have drugs. Maura saw them with prescription pill bottles." His eagerness radiated. I could see the boy still living within him for a moment, full of hope and wonder.

"Coal Creek?" Holli repeated, tilting her head, seemingly rolling the words over in her mind.

Eli nodded. "We could go back. Maura knows where. We could drive there today, get the antibiotics for Sid. We could—"

"Eli…" Her voice held a warning tone. She glanced at me, but I looked away, pressing myself against the wall beside the door. I wished he would leave me out of this.

"Holli, please! This is the answer. Maura's right — those prescriptions had to go somewhere. It only makes sense those men would take them. She said they've got a whole closet full."

"But we don't know if they have what we need."

"Does it matter? We've got more to go on than when we went to the city."

"Yes, but—"

"But what?"

"We had more time then," she said. "Sid's in a much worse state now. I don't know how much longer he has — I don't even know what good the antibiotics would do at this point."

Eli stepped forward. "We have to try. Come on! You

said if there were anything you could do, you'd do it! This is it! *This* is our best chance."

"Our best chance is staying right here and making him comfortable for the time he has left."

"No." Eli shook his head. "No. I don't accept it, Holli. I can't accept it."

Holli hung her head, closing her eyes as she steadied her breath. "Eli," she said slowly. "You're going to get yourself and Maura killed. And then what?" She looked up. "What will that mean for Mia and me? Without you and Sid?"

At the mention of her name, Mia clung to the back of Holli's legs, her thumb stuck between her lips.

"We won't. We'll be quick. We'll come back. I swear it to you."

"You can't!" she shouted, dropping the snacks she'd held beside the vending machine. "That's not something you can promise!"

"I have to try!" Eli exclaimed, his voice cracking. "Maybe we won't succeed, but we *have* to try. I won't—" he paused. "I won't be able to live with myself if I don't try."

"Eli," she warned.

"Hol, please. *Please.* I couldn't help Mom," he said, his shoulders tensing. "Everything happened so fast that she was gone by the time I was back. But right now I can help him. There's a *chance.*" His emotion swelled and peaked, cracking through his deep voice. "There's still a chance."

Conflict crossed her features. She pinched the loose skin at her throat, eyebrows drawn together as she seemed to play out the potential scenarios in her head. Finally, she brought her gaze up to Eli.

"You come back by tomorrow morning." Holli's voice was coated in fear. "Even if you don't have what you went for. You come back. Before it's too late."

Eli inhaled shakily and stepped forward, pulling Holli into his embrace, wrapping his arms around her head and squeezing. She closed her eyes, spilling tears down her cheeks, before he released her, and she looked up at him.

Guilt weighed heavy in my gut. I had caused this. I had prompted Eli's choice. Something I should've known he couldn't refuse.

"You come back," Holli ordered, her eyes shifting to me. "Both of you."

ELI HAD our things packed within minutes. It wasn't much: food to last us two days, a few medical supplies, his gun, and extra bullets. I hadn't revealed what Sid taught me back in the small cottage. I was still afraid of being responsible for a weapon. With Eli, there was no reason for me to volunteer that knowledge. I was likely safer without it.

My head spun. I wasn't sure if I'd done the right thing. What if Holli was right? What if the Coal Creek men killed us? What if Coal Creek didn't even have what we needed? This entire trip might be for nothing. But it didn't matter. Eli had barely spoken of anything else since I'd told him my thoughts. He would go to Coal Creek no matter what. But he'd never stepped foot in that wretched place, and without my insider knowledge, he'd be as good as dead.

Together, we climbed into the warm van, spreading the map across the center console. Coal Creek was south of East Lockwood. Scavenging had given me a good sense of direction, and I felt confident I could locate the house where Sid and I had found the car. From there, we could find the river near the cave where we'd slept, then travel southeast to the back of the lodge. The building was on a cliff overlooking the other mountains. At the very least, if we reached the mountain's edge, we could follow it to the lodge.

Eli took all of this information in stride, nodding enthusiastically, hanging on my every word. Hope filled his gaze as we mapped out the route we would take, but guilt made it difficult to meet his eyes. My directions were more strategic than a flat-out guess, but I still felt uneasy. The journey sounded simple in theory, but I knew it would be much different in practice. I thought of the flood light turning on us and the bullets hitting the trees as Sid and I scrambled to escape. The faith Eli held in my plan felt too strong. Too much relied on sheer memory, which was hazy from all the panic.

But Eli didn't seem to care.

I told him everything I remembered about the lodge — the overlook, the barbed wire fence, the makeshift showers, the stairs, the deck that wrapped around the place, and the hum of generators. The lobby would be difficult to enter, the drug closet even more so.

"I'll make a distraction," Eli promised, lifting his eyes from the map. "Maybe I can steal whatever gas they have for the generators and take it out to start a big fire in the woods. Cut off the generators and plunge them into darkness. They'll have no choice but to come outside, see the fire, and use their manpower to put it out."

"What if someone's guarding the generators?"

Eli's facial features tightened. "I'll take care of it."

I saw Sid in him at that moment — the viciousness of what it meant to survive. Of what love could make you do.

"So we'll sneak up the stairs and into the lobby," I said, trying to calm my swelling anxiety. "Into the closet and out."

Eli nodded. "You said you saw exactly where the door was?"

I nodded, grimacing at the memory. "Yes. Behind the desk."

"Did it have a lock on it?"

"I'm not sure."

"So we'll assume there is one. There might be a key, but we can't take that chance." He sat back in his seat, musing. "What kind of door was it?"

"Just a regular one."

"Wood?" I nodded. "And you don't remember *seeing* a lock?"

I shook my head.

"That's good," he said, tapping his fingers against the steering wheel. "It'll probably just be a hasp latch. Those are easy enough to pry off with a knife." He stared beyond me now, speaking to himself. "We can do that easily."

He stuck the key into the ignition and brought the van to life without casting me a second glance. Determination was written across his clenched jaw, and a small smile played on the edges of his lips. I had given him hope to cling to, but I didn't feel good about it.

"We'll stop in town to get gas," Eli told me as we pulled away from the motel parking lot. "Good thing I held onto my garden hose."

"What for?" I asked.

"Siphon," he answered. "Have to pull gas from the other cars to fill this one so we can make it to where we're going." He peered beneath the sun visor he'd pulled down over part of the windshield. "Sun's still high, too. We should be able to get there with just enough light to scope out the place. It'll be better to enter after the sun's set."

I felt nauseous at the thought. "They have flood lights, though," I whispered, glancing at him nervously.

"We're not going to be seen," he assured me, his gaze

narrowed on the road we traveled. "I'll distract them. Then we'll just slip inside." He made it sound so easy.

"They have guns."

"I have one too. We'll stay hidden. This will work." He glanced at me. "It has to work."

I pressed my lips together and looked at my lap.

"What?" he asked.

"Nothing, I'm just…worried. I—"

"Don't be worried. This is a good thing, Maura. A great thing. We'll be in and out with the antibiotics and come right back here to help Sid."

"But—"

"Maura," he said, stopping the van beside a washed-out green one. "I just…" He sighed. "Thank you."

It was enough to keep what I'd longed to say inside. Eli needed me. He wanted my help. He was *thanking* me. For once, I wasn't just a helpless burden. I had value. I could help him save Sid. We could get medication that might save not just his brother but all of us if we needed it.

Though the danger of the Coal Creek lodge still cautioned incessantly in the back of my mind, I pushed it away. My chest grew warm as I leaned against my seat, studying my companion. Finally, I could repay Eli for his kindness.

19

MAURA

ELI DROVE ON, unable to keep his hands still. He didn't seem happy, per se, but eager. And that scared me more than anything. He hadn't been to this place. He hadn't seen the men or the weapons they carried. If they hurt someone like Sid, Eli would be in just as much danger.

But I wouldn't voice these thoughts aloud — not when there was still hope for Sid, not while we were on our way into the lion's den. I kept myself occupied by staring out the window. Soft yellows and oranges peeked between the green foliage — the first signs that fall would soon be upon us. I found my reflection in the side mirror, startled to see my face so gaunt and pale.

With the map in my hands, I gave Eli directions to the best of my knowledge and told him everything I recognized between the tall pines — the occasional road sign, the broken-down motorbike, and a short fence — anything that confirmed we were still on the right path.

"Remember to stay low," he reminded me for the seventh time. "We'll draw as many of them out of the building before we move forward. The goal is to be stealthy. I'll pry the lock off. We grab the medicine and run."

"And we'll meet at the house—"

"If we get separated," he finished.

He nodded with certainty, an undeniable fire in his eyes. I wanted to feel what he felt, but the pit in my stomach remained. It would only disappoint him if I were to tell him how scared I was, how I didn't feel ready, and how my body was sore and exhausted from these past few days. He might insist I stay behind and try to go alone. I couldn't let him do that. After all, this had been my idea. An idea I'd put into Eli's head. I needed to see it through.

We curved around a bend in the road, and familiarity gripped me. I straightened in my seat, eyes on alert for the driveway I knew was here, somewhere between the trees. And sure enough, I saw it — the sunflower mailbox.

"There!" I exclaimed, and Eli slowed, turning into the long, steep driveway Sid and I had climbed. We bounced along the path until we reached the clearing. It was the same, single-story wooden home with a red metal roof I remembered, only it had been ransacked. The slim door was ripped from its hinges and thrown carelessly in the grass. All the windows were broken. Bullet holes split the wood and metal, casings still visible in the grass and between the walkway stones.

"They came looking for us," I whispered, horrified.

I wasn't sure why I hadn't considered the thought. The men seemed too sloppy to worry about chasing after Sid and me. We hadn't seemed worth it. But I'd watched Sid squeeze the life out of a man's lungs and leave him for dead in the middle of a field. And I supposed that called for revenge.

My blood ran cold as Eli rolled the van to a stop. Did he realize the danger we were stepping into? Did he understand the stakes? But my mouth wouldn't move. Obedience ran through my veins. And I knew, as he patted my arm from across the center console, there was no way I would back down from helping him try to save his brother.

———

DISTANT CLOUDS BLOCKED the setting sun, making the afternoon feel gloomy. On foot, the journey seemed both too long and impossibly fast. We reached the cave where Sid and I had slept in just under an hour, the walk much easier without a wounded man to support.

Sid had been adamant about us running northwest, so Eli and I followed the same path southeast. I didn't think Sid and I had diverted our path from our escape over the barbed wire fence, but my memory was muddled. As we walked, I tried to remind myself that adrenaline had fueled us. We'd been running. I didn't know for how long. It had felt like seconds, but it must have been much longer. The forest had no markers to assure me we were moving in the right direction. Fear followed me. Every few moments, I second-guessed my memory and intelligence. Had I remembered right? Were we walking towards nothing? Was all of this a waste of time?

Eli seemed nonplussed, carrying one of the van carpets over his arm as a barrier when climbing over the fence. He moved with purpose, relying on my poor memories to drive us onward. As we walked, he showed me how to use a spare pocketknife he'd brought for me, how to plow it up beneath someone's chin, into their eyeballs, the sides of their heads, though he promised to stay by my side the entire time. I didn't have the heart to tell him my go-to move when under duress was to freeze.

He kept the tone positive, but I struggled to match it. As

the sky darkened, a part of me hoped we wouldn't find it in time. But then, in the distance, I saw the unmistakable sight of barbed wire through the trees.

"There," I said, pointing.

Eli stopped, ran a hand through his beard, then knelt on one knee, opening the mouth of his pack, from which he pulled a lighter. He pocketed it, then gripped the gun, observing it, checking his ammo, before pocketing that too. "You still have your knife?" he asked.

I reached into my back pocket and produced it for him, thinking of Lee's arm around my neck. My skin had bruised. I hadn't been able to breathe, let alone *fight*. The knife felt too small to do any real damage.

"Good. Keep it in your hands. And—" Once again, he rifled through his pack, producing a black flashlight, which he handed me along with the empty backpack I'd carried when we had walked through the city. I slung the pack over my shoulders and pocketed the flashlight.

"You ready?" He was stone-faced, his jaw set, eyes narrowed and dark.

I nodded. He turned and began to walk.

Adrenaline took fear's place, pushing my feet forward even though all I wanted to do was turn around and run. In the light, however, the fence seemed less of a barrier than it had in the dark. We followed it until the trees cleared, giving us a view across the high grass field to the lodge beyond. On the other side of the fence stood a small weathered wooden structure — one I hadn't seen in the dark when Sid and I were running. It couldn't have been more than ten feet in either direction and, judging by the rot at its corners, it had seen better days.

The smell of yeast wafted between the wood, drying throat. I thought of the alcohol Lee and Ernie had forced me to drink, then glanced at Eli, who inspected the small building through the fence links.

"Well, well. This'll do nicely."

I raised my eyebrows. "What's that?"

"It's a moonshine cabin," he said. "This must be how they've maintained their supply. They're brewing it." A glimmer of satisfaction crossed his features before he met my eyes. "This is our distraction."

"Our distraction?"

He nodded, then waved me to follow as he continued along the fence. "I'll light it up. The whole thing'll be up in flames in seconds. Alcohol is flammable as hell. If we get lucky, there's enough in there to burn the whole fucking field down." His tone dripped with disdain and anger.

The gray clouds had turned a deep indigo in the last few moments. Dusk was here, and we needed to move fast if we wanted to execute our plan and get out before being seen. Eli continued around the fence, away from the small building. Fear numbed the courage I needed to ask what he was looking for. Once the moonshine cabin was a good distance from us, he paused at a break in the fence and looked up at the barbed wire.

"We'll climb here," he said, pointing up. "I'll leave the mat on top of the wire so you know where to come back out. We'll meet back here, a little bit into the trees." He pointed behind us. "You wait no more than two minutes for me before you start getting back to the house. Wait there. If I don't return by morning, get back to Holli. Okay?"

"Eli…" My heart hammered.

"Okay?" He tilted his head down, giving me a stern look.

"Okay."

"Up and over. Wait for me while I light the cabin up, then we'll get to the lodge to cut the generators."

I sucked in air through my nose, then nodded. It seemed too easy. Too good to be true. And I knew from experience how dangerous that was. I wanted to tell him that perhaps Sid's death was God's will. I wanted to hand the knife back, tell him I couldn't do it. I was too nervous, too fidgety, too irresponsible to handle something like this.

But hope lined his face and settled deep in his eyes. Didn't I owe Sid? Eli? I didn't leave the commune to be scared at every turn. On some level, I always knew what I was getting myself into.

I straightened. "I'm ready," I said.

Eli grabbed my hand. Surprised, I allowed mine to sit limply between his fingers as he squeezed, his dark brown eyes boring into mine. He pressed his lips together, and I squeezed his hand back.

"Let's go."

We approached the break in the fence. Eli hooked his fingers into the wire and began to climb, scaling the fence halfway before situating the van carpet over the wire, making it sag. Eli supported his weight on the fence poles, careful to carry his leg over the carpet. He came down the other side landing in a crouch. He looked at me, then glanced up. My turn. I hooked my fingers onto the wire to hoist myself up and over. The carpet helped the awkward placement of my legs, allowing me to swing over the side without having to worry about the wire. I took longer to get to the other side, but landed somewhat gracefully beside my companion.

Stars twinkled in the night sky as night fully settled over us. Red light glowed from the distant lodge windows, distorted by the slight breeze rippling through the tall grass. In the center of the field sat the makeshift showers

— a long, low building that made me shiver. I swallowed the pang of sadness that swelled in my memory of Bev. I wondered if she'd survived and if that was preferable to the alternative.

Eli breathed in my ear, fiddling with his gun by the sounds of it. But I only had eyes for the lodge. A plume of smoke rose near the trucks. A figure shifted, silhouetted in the red light. Far enough away that they wouldn't see us but still too close for comfort. Climbing that fence meant we were now in their territory.

"C'mon," Eli said, tugging my wrist. "This way."

He was a shadow now, features muddled in the dark as we moved along the fence toward the moonshine cabin. We reached it quickly, pressing our shoulders up against the wood. I smelled the alcohol now, so strong I was surprised how faint the scent had seemed on the other side of the fence. I tried not to gag.

Eli paused, bouncing on his heels. "Stay here," he said, glancing at me over his shoulder. Before I had time to respond, he disappeared around the front of the structure.

It was like getting the wind knocked out of me. The strange sense of being completely and utterly alone enveloped me. My vision tunneled, so I closed my eyes, counting my breaths, before I looked at the night sky. Sometimes, as kids, when the lights were out and the electricity stopped humming around us, Morgan and I would look at the stars to imagine what existed beyond. But Mother had caught us once and explained there was nothing up there but Heaven and that we were to stop making up stories. We never talked about it again.

My leg muscles ached, but I was afraid to move, so instead, I kneeled and leaned back on my heels, rolling the handle of the knife between my hands, waiting. I was good at waiting. It had been part of our training. As women, we were always waiting — for men to make the important decisions, to be given to our husbands for marriage, for them to come home and give us purpose. We waited in the wings, silent and obedient, until someone told us it was our turn or gave us permission for whatever we were useful for that day.

The faint smell of burning wood reached me just as Eli came around the corner of the building. He held different-sized bottles in his hands and beneath his arms. In one swift motion, he began dumping the contents all over the structure's walls, across the grass, and beyond. The smell of alcohol stung my nostrils, but I waited and watched as he emptied all the bottles, tossing them out into the grass, where they disappeared with a shatter.

Then he turned to me.

"Run."

He grabbed my bicep, and we took off together, crouching as we ran straight toward the lodge. The generators roared together in a mechanical symphony as we reached them — six in total, all haphazardly placed, wires hanging from their sides, stretching to different parts of the lodge. The stench of gasoline filled the air. Eli and I hovered behind them.

The smoke I'd seen earlier belonged to a man smoking a cigarette. He stood near the three parked trucks, idling between them. I didn't recognize him. He was lanky, his hair pulled back into a ponytail. The red light from the lodge made the angles of his body stand out harshly. He leaned on the hood of one of the trucks, finishing his cigarette, which he put out with his toe. He raised his head, and I followed his gaze to the glow in the distance. The moonshine cabin.

The wood had caught. Red, orange, and yellow flames licked up the sides of the structure, eating through the roof, and smoke rose from its belly into the night air. The man opened his mouth in surprise, and Eli moved beside me. I watched him yank every cord he could from its plug, flipping buttons, silencing the hum that had surrounded us.

Everything went black.

Above us, I heard screams and yells, angry moans and swearing. The man near the truck took off, sprinting up the creaky stairs. The whole lodge seemed to move, swaying on its posts as the rooms above devolved into chaos.

I looked at Eli. His wide eyes met mine. I clutched the knife, fingers digging into the side of the generator. What if they came down here to look at them? What if they didn't go straight to the cabin?

"Fuck!" A loud voice bounded down the stairs, belonging to the heavyset guard who had picked up Bev. He stopped on the bottom stair, looking out toward the fire, which had rapidly spread throughout the entire building, catching further on the tall, dead grass we'd trekked through. My jaw dropped. This whole place could go up in flames if they didn't put it out quickly. The grass was the perfect conduit.

I realized that was exactly what Eli had anticipated as I watched his lips curl into a sneer beneath his beard. I could hear a stampede of footfalls on the porch. From the stairs, I watched as man after man bounded down, past the trucks, into the field, yelling indistinct directions at one another. A fight broke out on our right, two men rolling around in the grass, drunk insults flying like bullets.

"We need *water*!" someone screamed.

"Get the water from the showers!" someone yelled, and the men took off in that direction.

Eli shifted behind me, toward the stairs. Terror gripped

my limbs. I knew I should follow him, but I felt frozen. Vulnerable. What had we done? He glanced over his shoulder, waving me forward urgently, and by the grace of God, I somehow got my feet to move.

The chaos had moved from the lodge out into the field. Shadows of men crowded the burning cabin, darting out from the showers, buckets held over their heads as they ran toward the fire. The lodge seemed quiet. Still.

Eli reached the bottom stair and looked up before he waved me forward again. I stood beside him, looking up at the dark prison I'd escaped from days ago. This was likely as empty as we were going to get it. This was our chance. And we didn't have much time. With an unsteady breath and my right hand gripping my knife, I followed Eli up the stairs.

20

MAURA

WITHOUT THE SPILL of light from the interior of the lodge, getting to the second floor was a precarious venture. Some stairs dipped and threatened to give way as we climbed them as silently as possible, eyes darting from side to side for any threat waiting in the shadows. I focused on Eli's crouched body, the way his muscles moved as he stalked up the stairs like a predator.

A predator. Was that what I had become? I couldn't help but think if the fire spread to the lodge, the people locked in their rooms would be innocent casualties, condemned to a fate they hadn't chosen.

The thought fell away as we reached the porch. Shadows moved in the distance, huddled against the far railing. Eli held a hand out, and I paused behind him, watching as his other hand reached for his gun. But even in the dark, I saw there was no danger. Nobody ambushed us or swore at us. They were skin and bones, some of them crying. They were afraid.

"Don't," I whispered, wrapping my fingers around his arm. "Leave them. They're okay."

He hesitated but gave a curt nod as we continued forward. We kept close to the wall of the building and approached the front door which hung open, the dark interior an uninviting mouth. From the threshold came the smell of unwashed bodies, liquor, and the stink of tobacco. Together, we entered.

It took a moment for my eyes to adjust to the penetrating darkness. There were more people than I expected, some sleeping, others gathered at the window to my right, peering through the glass at the fire that had taken hold of the field. From the corner of my eye, I saw men still running around, trying desperately to wash the blaze away with their buckets of water. It might have been comical if I hadn't been so terrified.

People took no notice of our entrance, perhaps assuming we were one of them. Eli moved toward the front desk, careful to step over a pile of what looked and smelled like vomit. The stench stung my nose and my stomach turned, threatening my own sick, but I swallowed it, moving behind the desk.

Between the lewd photographs of naked people, the door was hard to miss. As Eli had predicted, a metal lock was halfway down the frame. I averted my eyes from the images as Eli pried the lock free from the wood with his knife.

My body was on fire, my heart thudding painfully fast. The contrast of how I felt with the people lounging around disoriented me. After what I'd learned about this place, I still couldn't understand why they weren't all running to the fence. Didn't they want to escape? Didn't they want to be free from their prison? Did they understand they had a chance?

The sharp sound of wood cracking brought my attention back to Eli, who pried the rest of the lock away from the door with his fingers. He yanked the door open, and we both slipped inside.

There would be no adjusting to this punishing darkness. The closet smelled sterile, like bleach Abigail sometimes used to clean the kitchen. I found the textured flashlight handle in my pocket and pulled it into my grip. Light spilled from the tip, illuminating Eli, a cement floor, and rows of shelves that filled the closet from top to bottom. His eyes widened, mouth open as he pulled his backpack off his shoulders, staring at our bounty with awe.

"Look at this place," he hissed. "They must've robbed a dozen pharmacies for this stash." He shook his head, then pulled his backpack from his shoulders. I did the same. "Let's fill them up."

I shone the flashlight on the boxes, bottles, and baggies lining the shelves. Someone had labeled most of the boxes with scribbled letters that were hard to decipher — words I didn't quite understand: *barbiturates, stimulants, depressants, opioids.*

Eli approached the *opioids* first, inspecting the bottles for a moment before he swept half the shelf into his backpack. He moved to the next shelf, and I followed him with the light before my eyes landed on a large box at the end of the closet that read *antibiotics.*

"Eli."

But he'd already seen. He reached for my bag and I held it out for him as he filled it with pill bottles and small glass vials, packaged syringes, bottles of pink liquid. It was more than enough. Anger rose in my belly — these men may have been drunks and sinners, but they'd had the wherewithal to take something invaluable and stockpile it for themselves. All while Sid struggled to stay alive at the motel.

I fully grasped the irony. I knew how the Coutts

hoarded and how Father's greed had affected the Outside. It had been hard to fathom because I hadn't lived a day on this side. I'd never wanted for anything in my life. But this was what Father had been doing to the Outsiders — keeping them at bay with his guns, holding onto precious, life-saving medications distributed only to those who obeyed him.

How many had he condemned to death?

"Let's go," Eli whispered, handing me the full pack.

I pushed the thought away as I slung the backpack over my shoulders. There was no time for a philosophical reckoning about Father's actions now. I clicked off the flashlight, tucking it into my back pocket, and we plunged back into darkness.

Eli cracked the door, then paused, pressing himself up against the wall, his hand moving for the gun at his hip. Voices spilled through the lobby.

"Just get the fuckin' generators started!" someone shouted, their voice too close for comfort. "Can't see *shit.*"

Another muffled voice came from outside.

"I do *not* care!" the other voice retorted. "Figure it out!"

A door slam made me jump. I tilted my head forward, horrified to see a shadow move across the slit in the doorway.

I backed up, heart racing until my back met the shelf, rattling the bottles and baggies, the wire of the shelf itself. Clamping my free hand to my mouth, I squeezed my eyes closed, waiting for him to pull open the door to find us. What would he do? What would Eli do? My fist tightened around my knife.

The man outside the door grunted, and a glass clinked before I heard his heavy footsteps again. This was it. I braced myself against the shelf. My mind went blank, shamefully knowing I would do nothing but follow instructions if he found me. But his footfalls retreated, fading away, and when I heard the distinct hinges of the front door, I allowed myself to breathe.

Eli's face was visible from the crack in the door. I found his worried eyes and watched him take a breath before he approached the door again. His eyes studied the exterior before he waved me over.

We burst out from the door, around the side of the desk, beelining to the front of the lodge. A few people milling about turned now, eyes squinting in the darkness as they followed us. I knew I should've kept running, kept close behind Eli, but I paused as a woman walked up to me, her legs unsteady, reaching for my hair.

"Run," I told her, catching her distant gaze. She smiled at me, catching a strand of curls between her fingers. She rubbed them together, transfixed.

"Do you hear me?" I whispered, eyes darting to the door through which Eli had disappeared. "Run! They're all distracted! You can make it out of here."

Her eyes traveled from the curl to my gaze. She dropped my hair and tilted her head. "But where would I go?" she asked.

I opened my mouth, trying to think of something to say or a place to offer them, but I knew there was nothing. We could barely keep our own alive. And she was right — where was there to go? To Father? Condemned to a life like this? Sure, Father dressed it in better clothes, settled under the guise of God, but was it really all that different? We all lived in invisible shackles, whether or not we would admit it. I thought of that invisible border I'd been instructed not to go near. How terrified I had been to cross that line.

Could she then go to the Outside? To the blown-apart cities or the resource-sparse towns? To do what? Die alone? Starve to death? This place was filled with evil, but it was the devil this woman knew. And I understood, just by the look in her eyes, that trying to convince her somewhere else was better was a wishful dream. It might even be cruel to steal her from these walls, from the drugs she craved and the life she'd accepted.

"Maura!" Eli hissed from the doorway. His panicked gaze shifted from me to the stairs. My heart froze. "Leave her! Let's go!"

I cast one last glance back at the woman who'd retreated to a chair, grasping for a half-empty bottle on the table. She brought it to her lips and settled into her drink.

"Maura!" Eli's urgent voice sent chills up my spine. I met his gaze. "You can't help them. We need to go *now*."

"I'm sorry," I heard myself say as I hurried after my companion. "I'm so, so sorry."

MY HEART POUNDED in my ears as we raced back out into the night. The backpack's weight helped ground me as I followed Eli down the stairs and into the high grass. We moved in a low squat, half-running, half-walking. I used my hands to steady myself in the grass but kept my eyes on the figures in the field. Men hovered around the showers, handing off buckets to help put the fire out. They'd done considerably well since we'd been inside the lodge, but that meant our escape window was rapidly narrowing.

Adrenaline sharpened my vision. I watched the backpack bounce on Eli's shoulders as he ran ahead of me, turning every so often to make sure I was on his heels. My chest tightened, making it hard to suck in a breath. Despite my alertness, I had still pushed myself to the brink of exhaustion. My body was about ready to give out.

The fence came into view between the dark shadows, far enough away from the fire where we'd still have shadow cover as we climbed. I glanced up at the van mat, a black blemish on the wire. That was it — our ticket to freedom. We just had to get up and over.

A prickle of fear stung my spine as Eli straightened, waving me along so I could climb first. He held the gun between his hands, pointed at the ground, but ready. I thought of the floodlights that had blinded Sid and me as we ran and how lucky we'd been to make it out alive. Would we be so lucky again?

I gripped the fence, the wire digging into my skin as I scrambled up the side. My movements were slow, my biceps burning as I forced them to hoist my body weight up the incline. I cried out as my fingers brushed against the mat, gripping it as I plunged myself over the side.

My feet caught in the wire on the other side of the fence, and I lowered myself to the ground, squatting as Eli followed me over the mat. Fire still burned in the distance. I could smell moonshine and the burning of wood and grass. I glanced back at the still-dark lodge, hoping to see a few people running down the stairs. But the path behind us remained empty. I swallowed the lump in my throat.

Beside me, Eli gripped my arm and shook it, his grin wide and triumphant. "We did it!" he hissed into the night air, his breath warm on my cheek. "We friggin' did it!"

My eyes widened as I drank in his small celebration. We *had* done it. A nervous laugh bubbled in my chest at the thought. Eli and I had managed to break in and steal what we needed. To think I had been so afraid of these men, so willing to give up my newfound freedom only days ago. Pride settled in my hunched shoulders.

"Are you okay?" he asked, inspecting me.

I nodded. "I just—" I wanted to tell him how badly I felt

about leaving the prisoners behind and how easily I could've been one of them. How I wished that my circumstances were different so we could save them all. Instead, I gave a nervous laugh and said, "I can't believe we did it."

His grin widened, and he threw his arm around my shoulder, tugging me in step with him back into the dark forest. He squeezed my shoulders, and I glanced up at him, warmed at the sight of his happiness. I only hoped Sid was still alive to see it, too.

21

ELI

My ADRENALINE HAD FADED by the time we were nearly back at the van. Everything ached. But my pain was secondary to the lightness in my chest. We had two backpacks full of drugs that could help Sid. Hours ago, I had been trying to deal with his death. Now, we could heal him with something I thought we'd never find. If I believed in God, I'd call it a miracle.

Maura walked a few feet to my side, her breath heavy. It was difficult to see her in the forest's shadows, but I knew she must've been even more exhausted than me.

"Do you think the fire will burn down the lodge?" she asked, filling the quiet between us.

"Hope so."

"You don't think it's cruel?"

My steps faltered. I caught my balance and hung my hands on the straps of my backpack, confused by her question. Those men had kidnapped her, injured Sid so badly that he now sat on his deathbed, and she was worried about the barbarity of what we'd done?

"I think it was cruel what they did to you and Sid."

"I just mean…those people. Inside. They're innocent."

There it was. The naivety that lived inside her. Despite what that place represented, what she'd endured while she was there, she was still worried about morality. Likely about what her God would do if she did something sinful. It was compassionate, yes, but dangerous. She owed those people nothing. Why couldn't she just be happy with what we accomplished?

"Is that why you stopped in the lodge?" I asked. Silence filled the air between us. "Because you could've gotten us killed, you know."

She looked up, frowning. "I'm sorry. I just thought they should know there was a chance to escape."

I shook my head. "They're not your responsibility."

"So, that makes it right to leave them behind?"

"We didn't leave them behind."

"It feels like it."

"C'mon, Maura. It's not our job to save everyone."

"You saved me."

"That was—" I sighed. "That was different."

"Was it?" Skepticism filled her tone. "Just because they're ignorant of what's outside those walls? You don't think they're worth saving because they don't even realize they're trapped? Because they think a life of drugs and abuse is better than whatever's out here?"

"Maura—"

"They're still *people*, Eli! They're innocent people, and we may have just burned down the only place they can call home!" Her voice rose an octave. "What will they do now?"

"Jesus, Maura."

"And they're stuck there with those *horrible* men—"

I stopped in my tracks. "What's this really about?"

"What?" She turned in the dark, facing me. "It's about

those people back there!" She pointed back the way we'd come. "And *you* think they're not worth saving."

"Because," I said, starting to walk again, "I think this is about you."

"What?"

"Let's say before we met, I came into the commune while you were scavenging one day. Do you really think you'd welcome my presence? Let alone come *with* me?"

"What does this have to do—?"

"You probably would've run away and let everyone know there was an Outsider on your land. You would've laughed at the idea of leaving your life behind. You wouldn't have even been able to fathom it."

"So what?"

"So, that's what those people there probably feel. There's nowhere for them to go. They've accepted that life. To be honest, they may not know anything different. Otherwise, they'd have escaped just like you and Sid."

"So that makes it okay?"

"No!" I tightened my grip on my straps. "I'm not saying it's right. It's horrible what they're doing to those people. It's horrible that people like that exist. But that's the reality of this world, Maura. That was the reality of your world, too. Only now, you're on the other side of things. If you're going to survive out here, you need to understand and come to terms with the fact that not everyone can be saved. Not everyone *wants* to be saved."

She said nothing, and for a moment, I wondered if I'd gone too far.

"I left my whole family behind," she whispered into the night. "My mother and my siblings. I feel like I abandoned them. They must think terribly of me."

"You didn't abandon them," I reasoned. "You didn't have much of a choice."

"I still had a choice. What if I made the wrong one?"

"Listen, you were extremely loyal to the Coutts when I first met you. Your Mom and siblings had to know that. I'm sure they understand you didn't make your decision lightly. That you must've had a reason for it."

"I don't know about that. Father is pretty convincing…"

She was right, and I didn't have a good way to ease that fear. Her father was just about the most convincing person left on the planet.

"Have faith, Maura," I said, slowing my words in my best Peter Coutts impression.

She laughed at that, a bellow that echoed into the thinning trees. Stars twinkled in the sky above us. After a few more minutes, we emerged in the field behind the house, finding the van where we'd left it in front of the large garage. I began to breathe normally, allowing myself to feel a little of the hope I'd tucked away. This was good. No. More than good. It was great. Luck was on our side. All we needed to do was get back to Sid.

With the last of our energy, we sprinted across the property, heaving our bags into the backseat. I stashed the gun in between our seats and started the van.

Maura fell asleep before we even left the driveway, her head tilted against the window, breath already fogging up the glass. I smiled, watching her thick brows furrow together as she fell into a dream. She'd earned this rest. The very least I could do now was get her back to safety.

I DROVE down the dark road, wiping my hand down my face as I willed myself to focus. Exhaustion crept up my shoulders, weighing heavy on my back, but time was of the essence. Whether Sid lived or died could come down to a matter of seconds.

The main road from the house to the motel was tree-lined and curvy, making the drive precarious. A few minutes in, I found myself dozing, head resting against my hand, elbow against the van door. I straightened, slapped myself on the cheek, and opened the window.

Warm wind washed across my face. The smell of earth and nearby water was a familiar comfort. The seat beneath me felt like velvet — like a bed, easing the pain of my aching limbs and lower back. I settled deep into it, my hand resting on the steering wheel, weary eyes focused on the blurry yellow lines.

Sid and I had taken drives a lot when we were teenagers. The freedom of being on your own, on the road, was like nothing else we'd ever tasted. He'd speed past neighborhoods, the crappy stereo blaring whatever song was popular, our heads out the window. We'd smoke a joint and have a laugh until we tucked our tails between our legs as we pulled into Mom's driveway after curfew. I could see her face now, her angry, narrowed eyes that glowed.

Wait. That wasn't right. Mom's eyes were brown.

I blinked, displaced and confused, fumbling to emerge from the dream that had steered me off course. With a start, my hand gripped the wheel, and I inhaled as if rising out of water. Shock flooded through me as I squinted at the glow coming through the windshield — the glow that transformed into bright, urgent light.

Distracted and still weak from sleep, my hand jerked and pulled us to the right out of pure instinct. We needed to get away from those lights.

Headlights.

The realization hit me just as the tires left the road. The terrain shifted beneath the wheels before it dipped so drastically the entire vehicle tilted. I pulled the wheel back, frantically trying to get the van back on the road, but it was useless. Gravity turned the van on its side, and the steering wheel spun out of my grasp. I yelled for Maura, who had jerked awake, her hands fumbling for the door and her seatbelt, for something to hold on to as we rolled.

A deafening pop, followed by a sharp force, rammed into my face and chest. I lost the ability to breathe. Maura gasped beside me. I couldn't move, couldn't scream. Was I shot? I tried to take inventory of my body, but my limbs were stuck. The van came to a stop with a thunderous crash. My ears rang. I tasted blood on my tongue.

My vision steadied, and I took the next few moments to understand our surroundings better. Still in the van. Turned on our side. Windshield shattered. Maura was pressed backward by a large white—

The airbag.

I looked back at the steering wheel, which had begun to deflate, and laughed, hands grasping my chest in sweet relief that I was still in one piece. I moved both arms, stretched my legs, extended my fingers, and rolled my neck. No fatal wounds. Maura groaned beside me, and I reached for her, my hand pausing over the empty center console.

The gun. And more importantly, the *drugs*.

If I hadn't been awake before, I was now. A car had been driving toward us, their headlights on, unafraid of being seen. Could it have been the Coal Creek men? If so, we were in a whole lot of trouble. Cold fear washed over me. I turned in my seat, eyes searching the backseat. The rear window was cracked. The roof slightly caved in. I glimpsed our packs against the far door and leaned behind Maura's seat to reach them but couldn't.

I reassessed our situation through the windshield. One of the blinkers flashed orange against dead foliage and the incline we'd rolled down. The headlights were off, but even so, I saw smoke rising from the hood. If the car coming toward us stopped to look over the side of the road, they'd see us instantly.

"Maura," I croaked. "Are you hurt?"

"I'm okay." Her voice shook.

"Good. We need to move." I unbuckled my seatbelt. The strap came away from my chest, leaving behind a sharp sting from where it would later bruise. I awkwardly positioned my feet against the center console and reached for the door handle, pushing against gravity as I tried forcing the door up. It was no use. After limited sleep, the long trek to and from the lodge, and the crash, I was too weak to lift it. The heavy hunk of metal fell back against my hands, clicking closed.

"Shit." I needed to focus. Push through my exhaustion. We needed to get out of here.

Behind me, Maura had unbuckled herself, getting to her knees on the window, ready to follow me.

"Can you get the bags? Do you see the gun?" I asked, fear radiating through my tone. Her eyes widened.

"I'll look."

I went back to work on the door. With a heavy grunt and whatever remaining adrenaline I had left in my body, I managed to extend myself out of the van far enough to get the door up and open so it hung toward the van's hood. The cool night air and gasoline smell hit my senses, heightening my awareness. Light flashed from the blinker toward the trees, but otherwise, the forest was dark.

"Eli."

I glanced back. She kneeled on the center console, arm outstretched with my backpack. Carefully, I slipped it over my shoulders. Next, she handed me the gun, and I released a sharp breath, grateful she'd found it with such ease.

"I'm gonna climb out," I told her, eerily reminded of the instructions I'd given her the first time we'd met. "I'll pull you up once I'm out. Try to climb up to the window as far as possible."

She gave me a sort of pained look but followed it with a firm nod. Turning to the open door, I hoisted myself up onto the frame, gun still in hand. The van lay perpendicular on its side. I guessed we'd fallen maybe four feet from the road. We were lucky neither of us was hurt.

"Okay," I hissed, reaching back into the van. "Give me your—"

"Hello?" A voice broke through the silence to my left, and I hunched, trying to make myself small. It was useless. There was nothing to hide behind from where I stood.

"Wait," I whispered to Maura as her hand appeared on the side of the door. "Stay there!"

"Hey!" The same voice, closer now. I turned on my heel, grasping the gun, pointing wildly in the dark night.

Small beams of light bounced across the forest floor, illuminating the oil we'd spilled and the glass from the windshield. In the dim light, I could just make out three bodies. I could take them easily. I raised the gun, trying desperately to ease the quiver in my shoulders as I aimed.

But as soon as I'd pointed the weapon, I knew it wasn't the enemy I feared. They weren't men from Coal Creek. And they couldn't be Hunters, either. A petite woman was in their ranks, flanked by an average-sized man and a taller, broad-shouldered boy.

Their flashlights found me and my gun, and at once, the two men drew weapons. The woman kept her flashlight on me. I shifted my aim between the two men. Fear choked the breath from my lungs, making my knees tremble. Was this it? Was this how we met our end? I thought of Holli. And Mia. And Sid. No drugs to save him. No men to hunt, no able-bodies to protect them. And Maura, who had journeyed so far to find us. Survived a kidnapping. Brought Sid back to us. I had failed them all.

"Wait!" One of the men spoke. "Don't shoot."

Confusion rippled through me. Perhaps they *were* from Coal Creek. Perhaps they'd take Maura and me back to their lodge and keep us as prisoners, dooming Sid to an untimely death. We'd been so close. Too close. I bit my lip to keep my grief at bay.

"Eli?"

Did someone just say my name? I resisted the temptation to look at Maura — I'd told her to stay put. Surely, she wouldn't be foolish enough to give herself away. My breath caught in my throat, and I squinted against the flashlight's beam, releasing the grip on my gun. I held a hand over my eyes to see better.

"Is that Eli Bailey?"

"Who's that?"

My voice came out strangled with nerves. Who out here would know my name? The thought rattled me. I'd left everything I'd known behind at Mom's. Out here, the only chances of someone identifying me came from my time in prison — something, even now, I tried to forget.

"Eli." The voice softened. The smaller man stepped forward with a heavy limp. Upon further inspection, I realized he was walking with a cane. He came forward, away from the flashlight's beam but into enough light that I saw his face clearly. Recognition flickered through my brain — his thin face and sunken eyes gave him a perpetu- ally weary look. His hair had significantly receded since I'd seen him last, his face lined with wrinkles of worry.

I dropped my hand holding the gun, a gasp escaping my chest. He'd been as good as dead, I was sure of it.

Standing in front of us was Mia's father, Neil.

22

———

ELI

NEIL SPOKES and his wife had moved to Mom's neighborhood while I'd still been down in the cities serving my sentence. I'd gotten out in six months for good behavior but returned surly and humbled, not giving many people my attention. After so much time around others, seeing hardened men in vulnerable positions, and hearing the worst of humanity's gripes, I'd had enough of being social, aside from when it was absolutely necessary.

But Neil had always caught my eye. He was the kind of dad I'd have hoped to be if I ever wanted kids. I saw him outside with Mia on warm days, laying out on a picnic blanket or playing with dolls in the grass. He would draw colorful chalk paintings on the sidewalks, blow bubbles from soap suds, and tickle her until her little face turned pink.

He had loved his wife, who had just fallen sick when I'd returned. He would take her outside to feel the sunshine and the wind. And he was always the one running out to town for the shopping. I had gotten the sense he was a good man, even if I'd never taken the time to talk to him. I'd regretted that deeply after finding Mia.

Our last interaction on the bus showed me how dearly he cared for his daughter — how willing he had been to sacrifice himself for her safety. When I picked Mia up, I was so certain he'd been caught. And though we'd tried to keep hope alive for Mia's sake, in the depths of my soul, I always assumed him to be dead.

His lopsided stance showed he relied on the cane he carried in his left hand — something he hadn't had when I last left him. Neil looked to either side of him as his companions lowered their weapons, passing a confused gaze between them. Neil hobbled forward, avoiding forest debris or rocks until he approached the van and peered up at me.

"You hurt?" he asked, his gaze fixed on the vehicle. I could tell he wanted to ask, that his eyes were scanning the overturned vehicle for the daughter he'd left behind. He had no way of knowing that I'd scooped up Mia in that forest or that I'd taken her back to camp. I imagined he must've tried to find the spot where we'd fled from the bus, spending many sleepless nights worrying about his daughter's fate. The guilt he must have felt. The fear and grief he must have waded through.

"No," I said, still in awe. "Mia," I said, "she's—"

"Is she?" Neil stepped forward, his lower lip trembling as he looked towards the back seat.

"She's not with me," I said. "But she's alive. I found her after—" His face crumbled, and he reached his hands out towards me. "She's with our group, back at a lodge, due north. That's where we were heading. My brother, he—"

"She's...alive?" Neil's eyes shone with fresh tears as he gazed up at me on top of the van. "My Mia's alive?"

I nodded, overcome with emotion I couldn't swallow. Neil dropped his cane and fell to the ground, his head in his hands, shoulders shaking as he cried. I glanced at the two others who came forward, the woman placing her hand on Neil's shoulder before she looked up at me curiously. She was a petite woman with a hardened face — a scar ran from her cloudy left eye to her chin. Her black hair was tied away from her face in a thick braid. I placed her around her early-forties.

The dark-skinned man on the other side of Neil crossed his arms. He stood over a foot taller than the woman, and his youthful features suggested he was in his late teens. His eyes bored into me before a flicker of fear crossed his face. His hand went to his gun. Instinctively, I tightened the grip on my handgun before I realized Maura had begun climbing out of the van behind me.

"Who's that?" the man asked in a deep baritone.

"Maura," I said, intentionally omitting her last name. "She's with me."

I turned to help her, and she looked up at me for an explanation. My jaw dropped in disbelief. "It's Neil. Mia's father."

"Mia's — what?" Maura groaned as she grasped my hand to heave herself out. She joined me on the car's side before I slid down the side, helping her do the same.

Neil picked up his flashlight, leaning on his cane to stand.

"Wait," said the woman. She reached into her backpack and produced a device that looked like a security metal detector. Cold dread washed over me. I'd seen that the day Mom died. It was the same device the Hunters carried with them to scan us. I took a step back, the van at my back.

"What the hell is that?" I asked.

The woman handed the device to Neil, who held it up

to show me. "It's a scanner. We have to make sure you're not carrying anything contagious."

I had a million questions, but I knew Neil. And he knew me. Using his cane as support, he scanned me and Maura before pocketing the device. He broke into a wide grin and embraced me in a one-armed hug, his breath shuddering in my ear. I hugged him back. This poor man. All the pain and grief he must've felt losing Mia. Not being able to find her. Mia had significantly grown since I'd found her in the forest. Neil had missed so much.

"What the hell are you doing here, man?" I mumbled into his shoulder as he released me, holding me at arm's length. "We waited as long as we could back in the old neighborhood, but—" I shook my head, meeting his tired blue eyes. "We had to run."

He nodded. "I was hit by a bullet when we jumped off the bus. Caught me in the lower back, and I couldn't move my legs." He sighed, his breath shaky. "I thought I was paralyzed, so I told Mia to hide, to try to find you if she could. I figured she'd be safer out there than back with the Coutts." Maura stiffened beside me.

"They ran after us and found me lying in the woods. I have to assume they thought I was dead — I'd lost so much blood. Thankfully, they left me alone. I tried calling back for Mia once they'd gone, but she'd gone too deep into the woods. I was so weak from my injuries, I passed out, and the next thing I remember was waking up in Mick's office." He stifled a sob in his throat. "I thought the worst." He pressed his fingers to his mouth. "I thought I'd lost her forever."

"I found her. She was okay. She *is* okay," I said. "She's beautiful and healthy. Thriving."

He nodded, squeezing his eyes closed as tears leaked from the corners.

"Listen," I said, urgency plowing through our moment of relief. "We need to get back to the motel. I *have* to get these antibiotics to my brother. He'll die if we don't get back soon…He may already—"

"Yeah. Yes. Okay," Neil said, wiping tears from his cheek before picking up his cane and flashlight. He turned to his companions. "Darius. Gloria. You heard him," he said, clearing his throat. "Let's get moving."

Hope blossomed in my chest. I placed my hand on Neil's shoulder and gave it a squeeze. "Thank you," I said.

"No." He shook his head as we walked toward the dirt incline leading to the road. "Thank you. This is the least I can do. What you've done for me…for Mia. It can never be repaid."

The headlights of a silver SUV shone across the road. Its wheels tilted — half on dirt, half on pavement. Darius climbed into the driver's side, with Gloria accompanying him in the passenger seat. I held the door for Neil and Maura before closing us in.

"Where're we heading?" Darius grumbled, glancing at us in the rearview mirror.

"West," I said, pointing up the road where we were headed. "We're at a lodge up in Trahohill." He grunted, then began to drive.

Gloria turned to us in her seat. "Are y'all injured?" She inspected us with her good eye. "I have some medical supplies in the trunk if you need them."

I glanced at Maura, who shook her head. "We'll probably be pretty sore tomorrow, but nothing serious. I just have to get back to my brother," I said, trying to keep my voice steady.

"What happened to him?"

I launched into an abbreviated version of Sid's disappearance and his injury, carefully omitting Maura's part of escaping her commune and returning to us. She seemed to relax considerably at this, her body going slack as I told them about the Coal Creek men and how we'd raided them for antibiotics.

"Shit." Gloria's gaze swiveled to Neil. "We better tell Avi about them, then." Neil nodded.

"You're with a larger group, then, I assume?" I asked.

"A community," Neil specified. "There's maybe around four hundred of us now. Walls all around the place, decent armory, guards on duty twenty-four hours a day. And we've got all kinds of people — a physician, a dental hygienist, a few farmers who really know what they're doing. The guy running the place, Avi, he's ex-military. We're a scavenging team." He gestured to himself, Gloria, and Darius. "Well, mostly those two. They've been kind enough to let me tag along lately. It's taken me months to recover from my injury, and I'm still not completely right. But as long as I've been upright, I've been looking for Mia."

I nodded. "Wow. It sounds—"

"Too good to be true?" Gloria interjected, turning in her seat again. "It's not all sunshine and rainbows like Neil makes it sound."

"Well, compared to where we came from," Neil argued.

Gloria shrugged. "We're still able to only get an hour or two of electricity a day, sometimes less than that. Our water filtration system's been a bitch, and we're badly in need of more hands to harvest, cook, and scavenge. Not to mention more guards to relieve the ones we've got working twelve-hour shifts."

"Just the regular old ray of sunshine, Gloria is," Neil said. "She was one of the first in Avi's group, isn't that right?"

Gloria frowned. "We've come a long way," she admitted. "I'm just saying there's room for improvement."

"Well," Neil continued, "the point being, I'm sure Avi would be happy to welcome your group in. Especially after all you've done for Mia."

"He'll want to meet you first," said Darius, an edge of caution in his voice. "To make sure you fit his standards."

Maura tensed beside me again, and I knew it was because I'd left out arguably the most important thing about her. She was a Coutts. And I didn't know anyone out here who trusted them. If we were going to be assessed by this community leader, Avi, the truth would surface one way or another.

"Well, I hope we will," I said, giving both Gloria and Neil a grateful nod, trying to push the worry from my mind. We had bigger concerns right now. I had to focus on getting back to Sid. I had to get Holli the antibiotics. I had to make sure my brother stayed alive.

GRAVEL CRUNCHED beneath the SUV's tires as we approached the darkened lodge, headlights sweeping across the motel. I hoped Holli would assume it was us and not panic, but I knew the chances of that were slim. She'd be anxiously waiting at the window with a gun in hand, ready to shoot as soon as she saw the truck instead of the van.

Darius pulled the car into park and reached for the door handle.

"Wait." I touched his shoulder from the back seat. "Let Maura and I get out first. Holli's armed. If she doesn't recognize you, she might shoot on sight."

He grunted in response, leaning back in his seat. I had the distinct feeling he was disappointed there would be no confrontation.

We exited the car. Clouds still covered the night sky, obscuring the stars. Darius killed the engine, and the headlights faded, leaving us to adjust to the dark. Maura stood so close to me that I felt her shoulders move as she took a few deep breaths. Urgency nipped my heels as I approached the row of rooms, moving toward Room 7, a flickering light barely visible behind the flimsy curtain.

I brought my knuckles up to meet the wooden door, tapping them against it.

"Who is it?" Holli's voice sounded small.

"It's Eli," I said, hearing the latch rattle. "Don't panic," I added. "We have others with us. Friendlies."

Holli hesitated. I stared at the peephole, hoping she could read the sincerity on my face. Holli peeled the door back slowly, her tired eyes darting to the darkness behind us before she inspected Maura and me.

"Thank God," she said, pulling us through the door frame. Lantern light spilled from the room, washing over us like a warm bath. Holli had made a spot for herself on an armchair in the corner. Mia was huddled up on the bed closest to the door, her breathing slow as she slept.

"Sid?" I asked, studying Holli's lined face.

She gave me a grim smile. "Alive. And—?" She eyed our backpacks.

A shuddering breath escaped my chest. "We've got a whole lot of antibiotics," I said.

Her shoulders relaxed. "Good."

I turned to Maura, then glanced over her head at the dark truck in the distance. "Can you—?"

"I'll take care of Neil," she said without needing clarification. She shrugged off her backpack and handed it to me. "Go."

I didn't need her to tell me twice.

Taking one of the lanterns, Holli and I exited the room

to the strip of crumbling concrete connecting the motel doors. She unlocked Room 8, and we entered. Despite the cracked window, the dark room was stifling hot. It smelled of sickness, the onset of death, rot, iron, and sweat. I swallowed my disgust, hurrying to the dresser to deposit the lantern and drugs we'd found.

"We cleaned out most of their stash," I said, making a conscious decision not to look at Sid.

I pulled everything from the packs and organized them on the wooden surface. Holli looked like Christmas had come early, eyes wide, shining with some semblance of hope.

"Maybe," she muttered as her eyes soared across the labels. Her fingers turned some of the bottles before separating them into small piles.

Unable to avoid him any longer, I left Holli to her task and looked at Sid. He lay in the middle of the mattress, wrapped in layers of thin blankets up to his bearded chin. His eyes were closed, and his dark skin visibly clammy from fever. Beneath his dreads, a bandage covered almost the entire side of his face, clean and pristine, covering the infection. As I came closer, I could smell it — thick, unpleasant pus tinged with an open wound.

I sat beside him on the bed, bringing my hand to his shoulder. Mom had always been loving — unafraid to hug and kiss me and Sid to show us how much she loved us. But Sid and I were different. Brotherly and minimally affectionate. I regretted it now as I tried to make sense of what it would mean if we lost him.

If *I* lost him.

His unblemished skin was smooth to the touch, faded tattoos disappearing behind his good ear, down his neck, and beneath the blankets. I let my hand rest on his shoulder, heat radiating through my palm as I studied his face.

His normally trimmed facial hair had grown unruly, making his beard uneven, his mustache hiding the top of his lip from view. In the shadows, the scar down his nose made him appear older and wilder than when he was a child — any sign of boyhood had long since gone.

We'd all had things to contend with before the plague: hunger in our bellies and the fear that we may not survive a simple winter cold. But Sid's experience had been different. So much so that he'd left to be as far away from home as possible, venturing all the way to the California shores.

The west coast had withered away over decades, cities becoming full of homeless encampments, the business moguls and wealthy celebrities retreating to the Midwest, to their million-dollar bunkers that didn't rely on the Coutts power grid. And though we were deficient in many things, the closer we lived to the Coutts, the better resourced we could expect to be. Out in California, they were lucky to find clean water.

But he had gone, regardless, afraid of what the world had become for people like him here. It wasn't that the whole world disagreed with the existence of LGBTQ+ people; it was that voicing support earned you a spot on the Coutts' watch list. Sympathizers and pedophiles, they called them — supporting the Devil's ways.

So, even though I hadn't completely understood, and I hadn't agreed with his decision, I could rationalize the need to get away, even if it meant sacrificing everything he knew. Sid had said many times it wasn't even his safety he'd been worried about. It was the safety of those he loved who couldn't protect themselves. Sid had always been a fierce, loyal protector for Mom and me, and I knew it didn't end with us.

The lines on his face told more of his story — of the sleepless nights, of the atrocities he must have encountered, of the sacrifices he must have made to stay alive. He'd returned to Mom's a different man. A hardened man.

But it didn't matter. Beneath his hard shell and quick-to-anger attitude, my brother remained a selfless, honest, and loyal man. After everything he'd been through and given to the rest of us, we owed it to him to keep him alive.

23

SID

HE CAME to me in the darkness, his olive skin sun-kissed, a blush of sunburn across his nose, and muscular shoulders peeking through the arms of his sleeveless tee. He was the only bright thing in the endless sea of darkness I lay in.

Calix.

He smiled at me in a lazy sort of way, reaching his hand towards mine. Our fingers intertwined and he squeezed, sharing his warmth. I longed to speak, to say something, to tell him all the things I'd never managed to say.

Calix and I lived by the water at the back end of an old warehouse. It had been built decades prior to hold boxes of products that fed into whatever overconsumption humanity craved that year. The salt air had eaten away at its cheap exterior, rusting the edges until they browned and flaked, cracking and splintering until the ocean pulled chunks out to sea. We had duct-taped plastic sheets over the worst of it to keep out the mosquitos and flies.

At high tide, you could hear the water bump up against the building's edges, splash beneath the surface, and shift the sand brought up by its currents.

"It's like being in Mykonos," he'd joke as an homage to his Greek ancestry when we'd pass by on the way to our bed, a king-sized mattress we'd fished from a dumpster and hoisted up on wooden pallets, secured together with duct tape. Somewhere along the way, we'd collected an ugly orange afghan that lay over top. A bright spot in a dark room. Calix always seemed to find those.

Our warehouse was on the edge of Los Angeles, the once bright and bustling city filled with famous hopefuls and families with too much money. They'd moved on long ago, escaping the rising sea levels, the smog, and dwindling supply chains.

For us, this was a haven. We were as far away from the Coutts as humanly possible without fleeing the country, which was illegal for people like us. We could theoretically get to a border, but the risk of being found out was too great. We loved the wrong person, they'd say. We'd made a mistake. We'd given in to a life of sin. And we needed to be corrected.

The idea of it sent red-hot fury through both Calix and me. Peter Coutts continued to get stronger as sickness after sickness rolled through the world's population, and there was little we could do except try and keep ourselves healthy. But we were vengeful people, so we did the only thing we could think of doing to defy the powers that be. We opened our own black market and, through any means necessary, collected a decent inventory of things people needed to survive in the city.

At first, it was simple things — grams of weed, home-brewed liquor, and the occasional box of non-perishable food. Overconsumption had been an issue many decades before I'd been born, but the aftermath still existed. Many warehouses like ours were still filled to the brim with unopened boxes and packages never to be collected. With nearly nothing else to fill our time, we sifted through them, collected what was useful or enjoyable, and left the rest.

As people became accustomed to the idea of coming to us for things they needed, we also connected with suppliers in the area — people who had too much of one thing and were looking to diversify. Somehow, many people who had hoarded guns, which had been exceptionally cheap in recent years, had forgotten to hoard essential things like food or taken the time to understand how water filtration worked. A young woman we met in San Bernardino, who had all the knowledge of a small drug cartel, promised to keep importing and producing drugs in exchange for some of our supplies.

Over the course of a year, before the worst had hit, we'd racked up a small fortune. Of course, money was relatively useless at that point, but because the American Dream had been embedded so deeply within us, more than enough people were still willing to work for it. We installed two solar panels for electricity on our roof. We bartered for a compostable toilet. We constructed walls, weaved rugs, and got our hands on a camping stove, an ice box, and an old MacBook.

By the time the H5N1 came to our shores, Calix and I were living a life of relative luxury. It wasn't perfect. The seagulls woke us early. But we could see the sun rise and set, smell the warm ocean air, and provide products to the locals. We lived a life of purpose, away from Coutts rule. I should have known it wouldn't have lasted forever.

The day we were notified that the world was succumbing to yet another illness, Calix and I had woken to a gorgeous pink sky. His leg was curled up over the afghan, tangled between mine. I nuzzled into his warmth, kissing his salty chest and neck in bliss until our quiet room exploded with noise.

The alarms rang from everything we had connected to the Internet — the computer, both of our cell phones, and even the electronic doorbell security system we'd installed a few months back. Even though I was sure if someone had wanted to break in, they could just pull off a piece of the building. Sharp sounds blared, and we scrambled for our things to quiet the noise.

There wasn't much left to startle me anymore. I had seen bad things out here: the people dying of preventable illnesses, drug overdoses, small bodies washed up on our shores. I wasn't naive to the horrors that were out there in the world, but Calix and I did our best to ignore them inside our little bubble of a life. But the alarm made sure we listened.

Emergency Alert: All residents of the Los Angeles area must immediately shelter in place due to possible exposure to H5N1.

"The bird flu?" Calix looked up from his own phone, eyes still hooded with sleep.

I shrugged before stifling a yawn with the back of my hand. "What else is new? Coffee?"

He nodded, casting a worried look back down at his phone. I leaned forward and kissed him on the temple, my hand gripped tightly in his thick black hair, before I got up to pour hot water over instant coffee powder. It wasn't ever as good as the real stuff, but it was non-perishable, and we had loads of it.

"Don't worry about it babe," I called as I walked towards our makeshift kitchen, voice traveling over the empty warehouse space. "Those alerts don't mean shit."

But Calix worried, despite how many times I'd told him to stop looking at his phone, to stop talking in hushed whispers to worried customers. But as the evening fell and the last of our clientele rolled through the warehouse, it was apparent Calix wasn't the only one consumed with worry.

"Junior's fever's nearly 105," said a thin-haired woman, not looking so hot herself. "I can only hope he'll keep this down." She scurried away with a six-pack of apple juice.

We wore masks for the rest of the day, greeted by either sick people or those describing the illnesses of their family members. By the end of the night, we each stripped off the face coverings, dipped beneath the plastic of one of the warehouse walls, and sat out on the rotting floor. It had become a dock of sorts, the entire wall now missing, making way for a view of the twinkling night sky, the tide high enough that we could dip our toes into the warm ocean.

I sat beside Calix, resting my head on his shoulder, inhaling the sea breeze.

"Sid?"

"Hm?"

"I think we need to leave."

I straightened, my gaze fixed on Calix, studying his features to try and decipher if he was serious. "Leave?" I laughed. "To go where?"

"This one is bad," he said, pulling his phone from his pocket and waking it with his fingers.

I pushed his hand away. "I don't want to see it—"

"You can't just pretend it's not happening!" The nostrils on his wide nose flared.

"Jesus, Calix," I said, surprised by his anger. "We get notifications like that *all* the time. We've survived worse, haven't we? We've made it this far?"

He shook his head. "You don't get it. This one isn't like the others, they're saying."

"Who's saying?"

"Everyone, Sid! It's not a joke! There's a 15% survival rate. This isn't like COVID, or SARS —"

"Okay," I said, exasperated. "And what? We're going to try and run from it?"

His thick brow furrowed. "We need to get away from other *people*," he stressed. "Go somewhere isolated. Did you notice how many people were sick today? We keep that up, and we'll be dead in a month."

"But what about the business?" I countered, glancing back at our warehouse. What I really meant was *what about our life here*? I'd grown so fond of our mornings and evenings, of the way our days filled with excitement, of the purpose I felt of providing for the people in our city. I wasn't willing to give that all up just because of a few hysterical texts. "You want to leave behind everything here?"

Calix gazed at me, features falling. "If it meant us staying alive? If it meant not losing you?" He frowned. "Then yes, I want to leave it all behind."

"Cal," I warned, softening at his words.

He gripped my hand, fingernails sinking into my palm, eyes ablaze with worry. I looked out towards the sea, closing my eyes as I sucked in the sea breeze before I squeezed his fingers.

"Okay," I said. "We'll leave in the morning."

Calix's relief was palpable as we sat on the rotting wood, and we kissed lazily in bed later that evening after the sun sunk down and the tide retreated. But after Calix had fallen asleep, his breath heavy with snores, I lay awake, staring at the ceiling beams, wondering what life might look like away from here.

There'd been no warning besides the loud bang that startled us both from the bed. Sleep was our downfall, even though I slept with a loaded gun on the bedside table and even though I had it in my hands before they'd reached our bedroom.

Bullets swept through the space, shattering our things — lamps, glasses, and mirrors, splintering the wooden pallets, the bed, the plastic sheeting. I yelped, ducking behind the mattress, heart throbbing, hands shaking as I checked the chamber for bullets.

I wanted to scream for Calix, to tell him to get behind me, but my ears rang from the gunfire, distorting everything around me. I squeezed my eyes closed, centering myself, steadying my breath, before I came up to the top of the mattress and peered over.

Dust hovered in the dark air. In the distance, three shadowed figures ran through our warehouse, arms scooping up inventory strewn about in boxes, across the floor, and draped over furniture. I raised the pistol, but they were moving so quickly it was difficult to aim.

I shifted to the left, around the edge of the bed, eyes wide and frantic, looking for Calix. I found the dark pool first. The thick, hot liquid settled strangely against the concrete floor. There was a moment where I wondered whose blood it was and looked down at myself as though I had an injury I hadn't yet felt.

But I was intact. And I knew, somewhere in the depths of my mind, that the blood belonged to Calix. I swam through emotions like a slideshow, one after the other — panic, fear, grief, horror, until I finally settled into red-hot anger. I knew my odds. I knew what awaited me the moment I made the decision. I didn't care. Death meant I could remain with Calix.

I pulled the trigger on my pistol, shooting wildly at the men who yelled, pointing in my direction, brandishing their guns, and yelling at one another. I couldn't make out their words over the deafening noise of my shooting, yet somewhere in the middle of the chaos, I saw one crumple to the ground, his knees giving way until he was a pleading pile on the floor.

As a true testament to their character, his companions left him behind, rushing from the blown-apart door like scared rabbits. The man lay on the ground, his blood pooling around him. I stood above him, peering down into his wicked face — he was young, too young for something like this. But he was gaunt and hungry-looking, the shadows beneath his eyes dark and hollow, his cheekbones prominent beneath his sickly yellow skin.

"Who the fuck are you?" I'd growled, kneeling, bringing my hand to his throat and the gun to his head. "TELL ME!"

The man had whimpered so convincingly I'd hesitated. The knife glinted in his hand before I made a move. He caught me between my nose and cheek, slicing down to the top of my lip. I yelled in agony, hot blood running into my mouth, and before I could even make sense of it, I pulled the trigger.

Pain radiated through my nerves as I stumbled to the kitchen and found a rag to press against my face to slow the blood. My brain felt slow and foggy, still waking from sleep, still processing the events that had unfolded in seconds. I pushed past the pain, scrambling back into the bedroom, straining my one good eye to find Calix.

I found him propped up on his side of the bed, that ugly orange afghan covering his wounds. His green eyes stared, unblinking, his mouth still open in surprise. I found it both cruel and relieving that he hadn't lived long enough to suffer — that the bullets had ripped through him so completely he'd barely had time to register his fear.

For hours, I sat in his blood, holding his body, whispering words I wished I'd said sooner. If only we had left when he'd said. If only I hadn't been so afraid to leave it all behind.

After downing half a bottle of whiskey, I found enough strength to patch myself up with a needle and thread. I drank the rest before I buried Calix on the side of our home, in a shallow grave, wrapped in the afghan, beside the ocean he loved so dearly.

By the time nightfall came, I shivered on our bare mattress, covered in dried blood and sand. I wished for the virus to come and take me. To plague me with fever so I became delirious. To take me to wherever death had taken Calix. To ease me from the pain that somehow edged its way through the alcohol.

And here it was again. The welcome onset of death. I tried to reach back to the life before, which sat in my mind like a worry I couldn't quite remember. I had a pit in my stomach like I'd forgotten something. Like I'd left something behind. I wasn't sure how I'd ended up here in front of Calix, holding his warm, strong hands and gazing into his eyes. His handsome face and prominent Greek nose were as stunning as they had been the day I'd first met him.

His lips moved, and I watched them, shaking my head. I couldn't hear his voice, the one I'd known for so long. And then at once, as though I'd lifted my head from beneath water, I could hear him, clear as day.

"Not yet," he said, squeezing my hands. "They need you."

"Who?" I said desperately, clinging to him. "Calix, please."

"You look good," he said, eyes traveling over my features. "Older. More tired. *So* handsome." He turned over his shoulder. "Doesn't he?"

And from the depths of shadow behind him, my mother emerged. She was a good foot shorter than Calix, her wide smile shining against the darkness. She looked as I remembered her: unblemished skin, wide, healthy hips, her short hair framing her face. Her kind brown eyes studied me, as she had so many times over the years, inspecting me in a way only a mother could.

Her hands found my face as she leaned forward, eyes closed, inhaling. "That he does," she said, "but you're right. He's not ready yet."

"Ready for what?" I begged, but the pair kept their smiles on me as though they hadn't heard me.

"You go back now. They need you, Eli, and the others."

And I remembered. Memories came, crashing into me like waves — of Mom's home, of leaving because of the Coutts girl, of being ambushed by the Coal Creek men, the pain and unrelenting boom that came as I felt a piece of my ear blow off into the street. I remembered being prodded and bitten by the men who captured me, forced into a dark, dank room, and then escaping, the Coutts girl on my heels.

Fever had come then, I knew. Illness swam through my veins, infecting pieces of me that I needed. We had moved, I think. We had gone to a place near the water. A nice view. The rest of my memory came in fragments — Holli's hand on my head, Eli crying at my bedside, a vase of flowers picked by Mia on the table in my room.

"But," I said, searching for reason, "I *need you*," I said to both Calix and Mom. "I need you both. The pain," I cried. "It hurts too much. How can you expect me to live with this pain?" The words felt like knives in my throat.

Each of them touched the side of my face so I could nuzzle my cheeks against their palms.

"We are always with you, Sid," Mom said. "Even if you can't see us. Even if you aren't thinking of us. We are forever with you."

"There is more for you to do," Calix explained.

I broke, cracked beneath his words, voice, and touch, sobbing as I nuzzled into his hand that grew colder by the minute. "I'm sorry I couldn't protect you."

"You gave me the best years of my life," he whispered, lips suddenly at my ear. "You were the best thing to ever happen to me." He pulled back, and I met his eyes, narrowed sharply. "Now go," he said. "GO!"

Pain spilled across my chest. My body was on fire. I was sure of it. For one lucid moment, I sucked in a breath — a real breath, from the air around my body, and I saw Holli holding an empty needle, looking startled before I fell back into dreamless slumber once more.

24

—————

MAURA

THE NEWCOMERS EXITED the truck slowly, bodies tense and on alert for potential threats. Neil came across the gravel first, approaching me in the doorway. I glanced at Mia, sleeping in a huddle on the bed, fists at her chin. What would she think of her father's reappearance after being gone for so long?

I was vividly reminded of my youngest sibling, Matthew, and the way he'd once recoiled at Father's sudden appearance on Mother's threshold after being away for a long time. So many wives and so many children meant Father only had limited time to spend with his offspring. And as the numbers of both wives and children grew, the time he had shrunk. Mother mentioned that the last time Father had visited our family was after Matthew's birth. The next time he'd come was nearly two years later. I suppose we weren't high on his list of priorities.

Matthew had flinched at Father's touch, darting away from him to hide behind Mother's skirt. She had scolded him, urging him to embrace Father as we were all expected to. Father's smile had tightened as he forced a pat on his head. We ate Mother's meticulously prepared dinner together, but I didn't miss how he ignored little Matthew for the rest of the evening.

Gloria and Darius flanked Neil as he approached the doorway. Low lantern light flickered across his features. He had aged significantly from the young man I'd seen in the photograph Mia had shown me before we'd fled Eli's mother's home. Desperation filled his gaze as his eyes searched the area behind me. The scanner trembled in his grip.

"C'mon," I encouraged him, waving him into the room. He glanced at me before taking a few steps forward, crossing the threshold. A whimper escaped his lips as I moved aside to let him pass, his hands reaching out toward the small figure on the bed. The light illuminated the tears streaming down his cheeks, the tremble in his lower lip as he held the scanner over Mia.

The machine beeped, and he instantly put it in his pocket and sat beside his daughter. Neil leaned forward to brush Mia's hair from her face. The little girl stirred with a whine, tossing and turning as she awoke. For a moment, there was nothing but silence as I waited with bated breath for her eyes to blink open, to bulge with recognition before she wiggled free from her covers and onto her knees.

"Daddy?" Her whisper filled the silent room, and Neil's tears erupted into full-on sobs. His hands grasped his child, hand on the back of her head, cradling her tiny body to his chest as he wept into her hair. Mia's fingers dug into his flannel shirt so tight her little knuckles went white. Darius and Gloria stood at the door, whispering between themselves, but I was fixated on Neil and Mia. They were a bright light in a sea of dark, a moment of hope when there had been so much despair. These kinds of moments were pure and God-given.

A realization descended upon me as I watched Neil rub circles on Mia's back — that moments like this had been curated in the commune for as long as I could remember. Father bringing the healed to his altar, showcasing their wellness and taking the credit. Father presenting a reunited family, eager to explain how the new arrivals had seen the errors of their ways. Father displaying a changed follower who had spent the last six months on the Island of Repentance.

Emotion welled in my chest as I allowed my tears to spill. Some were for Mia and Neil, yes, but some were for selfish reasons, too. From knowing I may never see my Mother again. From knowing I would *never* have a reunion like this. Not unless it was commanded by Father.

It wasn't shock that I felt, but disgust at my sudden awareness. This beautiful moment had brought forth the reality of something so ugly. The anger I'd felt leaving the Island of Repentance reared its head once more.

I was alone again. Sid, Eli, and Holli were together in the room beside me, caring for one another. Neil and Mia were reunited. Gloria and Darius, I assumed, had a history of their own. And I stood in the corner of the room watching a moment not meant for me. Would moments like this ever be meant for me? Would I ever belong anywhere?

Unable to free myself from my constricting thoughts, I fled from the room, brushing past Gloria and Darius and back out into the night. The riptide of sadness, fear, and jealousy chased me, and just as I got past the office, I crumpled into a ball, pressing myself against the side of the building as I allowed grief to consume me.

25

ELI

SID'S FEVER broke two mornings later. The air was thick with hazy fog, clouds lingering over the dew-covered grass. I sat outside in a flimsy wooden chair I'd pulled out from my room, hands wrapped around a cup of tea I'd made from a stale tea bag Maura had found in one of the rooms. Holli bursted out of Sid's room, her head turning both directions before she spotted me, face breaking into a wide grin.

"Fever's down," she said, her voice lighter than I'd heard in weeks. "He's not awake yet, but the fever's down."

I stood up from my seat. "So they worked? The antibiotics?"

Holli nodded, her eyes welling with tears. "We still need to keep a careful eye on him. But for now, it looks like they may have done the trick."

My cheeks rose as I smiled back at her, rushing forward to pull her into a relieved hug.

"Thank you," I whispered, squeezing her smaller frame.

Holli patted me on the back before I released her. "Thank yourself, and thank Maura. Those antibiotics saved his life. He's a lucky man. Let's just hope that luck includes a full recovery."

I nodded.

"Anyone else awake yet?" she inquired.

"Neil and Mia went to the river to fill the water jugs." I glanced over my shoulder in the other direction through the fog. Darius stood at the edge of the row of rooms, his weapon slung across his back, staring out into the wilderness beyond. "And that guy," I said, pointing with my thumb. "I'm not sure he ever sleeps."

"Given any more thought to Neil's offer?"

I mused for a moment, rubbing my fingers across my beard. Neil and Gloria offered us to follow them back to their community the morning after they'd arrived. It made sense for Mia, but we still had one big problem. Maura.

Bringing a Coutts around new people was a dangerous gamble. Would we be able to convince them she was harmless? That we weren't complete fools for inviting her into our group?

"Yeah," I grumbled, sipping from the cooling tea. "What do you think?"

Holli hesitated, looking at her feet. "Well, I think Sid needs to go. He'll recover from this, but it'll take some time. He's going to be deaf in that ear for the rest of his life and he'll need to learn how to adapt before he even considers hunting again. Plus, he could certainly use the extra medical care." She swallowed. "And I think we need to, too. Fall is getting close. We have limited time to prepare for winter now. And with only you able to hunt, it'll be even more difficult. But in the community..." She left me to deduce the rest of her words.

"That's fair. But—"

"I know," she said, her gaze darkening. "Maura."

I sighed. "I mean, they've met her now. Been with her

for a few days. They should know she's not a threat," I reasoned.

"True. But the name is going to trigger *all* kinds of irrational feelings."

I didn't want to agree, but I knew she was right. I was living, breathing proof of that. "So what do we do?"

"So we have to tell them — Neil and the others. Tonight. Before we make the trek north. We *need* to know what our next steps are if we want to survive the winter."

"After dinner," I confirmed, my heart heavy in anticipation as I glanced sideways at Darius, now pacing across the gravel lot.

"Either they'll understand or they won't," Holli said. "That, we have no control over. But Eli?" I met her eyes. She chewed the side of her cheek. "For Sid's sake, you need to consider all sides of this decision."

"Meaning?"

"Meaning that if they say no to Maura, we should consider doing whatever it takes to make him go." She studied my face.

"You'll have a hell of a time trying to convince him to split up."

"Then you'll have to convince him."

I scoffed.

"At *least* until he recovers."

I tilted my head, then got back into my chair, draping my arms over my knees as I hunched forward, still gripping my cup of tea. I knew Holli was right. And I hated it.

"Just consider it," she said, walking back toward the office.

"Maybe."

"Stubborn man," she muttered under her breath with a shake of her head.

"I heard that!"

"Good!"

I tried shaking my worry as I checked in on Sid, who was still asleep, before I made a late breakfast with some berries Holli had found the day prior. Then, I set out to find Maura.

She sat beneath a large oak tree at the edge of the property. The massive tree's leaves hung limp from the brutal summer heat. Maura sat in the shade, a book in her hands, looping a strand of curly hair around her finger. She glanced up as I approached, shielding her eyes with her hand.

"Hey," I said, sitting beside her on the grass.

"Hi," she answered. "How's Sid?"

I smiled. "Better. Holli says his fever broke."

"Really?" Her cheeks rose into a grin. "That's incredible!"

I nodded, folding my hands in my lap.

"What?" she asked. I lifted my head and watched her study me. A breeze came through, disrupting her curls so they blew into her face. She tucked them behind her ear with a single swipe.

"Nothing," I said, rubbing blades of grass between my fingers.

"Not nothing."

"Neil and the others invited us back to their community," I said, looking down at my hands. "Holli said it'd be best for Sid to go, especially with his injury. She's worried about the cold weather and our ability to start a food supply in time for winter." I peered up at her. "So...Holli wants to go too."

"Oh." Her voice was soft, merely a breath. I could see the conflict behind her eyes as she processed what I'd said.

"We have to tell them about...your family," I said. "We have to be honest with them before we make the trip so they understand what they're getting into." Maura placed her elbows on her legs and put her head in her hands. My stomach rolled with guilt. "Listen, there's a chance they may not accept us all," I continued. "They may end up turning us all away. And even if they turn just you away, we would figure something else out."

She shook her head and looked up at me, eyes wide. "No," she said. "You won't."

"Of course we—"

"I won't let it be my fault. Joining a community would be a gift," she said. "If it would help Sid, you, Mia, and Holli, then I won't be the only thing holding you back."

"Maura…" My stomach dropped. "We can make them see," I said, softer this time. "We can make them understand that you're not like *them*." I tried to find her eyes, but she wouldn't meet my gaze. "You're nothing like them. They'll see," I pressed. "I'm sure of it."

Her eyes found mine, and she pressed her lips together, giving me a small nod. But I could tell she didn't believe me, not as badly as she wanted to.

I felt an inherent need to protect Maura — not just from bodily harm, but from the bad things people associated with her surname. I had once been that person who grouped all the Coutts in as one, but I now knew there was little truth to that. From what I knew of her history, she had endured enough ridicule for a lifetime.

I understood the danger of assuming one truth about an entire group of people. Both Maura and I held damaging views of one another before we met. But once we had, those walls had shattered. Those beliefs had broken. But I was one man, and she was one woman. We hadn't changed the beliefs of others — the beliefs Peter Coutts had worked so hard to establish. The ones he'd used to decimate the world.

Darius returned in the early afternoon with the first inklings of happiness I'd seen since we'd met him. He'd brought down a deer, so we headed out together to carry it back to the lodge to skin and cook up for dinner.

We ate like kings that night outside the office in the soft glow of the setting sun, a roaring fire in the middle of the gravel lot. We roasted chunks of venison, browning and charring the edges, tearing it away from the roasting sticks with our teeth. We laughed and talked with grease-covered faces until the last of the sunlight faded away and Mia whined for bed.

Holli took Mia back to her room to get settled with Neil on their heels. Though Mia had been thrilled to see her father, his presence would take some getting used to. Holli was still her comfort for now, but Neil didn't seem to mind in the least. I caught him staring at his little girl in awe many times, holding back his tears.

Darius, Gloria, and I dumped the deer remains far enough away from the motel that we wouldn't wake to bears. The fire had turned to embers by the time Neil and Holli joined us again, the warm air shifting to a cooler, less humid breeze. We sat in a circle with full bellies, sleep calling our name.

But my anxiety grew as I watched the last remnants of wood burn red. There was no more delaying the inevitable.

"We have something to tell you three," I announced. The chatter ceased and all five faces turned toward me.

"What's that?" Neil asked.

My chest tightened. "It's about Maura." She shifted beside me, casting me a desperate, pleading look. I placed my hand at her back to show her she could trust me. Her back muscles stretched beneath my fingers as she tensed.

"I pulled Maura out of a creek a few weeks ago," I said. "She'd gotten lost and had nearly drowned. She joined our group after some initial hesitation about her... background. But she's been with us for weeks and has shown us her true nature. She's kind and giving. I mean, Neil," I glanced at him, "you've seen her with Mia. She's great with her. And with her scavenging background, she's a valuable resource," I rambled, tripping over my words.

"What are you trying to say?" Gloria asked from across the coals.

"I guess what I mean to say is she's a member of our group. But we met under some...*unusual* circumstances." I looked at the dark sky, trying to avoid their perplexed gazes. "She's...well, she's a Coutts daughter." The last words slipped out of my mouth quickly, but there was no glazing over them.

Palpable silence followed my words. Determined not to make eye contact, I continued. "She's been a victim of that place since the day she was born. Believe me, we were all ready to throw her back out to the wolves when we first met her, but the more we've gotten to know her, the more we realized she had no idea what was going on outside those walls. She had no idea what a monster Peter Coutts was, what he'd done to all of us out here. In truth, she lived a simple life as a wife on the peak. She has played no part in their atrocities."

I allowed myself to look at all three of their faces. Gloria's mouth hung open, and she shook her head in disbelief. Neil looked at me blankly, hands folded together. He pressed the tip of his nose against them and looked down at the ground. Darius' expression hadn't noticeably changed, but his shoulders were more tense, his hands gripping his knees.

"Neil, we were just discussing your offer of coming to the community—"

"No." Darius' voice sliced through my anxious words, like a knife to the chest. I broke into a cold sweat as I let my hand curl around Maura's shoulder.

"No?" My voice was weak.

"Darius," Neil said, looking up over his hands. "Not your call to make."

"Not yours either," he grunted.

"A Coutts *daughter*?" Gloria asked. "As in, a direct descendant of Peter?" Her good eye inspected Maura critically. I glanced down at Maura, whose head dropped below her shoulders, chin to her chest. She looked like she had when I'd first brought her back to our camp. Like she was trying to disappear.

"Yes," I said.

"Mia really loves her," Neil mused, glancing at his two companions.

Darius scoffed. "You're blinded by your daughter," he said. "A Coutts descendant is dangerous."

"How so?" Neil pressed.

Darius rolled his eyes. "I can't believe I have to explain this to you. You'll never walk right again, and you want to show her mercy? What if she's been planted? What if we welcome her into our borders, and she escapes and returns to her commune with information that puts us in jeopardy? What about Mia?"

"I'm *not* a spy," Maura whispered beside me. I squeezed her shoulder.

"It's still not your call to make," Neil said.

"Listen, Maura saved our lives," I said. "We were being chased by Hunters. She returned to her commune and was placed in solitude. She escaped her prison and endured significant abuse to even get back to us." My voice rose in pitch, but I couldn't help it. "She saved Sid's life by getting him back to us. She helped me find the antibiotics that saved his life! If you think she went through all of that just to—"

"I don't know what the Coutts will do for power!" Darius shouted over me. "But I put *nothing* past them. I wouldn't doubt they'd send someone out here to infiltrate us."

"Ridiculous," Neil scoffed.

"Is it?" Darius practically shook with anger.

"No," Gloria said. "Neil's right, D. It's not our call to make." She turned toward Maura and me. "I say we bring everyone back and let Avi make the final call."

"You're being *stupid*," Darius spat.

"Your leader?" I asked, ignoring him.

"More like a guide. Avi has accepted other escapees from the Coutts commune, but never a blood relative. It'll change the circumstances. But he's fair. He'll give her a chance, determine if she'd be a good fit."

"And if she's not?"

Gloria's gaze darkened, and she narrowed her eyes at me, ignoring Maura. "Then, she's not. He won't beat around the bush." Her tone was one of finality.

Darius got to his feet, shaking his head as he retreated toward the motel. Gloria sighed. "Darius is right to be concerned," she said, getting to her feet with a groan. "But I know Avi well. I've been with him since the beginning. He wouldn't want us to turn anyone away."

I gave her a curt nod. "Thank you," I said.

"Don't thank me yet," she called over her shoulder.

I looked down at Maura, who finally turned to look up at me and Holli. She frowned. "I'm sorry," she whispered.

"You have no reason to be," Holli said. "All we can do is try."

"Okay."

Her voice sounded so small and far away. I wished there was something more comforting I could say, some solution to offer should Avi turn us away. But the alternative was even more brutal to think about and not at all comforting. And judging by the silence that passed between us, Holli and Maura knew it, too.

We were now at the mercy of a man we'd never met.

26

MAURA

Hope kept me going after I'd left the Island of Repentance. It had fueled me through hunger, bumps, bruises, and being kidnapped. It guided me back to Eli and helped me return to Coal Creek to get the antibiotics. But now, my hope had all but been extinguished.

I was naïve about how lucky I'd gotten when Eli had first fished me out of that river. He'd been kind and selfless. And even after he'd figured out I was a Coutts, he'd made the choice to save my life. Now I understood what a generous gift that had been, even if I hadn't appreciated it then. My surname spelled death and horrors for most of the Outside world. If it'd been anyone else but Eli, my body might've been rotting in a ditch right now.

Eli walked me back to my room in silence, his hands shoved in his front pockets, gaze distant. He chewed the side of his lip, occasionally shaking his head until we reached the door. He held it open as I found one of Holli's makeshift candle lanterns crafted from empty soda cans.

The candlelight flickered, illuminating only a small

area. Eli let the door close behind him and stood at the entryway as I sat on the bed.

"Maura…" The way he said my name made my chest tighten. I didn't want his pity.

"It's fine."

"It's not."

I sighed. "I can't force anyone to accept me, Eli. Darius isn't wrong."

"Yes, he is!" Eli shouted, slamming his hand against the wall. "He's wrong about *you*. He didn't even listen to me—"

"It doesn't matter!" I yelled, surprised by my conviction. "My father is a monster. Everyone recoils when they hear my name — that says a *lot*. He's hurt a lot of people. How can I blame them?" I shook my head and looked at my lap. "They don't know me. They don't know if they can trust me. His wicked deeds have tainted our name. I can't blame them."

"They're ignorant."

"They're afraid."

"Stop being so accepting!" he growled. "You aren't your family. You aren't your blood. Where we come from — that's not what makes us. It's the choices we make once we have freedom. That's what matters. The things we do when nobody's looking." He stepped forward and squatted, looking up at me through the candlelight. The flame danced across his features — his pleading eyes, his wild beard. "I know what you've been through to get here. You deserve a fair shot at safety. As fair of a shot as the rest of us."

"I'm not *like* the rest of you," I whispered, catching his gaze. "You know that."

"Jesus, Maura. Don't you *want* to be treated fairly?"

"Of course I do!"

"Then I don't understand how you can be so calm about this. Aren't you angry?"

"Maybe a little," I admitted. "But this is out of my control. I know you don't want to hear this, but I do believe God is on my side. And He will move me forward however He sees fit."

Eli groaned in frustration.

"What do you want me to do?" I asked. "Beg? Plead? Being angry or desperate isn't going to change their view of me, and that's okay. I can't change the outcome."

"I want you to fight for yourself," he said, his voice low. "I want you to value yourself more. I want *you* to want to believe that you deserve something better than that commune. Having faith is fine, but you need to have faith in yourself."

I let his words settle over me as I tried to make sense of them. Finally, I nodded. "I can try to do that."

Eli got to his feet. "Gloria said there's others there. From the commune. That's a good sign."

I nodded through the pit in my stomach. "I guess I'll just have to be really convincing."

Eli lifted his chin. "You will be. We've got your back, too. They can't ignore that." He turned, resting his hand on the door handle before he said, "Goodnight, Maura."

"Goodnight," I called.

He left, closing the door behind him. I laid down on the bed, fully clothed, feeling more alone than ever. I turned to blow out the candle and collected my thoughts in the dark, trying to push worry from my mind.

It was impossible. If this leader, Avi, rejected me, what then? Eli and Holli would have to choose between Sid and me, and I knew, at the very depths of my being, who they would choose. Of course, I didn't blame them, either. Had it been any of my own siblings, I'd choose them every time.

Still, I was ashamed of the hurt exploding in my chest at the thought of being abandoned. Logically, I knew they didn't owe me anything. But that didn't make it hurt less.

All that aside, I still had the problem of figuring out what to do if they rejected me from this new community. Perhaps they would throw me a few supplies out of pity. Perhaps, I could find a place like this one. I could live off plants and berries, maybe even trade with their community if they allowed that sort of thing.

I turned over on the bed, face squashed into the limp pillow, frustration welling in my throat. Eli wanted me to have faith in myself — but how? I'd been told for so long that my best hadn't been good enough, my failures highlighted at every turn. I'd defied my family and faith. I was an outcast — a vagrant.

A sinner.

And I feared what was yet to come.

MORNING CAME AFTER A SLEEPLESS NIGHT, announcing her arrival with bright sunlight through the sheer curtain. I squinted, turning beneath the covers as yesterday's worries flooded back. With a sigh, I sat up, easing my sore back with a few stretches. I couldn't stop thinking about the conversation I had with Eli. How adamant he'd been about me advocating for myself. The idea seemed laughable. Sticking up for myself blurred the lines of sin. It was disobedient. It went against everything I knew.

But that didn't mean I didn't want to. Perhaps I just didn't know *how*. I'd always given my power over to my faith. By leaving it in God's hands, was I letting things happen *to* me instead of having a say in them? If I made a choice, would it affect the outcome? Did God control those decisions? Or did I? Thoughts circled me like buzzards until I forced them to quiet.

Urgent and excited voices came from somewhere beyond my door, followed by footsteps. How long had I slept? I threw my legs over the side of the bed and stood, smoothing out the clothes I still wore from yesterday. After pressing some blood back into my cheeks in the dusty mirror, I moved to open my door, but before I could, someone knocked.

Anxiety reared its ugly head, and I tried hard to swallow it before I pulled it open. Eli stood on the other side, his face a far cry from the frustration he'd left me with last night. Instead, happiness filled his features, his eyes bright, lips pulled up in a lopsided grin. He had one arm up against the doorframe, leaning inward. I could smell his sweat.

"It's Sid," he said, eyes flashing to his brother's room down the row. "He's awake. C'mon."

A chill ran up my spine at his words, and I rushed to follow him down to Room 8. He pushed open the cracked door. Voices filled the warm space, and sunlight spilled from the window. Holli, Mia, and Neil sat crowded around Sid's bed. Eli leaned against the wall beside the door, and I remained in the threshold.

I hadn't seen much of Sid since we had come to the motel from the city, but it was clear he was on the road to recovery. His eyes were bright and focused, his skin clear of sweat. I smiled, and, as his gaze found mine, he grinned at me, dimples forming in his hollowed cheeks.

"Well, hi there," he said.

Every face in the room turned toward me. Mia ran up, wrapping her arms around my legs, and I scooped her up in one swift movement, hugging her to my side.

"Sid," I said, and before I knew it, every emotion I'd felt

since we'd stumbled out of Coal Creek came rushing to the surface.

"Don't cry," Mia said as she wiped my face with her small hands, making me cry harder. I placed the young girl back down on the ground and approached Sid's bedside, sitting beside him. Sid reached his hand across the comforter, and I took it, squeezing his fingers between my own.

"It's good to see you," I spluttered.

"Wouldn't be here if it wasn't for you."

I forced a laugh between my tears, shaking my head. "It was nothing—"

"It was nothing?" He laughed, glancing at Eli. "You hear her? She's more modest than you are."

"I know," Eli said with a laugh.

My heart swelled as I used my free hand to wipe the moisture from my face.

"We're thinking about leaving this afternoon," Eli said. "As long as Sid feels up to it. It's about a three-hour drive from here."

Immediately, a pit formed in my stomach as I looked around at the eager faces circling me. Tonight? Already? It wasn't as if we were established here, but I'd thought I would have at least another night to make a plan if they didn't accept me in the new community.

"Maura?" Sid leaned forward in the bed. "What's wrong?"

I looked at him, then at Eli, Holli, and Neil. They each exchanged nervous glances with each other, and I tried my best to force a smile.

"Nothing," I said. "It's fine—"

"They're just a little apprehensive," Holli said. "About her…background."

"Who's apprehensive?" Sid's face shifted, his jaw clenching as he narrowed his eyes at Neil.

"The others," Holli said. "Gloria and Darius."

"She saved my life."

"I know," Holli soothed. "It still doesn't change—"

"It changes a *lot*," Sid grumbled. "Let me talk to them."

"It's not up to them," Eli said. "And it's not up to us, either. We're going to go and see what happens. If Avi turns us away, then we'll figure it out."

"Hey," Sid whispered, squeezing my hand. I looked up, meeting his dark eyes. He gave me a stern nod. "Whatever happens, it'll be okay."

I pressed my lips together. "I know," I said as my stomach turned with anxiety. I looked at my hand, still gripped in Sid's. There was no way I'd let them not go to the community. They needed this. I had left the commune on my own, and it was my responsibility to take care of myself. I wouldn't allow them to sacrifice this gift for me.

27

MAURA

I BOUNCED in the third row of Gloria's truck beside Holli, my vision obscured by a piece of fabric. It was thin enough that occasional sunlight filtered through, but I couldn't see out the window. None of us could. Darius had blindfolded Eli, Sid, Holli, and me. He'd explained it was a precaution for all people from outside the community, but he'd given me the sternest look of all. I suspected we were getting special treatment because I was a Coutts.

All the jostling in the backseat reminded me of being on the scavenging bus in the commune, riding to my fate every day, consumed by worry. I pressed my head against the warm glass as we roared toward our destination. It was difficult to believe that I had been that girl only weeks ago — worried about an uncooperative womb, worried what Abigail and Joanna thought of me, worried about pleasing Andrew and Father.

Those things had seemed so important, as if there were nothing else in the world that I needed to focus on. Life had been uneventful, but I had learned that was how Father had constructed all our lives. To be simple and meaningless, forcing us to fight among ourselves so that we would turn a blind eye to the things that, perhaps, did not add up.

I felt a pang of guilt at the thought. I had cast my sister Morgan aside for so long. Her experiences on the Outside made little sense to me — they'd confused and scared me, and I'd silenced her into submission around me. After a while, she stopped trying to get me to listen.

My stomach growled offensively loud in the quiet car. I shifted in my seat. Holli slid her hand into mine and squeezed. A show of solidarity. It was hard to tell how long we'd been on the road. Gloria had said their community was a few hours north of the lodge, but it seemed like we'd been driving for most of the day.

Finally, the car began to slow, turning every few minutes before coming to a slow roll. A mechanical whir suggested Gloria had rolled down her window.

"Call Mick and Avi," she shouted. "Returning with five newcomers. Scanned and safe."

Someone outside the vehicle said something I couldn't hear.

"Only one," Gloria answered. "I'll bring the rest for a full assessment once I talk to Avi."

I heard the window roll back up. The car moved forward, and the sunlight beyond my blindfold blinked out, shrouding us in darkness.

We pulled to the left, rolling to a slow stop, where we sat idle for a moment before the engine cut. Muffled voices came from somewhere in the distance.

"Go ahead and take your blindfolds off," Neil said.

Holli released my hand, and I eagerly stripped the fabric away from my face. My eyes adjusted to the dim lighting, uncertain at first of our surroundings. The truck was inside a garage of some sort — a massive space with a tall, concrete ceiling. More vehicles were parked beside the spot we sat in. Sunlight filtered the room from high windows, pouring across the gray stone floor.

Darius and Gloria opened their doors.

"Stay put," Neil told Sid as Mia wiggled off his lap and out the door. We followed. Our footsteps echoed against the ceiling. It was notably cooler inside this space — a welcome relief from the stifling motel.

At the far end of the room, a pair of hinged doors burst forward by what looked like a bed on wheels. Two people navigated it on either side — an older man with gray hair and glasses and the other, a young brown-haired woman holding a clipboard. Both wore surgical masks.

"Where the hell did you get a gurney?" Eli mused.

"Oh, there were tons of them left behind at the makeshift medical center in town," Gloria answered, opening Sid's door and helping him out.

The individuals reached us, bringing the bed to a halt before unhooking one of the side rails. Sid got to his unsteady feet and collapsed in a heap on the bed, dirtying the crisp, white linens. It might've been comical had I not been so nervous. The woman with the clipboard began asking Sid questions about himself and his age, his medical history, and the wound on his ear while the doctor began wheeling the bed back toward the doors without so much as a glance toward us.

"Whoa, wait a minute," Eli said, stepping forward, trying to follow his brother. "Where're they taking him?"

"Doctor," Gloria said, holding her hand out to stop him. She studied Eli's worried face and gave him a small smile. "He'll be fine. Mick is a skilled physician."

Holli placed her hand on Eli's back. "I'm sure it'll be fine, E."

He looked down sharply at her but said nothing else.

"Before we do anything else, you'll need to meet Avi." She nodded at Neil and Darius before addressing us again. "Follow me."

The awe I'd felt at our arrival quickly dissipated as I remembered their words from the night prior. I tried to hold my nausea down as our group followed her across the empty room. She brought us to the wall and gestured for us to stand against it.

"Wait here," she said. "I'll grab Avi. Neil?" She raised an eyebrow and looked at the young father. Mia clung to Holli's legs as she leaned against the wall. "You should bring Mia in."

Conflict crossed Neil's features before he kneeled to get to Mia's height.

"Mia, honey, do you want to come see where Daddy lives? Where you'll live?" he asked.

Mia looked up at her father, then back at Holli. "Can you come?" the girl asked.

"Oh, love." Holli cupped Mia's face and smiled widely. "How about this? You go with Daddy, and I'll be there soon, okay? I have to talk to someone first."

"Why?"

"Well, they have to ask us some questions."

"What kind of questions?"

Holli tapped her fingers against her lips. "Probably what my favorite kind of candy is," she joked. "Maybe you can see if they have any M&M's!"

Mia's eyes brightened. "Do you?" she asked, turning toward her father.

Neil looked like he might cry. "I think we might."

"Let's go!" Mia said adamantly, tugging on Neil's hand.

Neil turned over his shoulder and mouthed a *thank you* to Holli before Mia led him out the doors, leaving us in silence.

"Where the hell do you think we are?" Eli whispered, glancing around the room.

"A warehouse, most likely," answered Holli. "Could be anywhere."

The doors opened again. Gloria came through first, followed by a heavy-set man. Avi was not at all what I imagined. I'd thought him to be someone like Father — thin, well-put-together, and clean-shaven. Instead, as he came closer, I saw Avi had broad shoulders, a handlebar mustache, and dark skin. His squashed nose took prominence on his blemished face. A dent in the middle suggested he had broken it at some point, but it had never healed correctly. He smiled, revealing a gold incisor and two boyish dimples in his cheeks.

"Afternoon," he said in a deep, raspy voice, approaching us. He stuck his hand out to each of us and shook them. "I'm Avi."

We took turns introducing ourselves. I had expected the leader to be annoyed by our arrival, but Avi looked pleased at our presence. His eyes studied me, then Eli, then Holli, and he nodded as if making notes.

"And one more is with Mick," Gloria added.

"Sid," Eli said. "My brother."

"And little Mia," Avi said, glancing back toward the door. "So. I typically do intakes in my office." He looked sideways at Gloria. "Is there an issue I should be aware of?"

"Sir," Gloria said hesitantly. "She's Coutts blood."

She did not look at me. Instead, she hung her head, clasped her hands behind her, and looked at the floor. My face flushed as embarrassment and shame washed through me once more at the sound of my name and the discussion it prompted. Following Gloria's lead, I looked at my shoes.

"Coutts *blood*, you say?" Avi said, the question rhetorical. He crossed his arms.

"Sir," Eli said, clearing his throat. I glanced up, horrified. "Please, before you make any judgments. We've been with her now for weeks. I rescued her from a river she found herself in by accident. She's trustworthy."

"Trustworthy?" Avi's voice had lost its edge of playfulness.

"Yes."

"She's a valuable asset," Holli interjected. "A scavenger. She's smart. Kind." She turned to me and smiled. "She's saved our lives more than once."

Avi rounded on me again. "And you married into the family or born within?"

"Born," I mumbled. "Sir."

"Married?"

My fingers came to rest on my wedding band. "Yes. To Andrew Coutts," I offered.

"Children?"

My stomach dropped at the question. "No."

"Where did you live in the commune?"

"Coutts Peak."

He seemed to ponder this before turning back to Eli. "And you said you found her in a river?"

Eli nodded, then launched into a long explanation of our time together. How he'd saved my life, and I had no idea where I was or how to return home. How he'd tried to deliver me back to the commune, only for us to run into danger. How I'd sacrificed my freedom to return to the confines of the commune so that they could escape. And then how I'd escaped to find them once more. He told them how I'd saved Sid's life and helped care for Mia. How I'd wanted nothing more than to help them.

I beamed at his words, in awe of the way he viewed me and surprised at my emotion at his description of what I'd accomplished since leaving the commune behind. Most of the time, I'd just felt like I was following the masses, that I was doing what needed to be done and nothing more. But the way Eli described it made me prideful — like I'd done something good in the world. That in some small way, I'd made up for the transgressions of Father's wrongdoings.

We stood in silence for a few minutes as Avi digested Eli's words, and I shifted my weight as I waited for someone to say something. I felt eyes on me but was determined to keep my gaze fixed on the floor.

"Well," Avi finally said, breaking the silence. "What do you have to say, Miss Maura?"

I looked up. I expected a stern glare or a narrowed gaze, but his eyes were relaxed, his features calm. He clasped his hands together casually, waiting for my answer.

"Well, I think after seeing my husband shoot an innocent man, not being believed by my own father, and then punished for something that was completely out of my hands, my feelings about my family have turned pretty sour." My stomach turned as my words fell from my mouth, but I knew as I heard them pour out that I meant them completely. I looked at Avi, whose head was tilted, still waiting expectantly.

"Listen, even if I wanted to go back — which I don't — I couldn't. I'll have been exiled by now. I'm a miscreant. They'll say I've abandoned my family and defied God. There's no life worth living back there," I said, my voice breaking as I thought of Mother and Morgan. And the truth was, if I'd ever had the opportunity to go back for them and the rest of my family, I might. But it wasn't something Avi needed to know.

"I think she's proven herself damn worthy," Eli started, but Avi held up a hand to silence him, his gaze still fixed on me.

"I believe you," he said, his voice stern and steady. "But

I'll say this. We do *not* tolerate treachery. We are honest and work together for the good of the community. If I find any wavering of your allegiance, you'll be outside this gate quicker than you can say, *Peter Coutts*."

He turned to Eli and Holli. His eyes darkened, gaze tensing as he continued speaking. "I am happy to welcome you into our home. We have plenty of space to house you, but what we ask in return is that you take up a job where you're needed and where your skills can contribute. Nothing here comes free. Nothing here comes without hard work. We are thriving because of these morals, and the moment I catch a whiff of someone who challenges them, there's a no-tolerance policy, and they're out."

Though his friendly demeanor had not completely faded, there was an air about Avi that told me it would not be smart to challenge him. We nodded at him, and his face broke into a wide grin.

"Great," he said, slapping his hands on his legs before looking at Gloria. "Why don't you show them around? I'll get someone to assign some of the spare living quarters for the four of you, as I assume Neil's daughter will be staying with him. You'll want to introduce her to Leo and the others," he added, nodding towards me.

"Thank you, sir," Eli said, "for your hospitality and kindness. It won't be forgotten. We'll be valuable assets for your community."

"Of that, I have no doubt," Avi answered, turning on his heel to exit the large room.

Disbelief settled in my chest. Our interaction with Avi somehow seemed too...easy. I had expected anger. Needing to pay penance. Some kind of expectation of Coutts secrets. But he had just...said yes. Momentary distrust flickered through me, but I shooed it away. This was what I'd wanted. This was the best possible outcome for all of us. There was no Plan B or need to figure out how to survive on my own. I should be happy.

"You okay?" Eli whispered, his hand flat on my back. I glanced at him, meeting his concerned gaze. My belly dropped an inch.

"Yes," I breathed, shaking my head. "This is wonderful news."

"Ready to see the rest of it?" Gloria asked, fiddling with a dial on the radio hooked to her belt.

"Absolutely," said Holli.

"Can we see Sid?"

Gloria nodded. "When Mick's finished with him, he'll let us know. His office is way on the other side of the building. Typically, we'd back the truck up to the other entrance, but..." She trailed off, avoiding my eyes.

"There's more than this?" Eli asked, looking around the large room in disbelief.

"Oh, this is just a warehouse for one of the larger stores," Gloria said with a smile. "You're standing at the back end of an old shopping mall."

"You're kidding," said Holli.

"I'm not," Gloria answered, waving us to fall in step with her. "Come on."

28

ELI

I'D NEVER SEEN a shopping mall, but I'd heard of them before. A place with hundreds of shops where people spent excess money, back when they weren't worried about clean water or finding food. Back when there were rules and order in the world. I often wondered what it would be like to have the luxury of time. To have enough money for things like televisions or sneakers instead of having barely enough for medicine and food. I'd always imagined these places to be extravagant. But *nothing* could have prepared me for the sheer size of the place we'd walked into.

Holli, Maura, and I followed Gloria down a walkway with a glass ceiling. Sunlight illuminated the cream floor, and dust particles floated in the air. Wide openings into small rooms with signs hung above them lined either side. Inside the small areas looked like living quarters — some separated with curtains, some decorated with different furniture, some tidy, and others a mess. Metal grates acted as a barrier to some.

Our footsteps echoed off the scuffed floor, mingled

with voices and occasional thuds from somewhere within the building. Maura grabbed my arm to steady herself after stumbling over her feet. I couldn't blame her. There was so much to look at and even more to listen to. After a year of mostly silent existence, the constant noises were unsettling.

A few people milled around us as we walked: a mother breastfeeding an infant, a young woman pushing a stroller, and two young teenage boys tossing a football back and forth. Each of them gave us a peculiar look as we strode past, and it was the first time I looked down to inspect my jeans since we'd left that morning. I could barely make out the denim between the deer blood and dirt.

"Why a shopping mall?" Holli asked, her gaze skyward.

"Plenty of space and resources," Gloria answered. "Easy to protect. Underground access. Not visible to the Coutts' drones. The roof is still in decent shape. Plus, there's an atrium we use for growing. It'll convert into a greenhouse once the weather gets cold enough."

We reached a cross in the walkway. Here, the ceiling expanded even higher, decorated with ornate metal detailing that cast shadows across the floor. Three more long hallways extended on all sides. It was hard to take everything in — there were so many *things* — signs, belongings, furniture, decorations, each a unique characteristic of the community-dwelling. The voices were louder here, echoing from all ends; an incessant buzzing.

"The barn, garden, and slaughterhouse are down at that end," Gloria said, pointing down the hallway to our right to a store labeled *Bargain Outlet*. "We raise chickens, pigs, and a small family of goats for cheese and milk. There's a gym, library, school, and clothing stalls on that end," she said, pointing in the opposite direction. "The armory, community center, and Mick and Avi's offices are down here," she said, pointing straight ahead of us as she continued to walk forward.

"In the warehouse on the opposite end, we have work-tables for metal and glass work and even small construction, should you need it. All resources are brought in via our scavengers or collected from what still exists in this building and surrounding areas. And then at the end of this hall—" She gestured vaguely at the open area we walked toward, "is our communal area. We call it the Mess Hall. It's where we eat and cook, but Avi also likes to have meetings here every week, and we throw the occasional celebration, too."

I tried to imagine Gloria celebrating anything and could not.

Maura looked over her shoulder at me, her brows raised as if she couldn't believe Gloria's words. I smiled. Meetings. Celebrations. Things we had taken for granted for so long — things I never thought we'd experience again.

"This is incredible," said Holli. "And all of this was built over the last year?"

"Actually, Avi started this place before the bird flu hit. It had been abandoned for years, and nobody seemed to care much about what was happening with it. After being in the military, he said he knew shit was going to go bad. That it was only a matter of time. Thank God someone was taking it seriously. Otherwise, I don't think most people here would've survived."

Furniture was scattered around the communal area we now paused in. Gloria led us to the right, where there was a smaller area with different stalls advertising a variety of different foods. The left side remained untouched, but the right side had been gutted to expose each stall. As we approached, I saw plastic curtains separating three areas.

"Showers," Gloria explained. "Rain barrels sit on the roof, and Avi and a few others implemented a water purification system that leads into the building. It's reliant on rain, of course. But they work okay. They're only available when the power is on," Gloria said, "usually in the evenings, after dinner for about two hours. There's a sign-up list," she said, pointing to a plastic-covered sheet with a pen attached that hung on one of the walls. "First come, first served."

"Power?" I asked.

"Yeah. We get some every other day for an hour or two. There are generators around the back of the building," she said, leading us past a few stalls. "But gas won't last forever, so we're working on getting solar up and running." She pointed toward a dark alcove beyond the showers. "A door out there leads outside to a few portable toilets." She sighed, hands on her hips as she looked around the room. "I think that's everything. You'll get a better tour once Mick gets you all checked out." She cast us a scrutinizing look with her good eye. "I suspect you're all dehydrated, but we also need a full workup on each of you. This way." She gestured for us to follow her again.

Gloria led us out of the shower area, through the community center, and into the large space at the end of the hall, which, according to its old signage, was a big-chain department store at one point. Though most of the space was dark, there was enough light that I saw piles of propane containers beside a large grill. Two shelves held plates, cups, and silverware. Folding tables and chairs were pushed to either side of the aisle through the store, unused, I assumed, until mealtime.

"Your food intake will depend on your body mass and your job here in the community. People working scavenging or security jobs typically get more to eat, while those working more sedentary jobs will get less," Gloria continued. "Mick will determine all of that. And once he's done with you, I'll have Nadia show you where you'll be staying. She's head of our security team."

She paused, corralling us through yet another door. This place was like a maze, and it was making my head hurt. I hoped we'd soon become accustomed to where everything was and how it all worked. Prison had been a large place, but still nothing like this. Was this how the commune was? I wondered if Maura felt as overwhelmed as I did. I cast her a curious glance. She stood beside Holli, arms crossed across her chest. Definitely overwhelmed.

The door led into a small area that looked like it may have once been a pharmacy. A few chairs and a small table furnished the room, but Gloria brushed right past them and through yet another door. This room was bright — brighter than any section we'd been in, and after a brief moment, I realized the overhead lights were on. I guess the hour or two of electricity didn't hold true everywhere.

The room comfortably accommodated six stationary beds. Plastic covered each mattress, with thin blankets draped over the ends of each unused one. Sid lay in the one closest to the door, the brown-haired nurse fiddling with an IV attached to his arm.

"Hey, Mick," Gloria said, holding the door as our group filtered in. The gray-haired doctor looked up, momentarily distracted by his patient — a small blonde girl with pigtails.

"Eli!" Mia exclaimed, reaching out her arms. "Holli! Maura!" Neil looked up from his seat beside Mia's bed, relief filling his features.

"Everything went okay with Avi?" he asked.

"Just fine," Holli said, planting a kiss on Mia's forehead. The doctor looked annoyed at the interruption.

"Oh good," said the nurse, patting Sid's shoulder. "Come on, you lot. On the beds," she instructed. We climbed onto the mattresses, crinkling with every shift of weight. I unlaced my boots and kicked them to the side, my stomach turning at the smell. My body didn't smell much better. Dirt and grime clung to almost every inch of my skin. I was sure the pristine nurse and doctor had seen worse than the likes of us, but I still felt a sliver of embarrassment as I laid back on the bed.

Though we'd gotten rest in the car, it was different being inside this place. It was secure. Guarded. There were heavy doors, blockades, and, according to what Gloria had told us back at the motel, guards on alert twenty-four hours a day. This was night and day compared to me and Sid watching our surrounding area from Mom's roof. At the thought, tension slipped from my shoulders, allowing my body to relax as I lay against the firm bed.

"I'll leave you to it," Gloria said to the nurse, waving a quick goodbye before she disappeared out the door.

Doctor Mick looked up at Neil. "Your daughter's body weight is low, and she's had some muscle loss. All typical signs of malnutrition which isn't surprising given the circumstances. However, all her other vitals look good. All in all, you have a very healthy six-year-old."

"Thank you," Neil spluttered as he stood, hugging Mia to his chest. He turned to us. "And thank you again, Eli. Holli. Sid. I—" He choked on his words momentarily before clearing his throat. "I dreamed about this day so many times."

"We love Mia," Holli said.

"And there's nothing to thank us for," I added. "You would've done it for any of us."

Neil pressed his lips together and nodded, wiping a few stray tears from his cheeks.

We weren't alone with the nurse and doctor for long. Shortly after Mick and the nurse had finished with Maura, a long-legged woman with blonde hair entered the room. She wore skin-tight jeans tucked into boots and a fitted tank top. A black radio hung from her belt loop beside a gun holster.

"Neil!" she exclaimed, crossing the room to pull Neil into a one-armed hug, her gaze fixed on Mia. "Is this her?" she asked him. "Oh, my goodness!" The woman squatted beside the bed, looking Mia straight in the eye. "Hello, Mia. My name's Nadia. We've been waiting for you for a long, long time. I'm *so* excited you're here. I can't wait for you to meet my daughter. She's about your age."

"Hi!" said Mia. "Do you have any M&M's?"

Nadia threw her head back and laughed before standing up straight. "You know, I might. I'll bring them to dinner tonight, okay?"

"Okay!" Mia said.

The woman turned and walked toward us, pausing by the foot of Maura's bed. "Hi there," she said. "I'm Nadia. Head of security and in charge of showing you to your living quarters once you're done here. But first..." She fixed her gaze on Maura. "Avi would like me to take you to meet Leo. He's a Coutts survivor, too."

Another Coutts survivor. Gloria had mentioned them after we'd told her about Maura. Their existence in this community was a glimmer of hope I'd clung to when I tried reassuring her about being accepted by Avi.

Maura glanced sideways at me. I caught her gaze and held it. This was a good thing. I liked to think I'd marginally helped Maura, though even that belief sometimes seemed flimsy. But another survivor here on the outside could do wonders for her. Help her work through her trauma. Help her understand that she wasn't alone. Help her navigate through something only another survivor could.

I gave her a supportive nod, wishing it could convey everything I felt. She flashed me a weak smile before hopping off the bed to follow Nadia out the door.

29

MAURA

THE MAN NAMED Leo sat in an upholstered chair in the corner of the community center. He was older, probably around Holli's age, with a deep-set brow wrinkle, a large mole on his purple cheeks, and twinkling green eyes. Gray weaved through his dark brown curls that hung over his ears. He smiled without his teeth as I sat down in the chair beside him, wondering if there were any remnants of our commune within him.

I wanted to feel comforted by his existence. There was someone here who, at least partially, understood what I'd been through. But his presence unsettled me. It seemed unnatural that there were others who had defied Father. It was something that was hard to fathom.

"I'll leave you two to it," Nadia said, but I didn't look up as she left. I was fixated on Leo and the gleaming gold cross around his neck.

"Hi, Maura," Leo said, his voice gentle. "I'm Leo. It's nice to meet you."

"You too," I said, meeting his eyes. He, too, reminded

me of Avi. There was a calmness in his gaze and I had the immediate feeling he was a very good listener.

"So," he began, drumming his fingers against the arm of his chair. "You're from the commune."

"You too?" I asked, hating that I sounded defensive.

He nodded. "Twelve years ago, I joined with my wife and two children, right after the SARS pandemic hit in 2024. I escaped a few months ago."

I glanced around as if expecting his family to appear out of nowhere, then glanced back at him for an explanation. He hung his head. "Unfortunately, none of them survived."

"Your whole—?" My mouth opened — in shock, awe, I wasn't sure. A death in the commune was a big deal. Father typically spared no expense, no matter where the person lived in the commune, no matter their rank. A death of one of our own was momentous — to be recognized and appropriately grieved.

"I didn't know," I said, my fingers at my lips as if they could help me make sense of this thing. "I'm so sorry, I didn't hear—"

"You wouldn't have," he said, shaking his head. "But that's a story for another day. That's not what we're here to talk about. We're here to talk about your deconstruction."

"My—what?"

"I imagine you have a lot of questions about your Father and the Coutts commune in general?" He asked, ignoring my question. I nodded. "And things might feel a little confusing — your relationship with God has been challenged?"

"Yes," I said with a sigh of relief. "Horribly so." I was confronted with how my belief had wavered over these past weeks. How Father's indifference to my plight forced me to revisit everything I'd known about him and, in turn, God.

Leo nodded. "Deconstruction is reanalyzing all of those things we were taught and believed for so long," he said. "For me, it might've been a little easier. You see, I had the world before as a reference for myself — I could return to that reality and understand I'd been roped into something dangerous. But you've grown up in that environment. It's been your entire world for so long. And now that you're out of it, the world and your relationship with God can come as a shock.

"I want to help you. I want you to understand that there's a way to still love God, to still have faith and believe in him without the influence of Peter Coutts. Sometimes, survivors reject God outright — they're angry at him. Sometimes, they're angry at others for what they've done to them. So, as you adjust to this new community and have enough downtime to sit in your feelings, know that all your emotions are valid and normal. If you're angry at God, so be it. If you're angry with your family, so be it. Allow yourself to feel those things."

I hesitated, looking down at my hands, then back up at him again. "It just feels so…sinful," I breathed, hating the words. "To think this way."

"Of course," Leo said. "Again, that's normal. And it will get easier over time."

I studied him for a brief moment before I crumbled. Somehow, he'd unearthed a mountain of emotion within me that seemed to cascade through my limbs and choke me until I released a sob. I reached across the distance between us, and his warm hands enveloped mine as I cried into my shoulder. There was so much — too much to grapple with. We had been running from danger for so long that I'd been able to silence most of it. I'd had other things to focus on — getting away from the commune, being kidnapped, getting Sid the help he so desperately needed.

But sitting here, in front of a man Father had also harmed was something I'd never expected when I swam away from the Island of Repentance. Eli and Holli and even Sid had been understanding with me since I'd arrived in their camp. But they hadn't *understood*.

Somehow, by God's grace, I'd fallen into a community with someone who had been through it too. Our journeys might not have been the same, but he could understand what Father was like and how much finding out these truths had complicated my relationship with God. I decided to take this as proof that God hadn't given up on me.

Not yet, anyway.

GLORIA ASSIGNED us an empty space near the barn. The smell wasn't pleasant, but it was something we would get used to. We split the large room into four separate quarters for each of us. When I arrived after my conversation with Leo, I found Holli and Eli setting up mattresses with sheets. Nadia had also left sleeping bags, towels, and hygiene products. By the time we'd assembled our beds, the sky outside the skylight windows was dark.

So much had happened over the past few days, and somehow we'd ended up here. This place wasn't perfect; it didn't have all the luxuries of the commune. But those luxuries, I'd learned, had come at such a price that they no longer felt like something I deserved. They had been given to me, Andrew, and the others at a terrible sacrifice.

No, I much preferred the peace of this new place. The

community I already felt welcomed into, despite being not just an Outsider, but someone who belonged to a group that had betrayed them all. They hadn't rejected me outright. They hadn't given in to sin and succumbed to the virus, as Father had once said. They had thrived in devastation without the guise of God keeping them obedient. They had done the very thing Father insisted they couldn't.

Eli sat at the edge of his bed, his face lined with exhaustion. He glanced around the room, at Holli peeling off her socks as she eased herself down on the mattress with a satisfied groan. With a smile, he met my eyes.

"Hey," he said, glancing around the room. "This is… kinda something, isn't it?"

I nodded. "It is."

"Oh!" he said, his eyes brightening. He turned to his backpack and pulled something out. "Here," he said, crossing the room to hand me a crayon drawing on loose-leaf paper. "Mia asked me to give this to you." He eyed it endearingly. "She wanted to make sure there was something pretty in our rooms."

I took it, my heart swelling at her depiction of her, Holli, Sid, Eli, and me. We stood in a line together, holding hands. "That was so sweet." I met his eyes. "Thanks for bringing it to me."

"You know she'd have my head if I didn't." He sat back on his bed, adjusting himself to get the covers out beneath him. "G'night, ladies. Get some sleep. We've earned it."

"Goodnight, Eli," both Holli and I said.

I kept the drawing at my side as I took my boots off, laying my socks beside them. I dressed in fresh clothes beneath the covers before blowing out the candle between Holli and me. As I laid my head on my pillow, I placed the drawing beside me on the floor, staring at Mia's gentle strokes, smiling at the thoughtful gesture. A small reminder that human connection thrived even in the wake of destruction.

And I would thrive too, wouldn't I? When I dwelled on my actions over the course of these last few weeks, I was rash and impulsive. I had left behind everything I'd ever known, everything I'd cared about for so long. Aside from Morgan and Mother, those things I had been so worried about now felt so ostentatious and meaningless. The idea of bringing a new child into this dangerous, dark world suddenly felt foolish. Irresponsible, even. Worrying about living up to Andrew's expectations and appeasing Abigail and Joanna, women who wanted nothing to do with me, seemed like a distant dream.

Still, my heart would ache for Mother, Morgan, and the rest of my siblings. I was sure a day would not go by without thinking of them. And perhaps, one day, they would understand. They would see. Perhaps, as Eli said, they already did. Life here, on my own, out in the freedom of the Outside world, was where I truly belonged.

30

———

THE PROPHET

THERE IT WAS AGAIN — the incessant ache in my temple. It persisted now more often than not. I thanked God for the two pain relievers I swallowed dry, glancing from my desk back out the window at the commune with a deep frown. Worry ate away at me from the inside.

You're losing them.

A lie! I pressed my palms into my eyelids, seeing stars. Let them go. Let the sinners flee. What was out there for them besides destruction, pain, and sin? The world outside these borders was not worth returning to. But if they wanted to abandon us — abandon God — then they should be free to do so.

Knuckles knocked at my door. I used my fingers to press life back into the skin beneath my eyes, feeling the soft muscle and the hard bone of my skull.

"Come in," I said.

The door creaked open, and he entered — a mop of blonde hair and muscle. Luke. He had the perpetual look of someone who had never developed a thought for himself. He was an obedient dog who would do my bidding for whatever I asked. Valuable and loyal, yes. Yet he lacked in innovation and decisiveness. But he was devout. Loyal. Devoted. And that was why I kept him at the helm of my Hunters.

"Father," he said, the door clicking closed behind him. "I have news from Command."

I lifted my head, observing him. His uniform was impeccable — no doubt cleaned by one of his three wives. How many kids did he have now? Six? Seven? And two of the wives were pregnant again. He was doing quite well for himself, the epitome of what a Coutts should be. What a shame he wasn't my blood descendant.

"What is it?"

He stepped forward once more, approaching slowly, cautiously, like quivering prey. He was afraid of me, I knew. I counted on it.

"Sir," he said, and I saw pride sweep across his face. He knew he was important. That he was the only one who could tell me the news. I straightened, eager in my anticipation. "There's been movement some two-hundred miles northwest of here."

I raised a brow. West remained untouched. Filled with empty flatlands and simple-minded people, it was not a priority. "What kind of movement?"

"Sir, Collins believes he's found a larger community out there."

My eyes widened. Now, this was news. Luke often delivered drivel he thought would interest me. A herd of elk. A couple of Outside stragglers. But this — this could be useful. After all, we were running low on our supply.

"How many?"

"He estimates a few hundred." He rocked on his heels, hands clasped behind his back. Eagerness was never acceptable, but we could bend the rules for this.

"What else?"

"He suspects they have some of ours. Or those who used to be ours."

"Is that so?" I tried to hide my shock at the fact that anyone who had escaped our borders was actually still alive. My own daughter could very well be dead in the river that kept the Islands of Repentance so secluded.

"Well then," I said, studying him, "by all means — gather all the information you can on them." I filled my tone with urgency. His eyes widened, and he gave a firm nod, turning on his heel.

"And Luke?" I called after him before he reached the door. He turned, features expectant. "You'll let me know straightaway if my heathen daughter is there, won't you?"

"Yes, sir," he answered before closing the door behind him

TO BE CONTINUED

ACKNOWLEDGMENTS

What a ride this book was. I had so much fun writing it but shaping it into its final form was a massive endeavor which wouldn't have been possible without the following people:

To my Hells Belles: Laura, Laura, and Liesl, the best critique partners I could ever ask for. Thank you for giving me invaluable feedback and helping me become a better writer every single week.

To Laura P, my proofreader. Thank you for being there for me in my moment of need and helping me fix this baby up in the final days leading to my launch.

To my WPC Coven: Michelle, my partner in crime, without whom I would not be writing today. Debbie and Jennifer, I'm not sure how I could have gotten through multiple edits without your help. Thank you for reading my work time and time again. To Monica, my sanity support partner. Thank you for letting me vent and cry. But most of all, thank you for helping me remember life is NEVER as serious as people on social media make it out to be. And of course, to Jason, for always making me laugh!

To my incredible team of beta readers, especially Emma, who gave me such helpful feedback on my first shared draft. To my amazing readers who have made me feel so lucky to share my stories. To my friends, who have showered me with amazing support and love.

And finally, to my insanely amazing family — Matt, Liam, and Devin. I love you, I love you, I love you. Thank

you for letting me hibernate in my office to make up
worlds and write them down on paper.

ABOUT THE AUTHOR

Caitlin Mazur is a multi-genre author whose works span science fiction, speculative fiction, horror, and supernatural genres. As a transracial adoptee, Caitlin's work often touches on themes of found family and self-discovery.

Caitlin co-founded the Writing, Prompts & Critiques (WPC) Facebook community with over 11k members, named one of Reedsy's 50 Best Places to Find a Critique Circle. She helped develop WPC Press, a spin-off independent publisher that publishes anthologies with stories from WPC group members. When she's not writing fiction, Caitlin is a freelance writer, wife to an incredibly supportive husband, and mom to two amazing kids. Caitlin holds a degree in English Communications with a minor in Marketing from Saint Joseph's University in Philadelphia, PA, and is now living her best life in Central Maine.

Follow Caitlin: https://linktr.ee/caitwritesstuff

facebook.com/caitlinwritesstuff

instagram.com/caitwritesstuff

tiktok.com/@caitlinwritesstuff

9 781960 864055